Jewel
A Chapter in Her Life

by

Clara Louise Burnham

Jewel
A Chapter in Her Life
by Clara Louise Burnham

ISBN: 978-93-62209-41-2

Published by

DOUBLE 9 BOOKS

2/13-B, Ansari Road
Daryaganj, New Delhi – 110002
info@double9books.com
www.double9books.com
Tel. 011-40042856

This book is under public domain

ABOUT THE AUTHOR

Clara Louise Burnham was an American novelist. Following the popularity of No Gentlemen (1881), further volumes appeared, including A Sane Lunatic (1882), Dearly Bought (1884), Next Door (1886), Young Maids and Old (1888), The Mistress of Beech Knoll (1890), and Miss Bagg's Secretary (1892). She is George Frederick Root's daughter and authored the text for several of his most successful cantatas. The 1923 film A Chapter in Her Life is based on Burnham's novel Jewel: A Chapter in Her Life, written in 1903. She was born in Massachusetts and died at her family's house in Maine in 1927. Clara Louise Root was born in Newton, Massachusetts, on May 25, 1854. She was the oldest of six children born to Dr. George Frederick Root, a musical composer, and the former Mary Woodman. Her father, who became a senior partner at Root & Cady in Chicago, relocated with his family to the city while Burnham was a child, and Chicago became her home from then on. A visit for numerous summers to the old homestead in North Reading, Massachusetts, combined with memories of her early upbringing, provided her with an understanding of New England dialect and character, which she later incorporated in her writing. She was primarily interested in music when she was little.

CONTENTS

CHAPTER I
THE NEW COACHMAN

"Now you polish up those buckles real good, won't you, 'Zekiel? I will say for Fanshaw, you could most see your face in the harness always."

The young fellow addressed rubbed away at the nickel plating good humoredly, although he had heard enough exhortations in the last twenty-four hours to chafe somewhat the spirit of youth. His mother, a large, heavy woman, stood over him, her face full of care.

"It's a big change from driving a grocery wagon to driving a gentleman's carriage, 'Zekiel. I do hope you sense it."

"You'd make a bronze image sense it, mother," answered the young man, smiling broadly. "You might sit and sermonize just as well, mightn't you? Sitting's as cheap as standing,"—he cast a glance around the clean spaces of the barn in search of a chair,—"or if you'd rather go and attend to your knitting, I've seen harness before, you know."

"I'm not sure as you've ever handled a gentleman's harness in your life, 'Zekiel Forbes."

"It's a fact they don't wear 'em much down Boston way."

His mother regarded his shock of light hair with repressed fondness.

"It was a big responsibility I took when I asked Mr. Evringham to let you try the place," she said solemnly, "and I'm going to do my best to help you fill it. It does seem almost a providence the way Fanshaw's livery fits you; and if you'll hold yourself up, I may be partial, but it seems to me you look better in it than he ever did; and I'm sure if handsome is as handsome does, you'll fill it better every way, even if he *was* a fashionable English coachman. Mrs. Evringham was so pleased with his style she tried to have him kept even after he'd taken too much for the second time; but Mr. Evringham valued his horses too highly for that, I can tell you."

"Thought the governor was a widower still," remarked Ezekiel as his mother drew forward a battered chair and dusted it with the huge apron that covered her neat dress. She seated herself close to her boy.

"Of course he is," she returned with some asperity. "Why should he get married with such a home as he's got? Fifteen years I've kept house for Mr. Evringham. I don't believe but what he'd say that in all that time he's never found his beef overdone or a button off his shirts."

"Humph!" grunted Ezekiel. "He looks as if he wouldn't mind hanging you to the nearest tree if he did. I heard tell once that there was a cold hell as well as a hot one. Think says I, when the governor was looking me over the other day, 'You've set sail for the cold place, old boy.'"

"Zeke Forbes, don't you ever let me hear you say such a thing again!" exclaimed Mrs. Forbes. "Mr. Evringham is the finest gentleman within one hundred miles of New York city. When a man has spent his life in Wall Street it's bound to show some in his face, of course; but what comfort has that man ever known?"

"Pretty scrumptious place he's got here in this park, I notice," returned the new coachman.

"Yes, he has a breath of fresh air before he goes to the city and after he gets back every day. Isn't that Essex Maid of his a beauty?" Mrs. Forbes cast her eyes towards the stalls where the shining flanks of two horses were visible from her seat by the wide-open doors of the barn. "His rides back there among the hills," — Mrs. Forbes waved her hand vaguely toward the tall trees waving in the spring sunshine, — "are his one pleasure; and he never tires of them. You will find the horses here something different to groom from those common grocery horses in Boston."

"Oh, I don't know," drawled 'Zekiel, teasingly.

"Then you'd better know, young man," emphatically. "And, Zeke, what's the names of those carriages?" pointing with sudden energy at two half shrouded vehicles.

"How many guesses do I get?"

"Guessing ain't going to do. Do you know, or don't you?"

"Know? Why," leniently, "bless your heart, mother, don't you s'pose I know a buggy and a carryall when I see 'em?"

"Oh, you poor benighted grocery boy!" Mrs. Forbes raised her hands. "What a mercy I mentioned it! Imagine Mrs. Evringham hearing you ask if she'd have the buggy or the carryall! 'Zekiel," solemnly, "listen to me. That tall one's a spider, and the other's a broom. There! Do you hear me? A *spider* and a *broom*!"

Ezekiel's merry eyes met the anxious ones with a twinkle.

"Who'd have thought it!" he responded.

"Now then, Zeke," anxiously, "it's my responsibility. I recommended you. I want you should say 'em off as glib as Fanshaw did. Now then, which is which?"

"Mother, didn't you tell me that the late lamented was not a prohibitionist?"

"Fanshaw drank like a fish, if that's what you mean."

"Well, just because he saw things in this barn you needn't expect me to! Poor chap! Spiders and brooms! He must have been glad to go."

Mrs. Forbes' earnest expression did not change. "'Zekiel, don't you tease, now! We haven't got time. I want you to make such a success of this that you'll stay with me. You can't think how I felt when I woke up this morning and thought the first thing, 'Zeke's here.' Why, I've scarcely kept acquainted with you for fifteen years. Scarcely saw you except for a few weeks in the summer time. Now I've got you again!"

"I ain't the only thing you've got again," grinned 'Zekiel, "if you're going to see things, same as Fanshaw did."

Thus reminded, the housekeeper looked back at the phaeton and the brougham. "Be a good boy, Zeke," coaxingly, "and don't forget now, because Mrs. Evringham is a great stickler—and a great sticker, too," added Mrs. Forbes in a different tone.

"Who *is* the old woman, if the governor isn't married?" asked Ezekiel with not very lively interest. "She don't seem popular with you."

"I'll tell you who she is," returned his mother in a low, emphatic tone. "she's just what I say—a sticker and an interloper."

"H'm! Shouldn't wonder if the green-eyed monster had got after mamma," soliloquized the youth aloud. "Somebody else sews on the buttons now, perhaps."

"'Zekiel Forbes, we must have an understanding right off. You've got to joke and tease, I s'pose, but it can't be about Mr. Evringham. This is like a law of the Medes and Persians, and I want you should understand it. The more you see of him the less you'll dare to joke about him."

"I told you he scared me stiff," acknowledged Zeke, running the harness through his hands to discover another dingy spot.

"Well, he'd *better*. Now I wouldn't gossip to you of my employer's affairs—I hope we're better than two common servants—but I want you to be as loyal to him as I am, and to understand a few of the reasons why he can't go giggling around like some folks."

"Great Scott!" interpolated the young coachman. "Mr. Evringham go giggling around! So would Bunker Hill monument!"

"Listen to me, Zeke. Mr. Evringham has had two sons. His wife died when the oldest, Lawrence, was fifteen. Well, both those boys disappointed him. Lawrence when he was twenty-one married secretly a widow older than himself, who had a little girl named Eloise. Mr. Evringham made the best of it, and helped him along in business. Lawrence became a broker and had made and lost a fortune when he died at the age of thirty-five."

"Broke himself, did he?" remarked the irrepressible 'Zekiel.

"Yes, he did. Here we were, living in peace and comfort,—my employer at sixty a man of settled habits and naturally very set in his ways and satisfied with his home and the way I had run it for him for fifteen years,—when three blows fell on him at once. Firstly his son Lawrence failed and was ruined; secondly he died; and thirdly his widow and her daughter nineteen years old came here a couple of months ago and settled on Mr. Evringham, and here they've stayed ever since! I don't think they have an idea of going away." Mrs. Forbes's eyes snapped. "Such an upset as it was! I couldn't show how I felt, of course, for it was so much worse for him than it was for me. He had never cared for Mrs. Evringham, and scarcely knew the girl who called him 'grandfather' without an atom of right."

"Hard lines," observed 'Zekiel. "Does the girl call herself Evringham?"

"Does she?" with scorn. "Well I guess she does. Of course she was only four when her mother married Lawrence, and I guess she was fond of her stepfather and he of her, because he never had any children; but sometimes I ask myself, is it going on forever? I only hope Eloise'll get married soon."

'Zekiel dropped the harness to arrange imaginary curls on his temples and pat the tie on his muscular neck. "If she's pretty I'm willing," he responded.

His mother shook her head absently. "Then there was Mr. Evringham's younger son, a regular roving ne'er-do-well. He didn't like Wall Street and he went West to Chicago. He was a rolling stone, first in one position and then in another; then he got married, and after a few years he rolled away altogether. All Mr. Evringham knows about him and his family is that he had one child. Harry wrote a few letters about his wife Julia and the baby, at the time it was born, and Mr. Evringham sent a present of money; then the letters ceased until one day the wife wrote him frantically that her husband had disappeared and begged to know where he was. Mr. Evringham knew nothing about him and wrote her so, and that is the last he's heard. So you see if he looks cold and hard, he's had enough to make him so."

"H'm!" ejaculated 'Zekiel. "He don't give the impression of lyin' awake nights wondering how his deserted daughter-in-law and the kid make out."

"Why should he?" retorted Mrs. Forbes sharply. "His two boys acted as selfish to him as boys could. He's a disappointed, humiliated man in that proud heart of his. He's been hunted out and harrowed up in this peaceful retreat, when all he asked was to be let alone with his horses and his golf clubs, and I think one daughter-in-law's enough under the circumstances. I have some respect for Mrs. Harry, whoever she is, because she lets him alone. In all the long years we've spent here, when he often had no one to talk to but me, he's let me have a glimpse of these things, and I've told you so's you'd think right about him and serve him all the better."

"He's got a look in his eyes like cold steel," remarked Ezekiel, "and lines under 'em like they'd been drawn with steel; and his back's as flat and straight as if a steel rod took the place of a spine. That thick gray hair and mustache of his might be steel threads."

"He's a splendid sight on horseback," responded Mrs. Forbes devoutly. "His sons were neither of 'em ever the man he is. I'd like to protect him from being imposed upon if such a thing was possible."

"Sho!" drawled 'Zekiel. "Might's well talk about protecting a battleship."

"Well, 'Zekiel Forbes," returned his mother, her eyes bright, "can't you imagine a battleship hesitating to run down a little pleasure yacht with all its flags flying? And can't you imagine that hesitation costing the battleship considerable precious time and money? You've said a good deal about my sacrificing my room in the house and coming out here to fix a little home for us both, upstairs in the barn chambers, but perhaps you can see now that it isn't all sacrifice, that perhaps I'm glad of an excuse to get out of the house, where things are so different from what they used to be, and to have a cosy home with my own boy. Now then, 'Zekiel," coaxingly, these words recalling her boy's responsibilities, "look over there once more and tell me which of those is the spider."

Zekiel dropped the harness and laid his hand gently on his mother's forehead. "There isn't anything there, dear mother," he said soothingly.

"Zeke!" she exclaimed, jerking away with a short reluctant laugh.

"'Mother, dear mother, come home with me now,'" he roared sentimentally, so that Essex Maid lifted her beautiful head and looked out in surprise. "Remember Fanshaw, and put more water in it after this," he added, dropping his arm to his mother's neck and capturing her with a hug.

"'Zekiel!" she protested. "'Zekiel!"

CHAPTER II
THE CHICAGO LETTER

The mother was still laughing and struggling in the irresistible embrace when both became aware that a third person was regarding them in open-mouthed astonishment.

"'Zekiel, let me *go!*" commanded the scandalized woman, and pushed herself free from her tormentor, who forthwith returned rather sheepishly to his buckles.

The young man with trim-pointed beard and mirthful eyes, who stood in the driveway, had just dismounted from a shining buggy. Doubt and astonishment were apparently holding him dumb.

The housekeeper, smoothing her disarranged locks and much flushed of face, returned his gaze, rising from her chair.

"I couldn't believe it was you, Mrs. Forbes!" declared the newcomer. "Fanshaw isn't—" He looked around vaguely.

"No, he isn't, Dr. Ballard," returned Mrs. Forbes shortly. "He forgot to rub down Essex Maid one evening when she came in hot, and that finished him with Mr. Evringham."

The young doctor's lips twitched beneath his mustache as he looked at 'Zekiel, polishing away for dear life.

"You seem to have some one else here—some friend," he remarked tentatively.

"Friend!" echoed the housekeeper with exasperation, feeling to see just how much Zeke had rumpled her immaculate collar. "We looked like friends when you came up, didn't we!"

"Like intimate friends," murmured the doctor, still looking curiously at the big fair-haired fellow, who was crimson to his temples.

"I don't know how long we shall continue friends if he ever grabs me again like that just after I've put on a clean collar. He's got beyond the place where I can correct him. I ought to have done it oftener when I had the chance. This is my boy 'Zekiel, Dr. Ballard," with a proud glance in the direction of the youth, who looked up and nodded, then continued his labors. "Mr. Evringham has engaged him on trial. He's been with horses a couple of years, and I guess he'll make out all right."

"Glad to know you, 'Zekiel," returned the doctor. "Your mother has been a good friend of mine half my life, and I've often heard her speak of you. Look out for my horse, will you? I shall be here half an hour or so."

When the doctor had moved off toward the house Mrs. Forbes nodded at her son knowingly.

"Might's well walk Hector into the barn and uncheck him, Zeke," she said. "They'll keep him more'n a half an hour. That young man, 'Zekiel Forbes, — that young man's my *hope*." Mrs. Forbes spoke impressively and shook her forefinger to emphasize her words.

"What you hoping about him?" asked 'Zekiel, laying down the harness and proceeding to lead the gray horse up the incline into the barn.

"Shouldn't wonder a mite if he was our deliverer," went on Mrs. Forbes. "I saw it in Mrs. Evringham's eye that he suited her, the first night that she met him here at dinner. I like him first-rate, and I don't mean him any harm; but he's one of these young doctors with plenty of money at his back, bound to have a fashionable practice and succeed. His face is in his favor, and I guess he knows as much as any of 'em, and he can afford the luxury of a wife brought up the way Eloise Evringham has been. That's right, Zeke. Unfasten the check-rein, though the doctor don't use a mean one, I must say. I only hope there's a purgatory for the folks that use too short check-reins on their horses. I hope they'll have to wear 'em themselves for a thousand years, and have to stand waiting at folks' doors frothing at the mouth, and the back of their necks half breaking when the weather's down to zero and up to a hundred. That's what I hope!"

'Zekiel grinned. "You want 'em to try the cold place and the hot one too, do you?"

"Yes I do, and to stay in the one that hurts the most. The man that uses a decent check-rein on his horse," continued Mrs. Forbes, dropping into a philosophizing tone, "is apt to be as decent to his wife. The doctor would be a great catch for that girl, and I *think*," dropping her voice, "her mother'd be liable to live with 'em."

"You're keeping that dark from the doctor, I s'pose?" remarked 'Zekiel.

"H'm. You needn't think I go chattering around that house the way I do out here. I've got a great talent, if I do say it, for minding my own business."

"Good enough," drawled 'Zekiel. "I heard tell once of a firm that made a great fortune just doing that one thing."

"Don't you be sassy now. I've always waited on Mr. Evringham while he ate his meals, and that's the time he'd often speak out to me about things if he felt in the humor, so that in all these years 't isn't any wonder if I've come to feel that his business is mine too."

"Just so," returned 'Zekiel, with a twinkle in his eye.

"It's been as plain as your nose that the interlopers don't like to have me there. Not that they have anything special against me, but they'd like to have someone younger and stylisher to hand them their plates. I'll never forget one night when they'd been here about a week, and I think Mr. Evringham had begun to suspect they were fixtures,—I'd felt it from the first,—Mrs. Evringham said, 'Why father, does Mrs. Forbes always wait on your table? I had supposed she was temporarily taking the place of your butler or your waitress.'"

The housekeeper's effort to imitate the airy manner she remembered caused her son to chuckle as he gathered up the shining harness.

"You should have seen the look Mr. Evringham gave her. Just as if he didn't see her at all. 'Yes,' he answered, 'I hope Mrs. Forbes will wait on my table as long as I have one.' And I will if I have my health," added the speaker, bridling with renewed pleasure at the memory of that triumphant moment. "They think I'm a machine without any feelings or opinions, and that I've been wound up to suit Mr. Evringham and run his establishment, and that I'm no more to be considered than the big Westminster clock on the stairs. Mrs. Evringham did try once to get into my employer's rooms and look after his clothes." Mrs. Forbes shook her head and tightened her lips at some recollection.

"She bucked up against the machine, did she?" inquired Zeke.

The housekeeper glanced around to see if any one might be approaching.

"I saw her go in there, and I followed her," she continued almost in a whisper. "She sort of started, but spoke up in her cool way, 'I wish to look over father's clothes and see if anything needs attention.' 'Thank you, Mrs. Evringham, but everything is in order,' I said, very respectful. 'Well, leave it for me next time, Mrs. Forbes,' she says. 'I shall take care of him while I am here.' 'Thank you,' says I, 'but he wouldn't want your visit interfered with by that kind of work.' She looked at me sort of suspicious and haughty. 'I prefer to do it,' she answers, trying to look holes in me with her big eyes. 'Then will you ask him, please,' said I very polite, 'before I give you the keys, because we've got into habits here. I've taken care of Mr. Evringham's clothes for fifteen years.' She looked kind of set back. 'Is it so long?' she asks. 'Well, I will see about it.' But I guess the right time for seeing about it never came," added the housekeeper knowingly.

"You're still doing business at the old stand, eh?" rejoined Zeke. "Well, I'm glad you like your job. It's my opinion that the governor's harder—"

"Ahem, ahem!" Mrs. Forbes cleared her throat with desperate loudness and tugged at her son's shirt sleeve with an energy which caused him to wheel.

Coming up the sunny driveway was a tall man with short, scrupulously brushed iron-gray hair, and sweeping mustache. The lines under his eyes were heavy, his glance was cold. His presence was dignified, commanding, repellent.

The housekeeper and coachman both stood at attention, the latter mechanically pulling down his rolled-up sleeves.

"So you're moving out here, Mrs. Forbes," was the remark with which the newcomer announced himself.

"Yes, Mr. Evringham. The man has been here to put in the electric bell you ordered. I shall be as quick to call as if I was still in the house, sir, and I thank you—'Zekiel and I both do—for consenting to my making it home-like for him. Perhaps you'd come up and see the rooms, sir?"

"Not just now. Some other time. I hope 'Zekiel is going to prove himself worth all this trouble."

The new coachman's countenance seemed frozen into a stolidity which did not alter.

"I'm sure he'll try," replied his mother, "and Fanshaw's livery fits him to such a turn that it would have been flying in the face of Providence not to try him. Did you give orders to be met at this train, sir?" Mrs. Forbes looked anxiously toward the set face of her heir.

"No—I came out unexpectedly. I have received news that is rather perplexing."

The housekeeper had not studied her employer's moods for years without understanding when she could be of use.

"I will come to the house right off," was her prompt response. "It's a pity you didn't know the bell was in, sir."

"No, stay where you are. I see Dr. Ballard is here. We might be interrupted. You can go, 'Zekiel."

The young fellow needed no second invitation, but turned and mounted the stairway that led to the chambers above.

Mr. Evringham took from his pocket a bunch of papers, and selecting a letter handed it to Mrs. Forbes, motioning her to the battered chair, which was still in evidence. He seated himself on the stool Zeke had vacated, while his housekeeper opened and read the following letter:—

CHICAGO, April 28, 19—.

DEAR FATHER,—The old story of the Prodigal Son has always plenty of originality for the Prodigal. I have returned, and thank Heaven sincerely I do not need to ask you for anything. My blessed girl Julia has supported herself and little Jewel these years while I've been feeding on husks. I don't see now how I was willing to be so revoltingly cruel and cowardly as to leave her in the lurch, but she has made friends and they have stood by her, and now I've been back since September, doing all in my power to make up what I can to her and Jewel, as we call little Julia. They were treasures to return to such as I deserved to have lost forever; but Julia treats me as if I'd been white to her right all along. I've lately secured a position that I hope to keep. My wife has been dressmaking, and this is something in the dry goods line that I got through her. The firm want us to go to Europe to do some buying. They will pay the expenses of both; but that leaves Jewel. I've heard that Lawrence's wife and daughter are living with you. I wondered if you'd let us bring Jewel as far as New York and drop her with you for the six weeks that we shall be gone. If we had a little more ahead we'd take the child with us. She is eight years old and wouldn't be any trouble, but cash is scarce, and although we could board her here with some friend, I'd like to have her become acquainted with her grandfather, and I thought as Madge and Eloise were with you, they would look after her if Mrs. Forbes is no longer there. This has all come about very suddenly, and we sail next Wednesday on the Scythia, so I'll be much obliged if you will wire me. I shall be glad to shake your hand again.

Your repentant son,

HARRY.

Mrs. Forbes looked up from the letter to find her employer's eyes upon her. Her lips were set in a tight line.

"Well?" he asked.

"I'd like to ask first, sir, what you think of it?"

"It strikes me as very cool. Harry knows my habits."

The housekeeper loosened the reins of her indignation.

"The idea of your having a child here to clatter up and down the stairs at the very time you want to take a nap!" she burst forth. "You've had enough to bear already."

"A deal of company in the house as it is, eh?" he rejoined. It was the first reference he had ever made to his permanent guests.

"It's what I was thinking, sir."

"You're not for it, then, Mrs. Forbes?"

"So far as taking care of the child goes, I should do my duty. I don't think Mrs. Evringham or her daughter would wish to be bothered; but I know very little about children, except that your house is no place for them to be racing in. One young one brings others. You would be annoyed, sir. Some folks can always ask favors." The housekeeper's cheeks were flushed with the strength of her repugnance, and her bias relieved Mr. Evringham's indecision.

"I agree with you," he returned, rising. "Tell 'Zekiel to saddle the Maid. After dinner I will let him take a telegram to the office."

He returned to the house without further words, and Mrs. Forbes called to her son in a voice that had a wrathful quaver.

"What you got your back up about?" inquired Zeke softly, after a careful look to see that his august master had departed.

"Never you mind. Mr. Evringham wants you should saddle his horse and bring her round. I want he should see you can do it lively."

"Ain't she a beaut'!" exclaimed Zeke as he led out the mare. "She'd ought to be shown, she had."

"Shown! Better not expose your ignorance where Mr. Evringham can hear you. That mare's taken two blue ribbons already."

"Showed they knew their business," returned Zeke imperturbably. "I s'pose the old gent don't care any more for her than he does for his life."

"I guess he loves her the best of anything in this world."

"Love! The governor love anything or anybody! That's good," remarked the young fellow, while Essex Maid watched his movements about her with gentle, curious eyes.

"I do believe she misses Fanshaw and notices the difference," remarked Mrs. Forbes.

"Glad to, too. Ain't you, my beauty? She's going to be stuck on me before we get through. She don't want any Britishers fooling around her."

"You've certainly made her look fine, Zeke. I know Mr. Evringham will be pleased. She just shines from her pretty little ears to her hoofs. Take her around and then come back. I want to talk to you."

"If I don't come back," returned the boy, "you'll know the governor's looked at me a little too hard and I've been struck so."

"Don't be any foolisher than you can help," returned Mrs. Forbes, "and hurry."

On 'Zekiel's return to the barn he saw that his mother's face was portentous. "Lawrence was at least handsome like his father," she began without preamble, looking over Zeke's shoulder, "but Harry was as homely as he was no account. I should think that man had enough of his sons' belongings hanging on him already. What do you think, 'Zekiel Forbes? Mr. Evringham's youngest son Harry has turned up again!"

"I should think it was the old Harry by your tone," rejoined Zeke equably.

"He and his wife, poor as church mice, are getting their expenses paid to Europe on business, and they have the nerve—yes, the cheek—to ask Mr. Evringham to let them leave their young one, a girl eight years old, with him while they're gone."

"I hope it's a real courageous youngster," remarked Zeke.

"A child! A wild Western dressmaker's young one in Mr. Evringham's elegant house!"

"Is the old Harry a dressmaker?" asked Zeke mildly.

"No, his wife is. His Julia! They've named this girl for her, and I suppose they called her Jule, and then twisted it around to Jewel. Jewel!"

"When is she coming?" asked Zeke, seeing that he was expected to say something.

"Coming? She isn't coming," cried his mother irefully. "Not while Mr. Evringham has his wits. They haven't a particle of right to ask him. Harry has worried him to distraction already. The child would be sure to torment him."

"He'd devour her the second day, then," returned Zeke calmly. "It would be soon over."

CHAPTER III
MOTHER AND DAUGHTER

Dr. Ballard had gone, and his hostesses were awaiting the summons to dinner. Mrs. Evringham regarded her daughter critically as the girl sat at the piano, idly running her fingers over the keys.

The listlessness expressed in the fresh face and rounded figure brought a look of disapproval into the mother's eyes.

"You must practice that nocturne," she said. "You played it badly just now, and there is no excuse for it, Eloise."

"If you will let me give lessons I will," responded the girl promptly, without turning her graceful, drooping head.

The unexpected reply was startling.

"What are you talking about?" asked Mrs. Evringham.

"Oh, I'm so tired of it all," replied the girl wearily.

A frown contracted her mother's forehead. "Tired of what? Turn around here!" She rose and put her hands on the pretty shoulders and turned her child until the clear gray eyes met hers. "Now then, tired of what?"

Eloise smiled slightly, and sighed. "Of playing nocturnes to Dr. Ballard."

"And he is quite as tired of hearing you, I dare say," was the retort. "It seems to me you always stumble when you play to the doctor, and he adores Chopin."

Eloise continued to meet her mother's annoyed gaze, her hands fallen in her lap, all the lines of her nut-brown hair, her exquisite face, and pliable, graceful figure so many silent arguments, as they always were, against any one's harboring annoyance toward her.

"You say he does, mother, and you have assured him of it so often that the poor man doesn't dare to say otherwise; but really, if you'd let him have the latest Weber and Field hit, I think he would be so grateful."

"Learn it then!" returned Mrs. Evringham.

Eloise laughed lazily. "Intrepid little mother!" Then she added, in a different tone, "Don't you think there is any danger of our being too obliging? I'm not the only girl in town whose mother wishes her to oblige Dr. Ballard. May we not overreach ourselves?"

"Eloise!" Mrs. Evringham's half-affectionate, half-remonstrating grasp fell from her child's shoulders. "That remark is in very bad taste."

The girl shook her head slowly. "I never can understand why it is any satisfaction to you to pretend. You find comfort in pretending that Mr. Evringham likes to have us here, likes us to use his carriages, to receive his friends, and all the rest of it. We've been here seven weeks and three days, and that little game of pretending is satisfying you still. You are like the ostrich with its head in the sand."

Mrs. Evringham drew her lithe figure up. "Well, Eloise, I hope there are limits to this. To call your own mother an—an ostrich!"

"Don't speak so loud," returned the girl, rising and patting her mother's hand. "Grandfather has returned from his ride. I just heard him come in. It is too near dinner time for a scene. There is no need of our pretending to each other, is there? You have always put me off and put me off, but surely you mean to bring this to an end pretty soon?"

"You could bring it to an end at once if you would!" returned Mrs. Evringham, her voice lowered. "Dr. Ballard has nothing to wait for. I know all about his circumstances. There never was such a providence as father's having a friend like him ready to our hand—so suitable, so attractive, so rich!"

"Yes," responded the girl low and equably, "it is just five weeks and two days that you have been throwing me at that man's head."

"I have done nothing of the kind, Eloise Evringham."

"Yes you have," returned the girl without excitement, "and grandfather sneering at us all the time under his mustache. He knows that there are other girls and other mothers interested in Dr. Ballard more desirable than we are. Oh! how easy it is to be more desirable than we are!"

"There isn't one girl in five hundred so pretty as you," returned Mrs. Evringham stoutly.

"I wish my prettiness could persuade you into my way of thinking."

"What do you mean?" The glance of the older woman was keen and suspicious.

"We would take a cheap little apartment to-morrow," said the girl wistfully.

Mrs. Evringham gave an ejaculation of impatience. "And do all our own work and live like pigs!" she returned petulantly.

Eloise shrugged her shoulders. "I may flatter myself, but I fancy I should keep it rather clean."

"You wouldn't mind your hands then." Mrs. Evringham regarded the hands worthy to be imitated by a sculptor's art, and the girl raised them and inspected the rose-tints of their tips. "I've read something about rubber gloves," she returned vaguely.

"You'd better read something else then. How do you suppose you would get on without a carriage?" asked her mother with exasperation. "You have never had so much as a taste of privation in any form. Your suggestion is the acme of foolishness."

"I think I could do something if you would let me," rejoined the girl as calmly as before. "I think I could teach music pretty well, and keep house charmingly. If I had any false pride when we came out here, the past six weeks have purified me of it. Will you let me try, mother? I'm asking it very seriously."

"Certainly not!" hotly. "There are armies of music teachers now, and you would not have a chance."

"I think I could dress hair well," remarked Eloise, glancing at the reflection in a mirror of her own graceful coiffure.

"I dare say!" responded Mrs. Evringham with sarcastic heat, "or I'm sure you could get a position as a waitress. The servant problem is growing worse every year."

"I'd like to be your waitress, mother." For the first time the girl lost her perfect poise, and the color fluctuated in her cheek. She clasped her hands. "It would be heaven compared with the feeling, the sickening, appalling suspicion, that we are becoming akin to the adventuresses we read of, the pretty, luxurious women who live by their wits."

"Silence!" commanded Mrs. Evringham, her eyes flashing and her effective black-clothed figure drawn up.

Eloise sighed again. "I didn't expect to accomplish anything by this talk," she said, relapsing into listlessness.

"What did you expect then? Merely to be disagreeable? I hope you may be as successful in worthier undertakings. Now listen. Some of the plans you have suggested at various times might be sensible if you were a plain girl. Your beauty is as tangible an asset as money would be; but beauty requires money. You must have it. Your poor father might have left it to you, but he didn't; so you will marry it—not unsuitably," meeting an ominous look in her child's eyes, "not without love or under any circumstances to make a martyr of you, but according to common sense; and as a certain young man is evidently more and more certain of himself every time he comes"—she paused.

"You think there is no need for him to grow more certain of me?" asked Eloise.

"You might have saved us the disagreeables of this interview. And one thing more," impressively, "you evidently are not taking into consideration, perhaps you never knew, that it was your grandfather's confidence in a certain course which induced your poor father to take that last fatal flyer. Your grandfather feels—I'm sure he feels—that much reparation is due us. The present conditions are easier for him than a separate suitable home would be, therefore"—Mrs. Evringham waved her hand. "It is strange," she added, "that so young a girl should not repose more trust in her mother's judgment. And now that we are on the subject, I wish you would make more effort with your grandfather. Don't be so silent at table and leave all the talking to me. A man of his age likes to have merry young people about. Chat, create a cheerful atmosphere. He likes to look at you, of course, but you have been so quiet and lackadaisical of late, it is enough to hurt his feelings as host."

"He has never shown any symptoms of anxiety," remarked Eloise.

"Well, he is a very self-contained man."

"He is indeed, poor grandfather; I don't know how you will manage, mother, when you have to play the game of 'pretend' all alone. He is growing tired of it, I can see. His courtesy is wearing very thin. I'm sorry to make it harder for you by taking away what must have been a large prop and support, but I heard papa say to himself more than once in those last sad days, 'If I had only taken my father's advice.'"

"Eloise," very earnestly, "you misunderstood, you certainly misunderstood."

The girl shook her head wearily. "No, alas! I neither misunderstand nor forget, when it would be most convenient to do so."

Mrs. Evringham's fair brow contracted as she regarded her daughter with exasperation. "And you are only nineteen! One would think it was you instead of me to whom the next birthday would bring that detested forty."

The girl looked at her mother, whose youthful face and figure betrayed the source of her own heritage of physical charm.

"I long ago gave up the hope of ever again being as young as you are," she returned sadly. "Oh!" with a rare and piteous burst of feeling, "if dear papa could have stayed with us, and we could have had a right somewhere!"

Mrs. Evringham threw her arms about the young creature, welcoming the softened mood. "You know I took you right to my own people, Eloise," she said gently. "We stayed as long as I thought was right; they couldn't afford to keep us." A sound at the door caused her to turn. The erect form of her father-in-law had just entered the room.

"Ah, good evening, father," she said in tones whose sadness was not altogether feigned, even though she secretly rejoiced that Eloise should for once show such opportune emotion. "Pardon this little girl. She was just feeling overwhelmed with a pang of homesickness for her father."

"Indeed!" returned Mr. Evringham. "Will you walk out? Mrs. Forbes tells me that dinner is served."

Eloise, hastily drawing her handkerchief across her eyes, passed the unbending figure, her cheeks stinging. His hard voice was in her ears.

That she was not his son's child hurt her now as often before in the past two months, but that he should have discovered her weeping at a moment when he might have been expected to enter was a keen hurt to her pride, and her heart swelled with a suspicion of his unspoken thoughts. She had never been effusive, she had never posed. He had no right to suspect her.

With her small head carried high and her cheeks glowing, she passed him, following her mother, who floated on before with much satisfaction. These opportune tears shed by her nonconforming child should make their stay good for another two months at least.

"You must have had a beautiful ride, father," said Mrs. Evringham as they seated themselves at table. She spoke in the tone, at once assured and ingratiating, which she always adopted toward him. "I noticed you took an earlier start than usual."

The speaker had never had the insight to discover that her father-in-law was ungrateful for proofs that any of his long-fixed, solitary habits were now observed by feminine eyes.

"I did take a rather longer ride than usual," he returned. "Mrs. Forbes, I wish you would speak to the cook about the soup. It has been served cool for the last two days."

Mrs. Forbes flushed as she stood near his chair in her trim black gown and white apron.

"Yes, sir," she replied, the flush and quiet words giving little indication of the tumult aroused within her by her employer's criticism. To fail to please Mr. Evringham at his meals was the deepest mortification life held for her.

"I'm sure it tastes very good," said Mrs. Evringham amiably, "although I like a little more salt than your cook uses."

"You can reach it I hope," remarked the host, casting a glance at the dainty solitaire salt and pepper beside his daughter's plate.

"But don't you like it cooked in?" she asked sweetly.

"Not when I want to get it out," he answered shortly.

"How can mother, how can mother!" thought Eloise helplessly.

"There is decided spring in the air to-day," said Mrs. Evringham. "I remember of old how charmingly spring comes in the park."

"You have a good memory," returned Mr. Evringham dryly.

"Why do you say that?" asked the pretty widow, lifting large, innocent eyes.

"It is some years since you accompanied Lawrence in his calls upon me, I believe."

"Poor father!" thought Mrs. Evringham, "how unpleasantly blunt he has grown, living here alone!"

"I scarcely realize it," she returned suavely. "My recollection of the park is always so clear. It is surprising, isn't it, how relatives can live as near together as we in New York and you out here and see one another so seldom! Life in New York," sighing, "was such a rush for us. Here amid the rustle of the trees it seems to be scarcely the same world. Lawrence often said his only lucid intervals were during the rides he took with Eloise in Central Park. Do you always ride alone, father?"

"Always," was the prompt rejoinder, while Eloise cast a glance full of appeal at her mother.

The latter continued archly, "If you could see Eloise on a horse you would not blame me for trying to screw up my courage, as I have been doing for days past, to ask you if she might take a canter on Essex Maid in the morning, sometimes, while you are away. Fanshaw assured me that she would be perfectly safe."

Mr. Evringham's cold eyes stared, and then the enormity of the proposition appeared to move him humorously.

"Which maid did Fanshaw say would be safe?" he inquired, while Eloise glowed with mortification.

"Well, if you think Eloise can't ride, try her some time!" exclaimed the widow gayly. It had been a matter of surprise and afterward of resentment that Mr. Evringham could remain deaf to her hints so long, and she had determined to become frank. "Or else ask Dr. Ballard," she went on; "he has very kindly provided Eloise with a horse several times, but the child likes a solitary ride, sometimes, as well as you do."

The steely look returned to the host's eyes. "No one rides the Maid but myself," he returned coldly.

"I beg you to believe, grandfather, that I don't wish to ride her," said Eloise, her customary languor of manner gone and her voice hard. "Mother is more ambitious for me than I am for myself. I should be very much obliged if she would allow me to ask favors when I want them."

Mrs. Forbes's lips were set in a tight line as she filled Mrs. Evringham's glass.

That lady's heart was beating a little fast from vexation, and also from the knowledge that a time of reckoning with her child was coming.

"Oh, very well," she said airily. "No wonder you are careful of that beautiful creature. I caught Eloise with her arms around the mare's neck the other day, and I couldn't help wishing for a kodak. You feed her with sugar, don't you Eloise?"

"I hope not, I'm sure!" exclaimed Mr. Evringham sternly.

"I'll not do it again, grandfather," said the girl, her very ears burning.

Mrs. Evringham sighed and gave one Parthian shot. "The poor child does love horses so," she murmured softly.

The host scowled and fidgeted in his chair with a brusque gesture to Mrs. Forbes to remove the course.

"Harry has turned up again," he remarked, to change the subject.

"Really?" returned his daughter-in-law languidly. "For how long I wonder?"

"He thinks it is permanent."

"He is still in Chicago?"

"Yes, for a day or two. He and his wife sail for Europe immediately."

"Indeed!" with a greater show of interest. Then, curiously, "Are you sending them, father?"

"Scarcely! They are going on business."

"Oh," relapsing into indifference. "They have a child, I believe."

"Yes, a girl. I should think perhaps you might have remembered it."

"I hardly see why, if Harry didn't—a fact he plainly showed by deserting the poor creature." The insolence of the speaker's tone was scarcely veiled. Her extreme disapproval of her father-in-law sometimes welled to the surface of her suave manner.

Mr. Evringham's thoughts had fled to Chicago. "Harry proposed leaving the girl here while they are gone," he said.

Mrs. Evringham straightened in her chair and her attention concentrated. "With you? What assurance! How like Harry!" she exclaimed.

The words were precisely those which her host had been saying to himself; but proceeding from her lips they had a strange effect upon him.

"You find it so?" he asked. The clearer the proposition became to Mrs. Evringham's consciousness the more she resented it. To have the child in the house not only would menace her ease and comfort, but meant a possibility that the grandfather might take an interest in Harry's daughter which would disturb Eloise's chances.

"Of course it does. I call it simply presumptuous," she declared with emphasis.

"After all, Harry has some rights," rejoined Mr. Evringham slowly.

"His wife is a dressmaker," went on the other. "I had it directly from a Chicago friend. Harry has scarcely been with the child since she was born. And to saddle a little stranger like that on you! Now Eloise and *her* father were inseparable."

There was an ominous glitter in Mr. Evringham's eyes. "Eloise's father!" he returned slowly. "I did not know that she remembered him."

The hurt of his tone and words sank deep into the heart of the girl, but she looked up courageously.

"Your son was my father in every best sense," she said. "We were inseparable. You must have known it."

"You appeared to be separable when your father made his visits to Bel-Air Park," was the rejoinder. "Pardon me if I knew very little of what took place in his household. A telegraph blank, please, Mrs. Forbes, and tell Zeke to be ready to go to the office."

There was a vital tone in the usually dry voice. Mrs. Evringham looked apprehensively at her daughter; but Eloise gave her no answering glance; her eyes were downcast and her pretense of eating continued, while her pulses beat.

CHAPTER IV
FATHER AND SON

When later they were alone, the girl looked at her mother, her eyes luminous.

"You see," she began rather breathlessly, "even you must see, he is beginning to drive us away."

"I do hope, Eloise, you are not going to indulge in any heroics over this affair," returned Mrs. Evringham, who had braced herself to meet an attack. "Does the unpleasant creature suppose we would stay with him if we were not obliged to?"

"If we are obliged to, which I don't admit, need you demand further favors than food and shelter? How could you speak of Essex Maid! How can you know in your inmost heart, as you do, that we are eating the bread of charity, and then ask for the apple of his eye!" exclaimed Eloise desperately.

"Go away with your bread and apples," responded Mrs. Evringham flippantly. "I have a real worry now that that wretched little cousin of yours is coming."

"She is not my cousin please remember," responded the girl bitterly. "Mr. Evringham reminded us of that to-night."

"Now don't you begin calling him Mr. Evringham!" protested her mother. "You don't want to take any notice of the man's absurdities. You will only make matters worse."

"No, I shall go on saying grandfather for the little while we stay. Otherwise, he would know his words were rankling. It *will* be a little while? Oh mother!"

Mrs. Evringham pushed the pleading hand away. "I can't tell how long it will be!" she returned impatiently. "We are simply helpless until your father's affairs are settled. I thought I had told you that, Eloise. He worshipped you, child, and no matter what that old curmudgeon says, Lawrence would wish us to remain under his protection until we see our way clear."

"Won't you have a business talk with him, so we can know what we have to look forward to?" The girl's voice was unsteady.

"I will when the right time comes, Eloise. Can't you trust your mother? Isn't it enough that we have lost our home, our carriages, all our comforts and luxuries, through this man's bad judgment—"

"You will cling to that!" despairingly.

"And have had to come out to this Sleepy Hollow of a place, where life means mere existence, and be so poor that the carfare into New York is actually a consideration! I'm quite satisfied with our martyrdom as it is, without pinching and grinding as we should have to do to live elsewhere."

"Then you don't mean to attempt to escape?" returned Eloise in alarm.

"Hush, hush, Goosie. We will escape all in good time if we don't succeed in taming the bear. As it is, I have to work single handed," dropping into a tone of reproach. "You are no help at all. You might as well be a simpering wax dummy out of a shop window. I would have been ashamed at your age if I could not have subjugated any man alive. We might have had him at our feet weeks ago if you had made an effort."

"No, no, mother," sadly. "I saw when we first came how effusiveness impressed him, and I tried to behave so as to strike a balance—that is, after I found that we were here on sufferance and not as welcome guests."

"Pshaw! You can't tell what such a hermit is thinking," returned Mrs. Evringham. "It is the best thing that could happen to him to have us here. Dr. Ballard said so only to-day. What is troubling me now is this child of Harry's. I was sure by father's tone when he first spoke of her that he would not even consider such an imposition."

"I think he did feel so," returned Eloise, her manner quiet again. "That was an example of the way you overreach yourself. The word presumption on your lips applied to uncle Harry determined grandfather to let the child come."

"You think he really has sent for her then!" exclaimed Mrs. Evringham. "You think that is what the telegram meant! I'm sure of it, too." Then after a minute's exasperated thought, "I believe you are right. He is just contrary enough for that. If I had urged him to let the little barbarian come, he couldn't have been induced to do so. That wasn't clever of me!" The speaker made the admission in a tone which implied that in general her cleverness was unquestioned. "Well, I hope she will worry him out of his senses, and I don't think there is much doubt of it. It may turn out all for the best, Eloise, after all, and lead him to appreciate us." Mrs. Evringham cast a glance at the mirror and patted her waved hair. "And yet I'm anxious, very anxious. He might take a fancy to the girl," she added thoughtfully.

"I'm such a poor-spirited creature," remarked Eloise.

"What now?"

"I ought to be strong enough to leave you since you will not come; to leave this roof and earn my own living, some way, any way; but I'm too much of a coward."

"I should hope so," returned her mother briefly. "You'd soon become one if you weren't at starting. Girls bred to luxury, as you have been, must just contrive to live well somehow. They can't stand anything else."

"Nonsense, mother," quietly. "They can. They do."

"Yes, in books I know they do."

"No, truth is stranger than fiction. They do. I have been looking for that sort of stamina in myself for weeks, but I haven't found it. It is a cruel wrong to a girl not to teach her to support herself."

"My dear! You were going to college. You know you would have gone had it not been for your poor father's misfortunes."

Eloise's eyes filled again at the remembrance of the young, gay man who had been her boon companion since her babyhood, and at the memory of those last sad days, when she knew he had agonized over her future even more than over that of his volatile wife.

"My dear, as I've told you before, a girl as pretty as you are should know that fortune cannot be unkind, nor the sea of life too rough. In each of the near waves of it you can see a man's head swimming toward you. You don't know the trouble I have had already in silencing those who wished to speak before you were old enough. They could any of them be summoned now with a word. Let me see. There is Mr. Derwent—Mr. Follansbee—Mr. Weeks—"

"Hush, mother!" ejaculated the girl in disgust.

"Exactly. I knew you would say they were too old, or too bald, or too short, or too fat. I've been a girl myself. Of course there is Nat Bonnell, and a lot more little waves and ripples like him, but they always *were* out of the question, and now they are ten times more so. That is the reason, Eloise," the mother's voice became impressive to the verge of solemnity, "why I feel that Dr. Ballard is almost a providence."

The girl's clear eyes were reflective. "Nat Bonnell is a wave who wouldn't remember a girl who had slipped out of the swim."

"Very wise of him," returned Mrs. Evringham emphatically. "He can't afford to. Nat is—is—a—decorative creature, just as you are,—decorative. He must make it pay, poor boy."

Meanwhile Mrs. Forbes had sought her son in the barn. He and she had had their supper in time for her to be ready to wait at dinner.

"Something doing, something doing," murmured Zeke as he heard the impetuosity of her approaching step.

"That soup *was* hot!" she exclaimed defiantly.

"Somebody scald you, ma? I can do him up, whoever he is," said Zeke, catching up a whip and executing a threatening dance around the dimly lighted barn.

His mother's snapping eyes looked beyond him. "He said it was cold; but it was only because he was distracted. What do you suppose those people are up to now? Trying to get Essex Maid for Mamzell to ride!"

Zeke stopped in his mad career and returned his mother's stare for a silent moment. "And not a dungeon on the place probably!" he exclaimed at last. "Just like some folks' shiftlessness."

"They *asked* it. They asked Mr. Evringham if that girl couldn't ride Essex Maid while he was in the city!"

'Zekiel lifted his eyebrows politely. "Where are their remains to be interred?" he inquired with concern.

"Well, not in *this* family vault, you may be sure. He gave it to them to-night for a fact." Mrs. Forbes smiled triumphantly. "'I didn't know Eloise remembered her father,'" she mimicked. "'I'll bet that got under their skin!"

"Dear parent, you're excited," remarked Zeke.

She brought her reminiscent gaze back to rest upon her son. "Get your coat quick, 'Zekiel. Here's the telegram. Take the car that passes the park gate, and stop at the station. That's the nearest place."

Ezekiel obediently struggled into the coat hanging conveniently near. "What does the telegram say?—'Run away, little girl, the ogre isn't hungry'?"

"Not much! She's coming. He's sending for the brat."

"Poor brat! How did it happen?"

"Just some more of my lady's doings," answered Mrs. Forbes angrily. "Of course she had to put in her oar and exasperate Mr. Evringham until he did it to spite her."

"Cutting off his own nose to spite his face, eh?" asked Zeke, taking the slip of paper.

"Yes, and mine. It's going to come heavy on me. I could have shaken that woman with her airs and graces. Catch her or Mamzell lifting *their* hands!"

"Yet they want her, do they?"

"No, Stupid! That's why she's coming. Can't you understand?"

"Blessed if I can," returned the boy as he left the barn; "but I know one thing, I pity the kid."

Mr. Evringham received a prompt answer to his message. His son appointed, as a place of meeting, the downtown hotel where he and his wife purposed spending the night before sailing.

Father and son had not met for years, and Mr. Evringham debated a few minutes whether to take the gastronomic and social risk of dining with Harry *en famille* at the noisy hotel above mentioned, or to have dinner in assured comfort at his club—finally deciding on the latter course.

It was, therefore, nearly nine o'clock before his card was presented to Mr. and Mrs. Harry, to whom it brought considerable relief of mind, and they hastened down to the dingy parlor with alacrity.

"You see we thought you might accept our invitation to dinner," said Harry heartily, as he grasped his parent's passive hand; "but your business hours are so short, I dare say you have been at home since the middle of the afternoon." As he spoke the hard lines of his father's impassive face smote him with a thousand associations, many of them bringing remorse. He wondered how much his own conduct had had to do with graving them so deeply.

His wife's observant eyes were scanning this guardian of her child from the crown of his immaculate head to the toes of his correct patent leathers. His expressionless eyes turned to her. "This is your wife?" he asked, again offering the passive hand.

"Yes, father, this is Julia," responded Harry proudly. "I'm sorry the time is so short. I do want you to know her."

The young man's face grew eloquent.

"That is a pleasure to come," responded Mr. Evringham mechanically. He turned stiffly and cast a glance about. "You brought your daughter, I presume?"

"Yes, indeed," answered Mrs. Evringham. "Harry was so glad to receive your permission. We had made arrangements for her provisionally with friends in Chicago, but we were desirous that she should have this opportunity to see her father's home and know you."

Mr. Evringham thought with regret of those friends in Chicago. Many times in the last two days he had deeply repented allowing himself to be exasperated into thus committing himself.

"Do sit down, father," said Harry, as his wife seated herself in the nearest chair.

Mr. Evringham hesitated before complying. "Well," he said perfunctorily, "you have gone into something that promises well, eh Harry?"

"It looks that way. I'm chiefly occupied these days in being thankful." The young man smiled with an extraordinary sweetness of expression, which transfigured his face, and which his father remembered well as always promising much and performing nothing. "I might spend a lot of time crying over spilt milk, but Julia says I mustn't," —he glanced across at his wife, whose dark eyes smiled back, — "and what Julia says goes. I intend to spend a year or two doing instead of talking."

"It will answer better," remarked his father.

"Yes, sir," Harry's voice grew still more earnest. "And by that time, perhaps, I can express my regret to you, for things done and things left undone, with more convincingness."

The older man made a slight gesture of rejection with one well-kept hand. "Let bygones be bygones," he returned briefly.

"When I think," pursued Harry, his impulsive manner in strange contrast to that of his listener, "that if I had been behaving myself all this time, I might have seen dear old Lawrence again!"

Mr. Evringham kept silence.

"How are Madge and Eloise? I thought perhaps Madge might come in and meet us at the train."

"They are in the best of health, thank you. Eh—a—I think if you'll call your daughter now we will go. It's rather a long ride, you know. No express trains at this hour. When you return we will have more of a visit."

Harry and his wife exchanged a glance. "Why Jewel is asleep," answered the young man after a pause. "She was so sleepy she couldn't hold her eyes open."

"You mean you've let her go to bed?" asked Mr. Evringham, with a not very successful attempt to veil his surprise and annoyance.

"Why—yes. We supposed she would see us off, you know."

"Your memory is rather short, it strikes me," returned his father. "You sail at eight A.M., I believe. Did you think I could get in from Bel-Air at that hour?"

"No. I thought you would naturally remain in the city over night. You used to stay in rather frequently, didn't you?"

"I've not done so for five years; but you couldn't know that. Is it out of the question to dress the child again? I hope she is too healthy to be disturbed by a trifle like that."

Mrs. Evringham cast a startled look at her father-in-law. "It would disappoint Jewel very much not to see us off," she returned.

Mr. Evringham shrugged his shoulders. "Let it go then. Let it go," he said quickly.

Harry's plain face had grown concerned. "Is Mrs. Forbes with you still?" he asked.

"Oh, yes. I couldn't keep house without Mrs. Forbes. Well," rising, "if you young people will excuse me, I believe I will go to the club and turn in."

"Couldn't you stand it here one night, do you think?" asked Harry, rising. "The club is rather far uptown for such an early start."

"No. I'll be on hand. I'm used to rising early for a canter. I'll take it with a cab horse this time. That will be all the difference." And with this attempt at jocularity, Mr. Evringham shook hands once more and departed, swallowing his ill-humor as best he could. Any instincts of the family man which might once have reigned in him had long since been inhibited. This episode was a cruel invasion upon his bachelor habits.

Left alone, Harry and his wife without a word ascended to their room and with one accord approached the little bed in the corner where their child lay asleep.

The man took his wife's hand. "I've done it now, Julia," he said dejectedly. "It's my confounded optimism again."

"Your optimism is all right," she returned, smoothing his hand gently, though her heart was beating fast, and the vision of her father-in-law, with his elegant figure and cold eyes, was weighing upon her spirit.

Harry looked long on the plain little sleeping face, so like his own in spite of its exquisite child-coloring, and bending, touched the tossed, straight, flaxen hair.

"We couldn't take her, I suppose?" he asked.

"No," replied the yearning mother quietly. "We have prayed over it. We must know that all will be right."

"His bark is worse than his bite," said Harry doubtfully. "It always was; and Mrs. Forbes is there."

"You say she is a kind sort of woman?"

"Why, I suppose so," uncertainly. "I never had much to do with her."

"And your sister? Isn't it very strange that she didn't come in to meet us? I was so certain I should put Jewel into her hands I feel a little bewildered."

"You're a trump!" ejaculated Harry hotly, "and you've married into a family where they're scarce. Madge might have met us at the train, at least."

"Perhaps she is very sad over her loss," suggested Julia.

"In the best of health. Father said so. Oh well, she never was anything but a big butterfly and Eloise a little one. I remember the last time I saw the child, a pretty fairy with her long pink silk stockings. She must have been just about the age of Jewel."

The mother stooped over the little bed and the dingy room looked pleasanter for her smile. "Jewel hasn't any pink silk stockings," she murmured, and kissed the warm rose of the round cheek.

The little girl stirred and opened her eyes, at first vaguely, then with a start.

"Is it time for the boat?" she asked, trying to rise.

Her father smoothed her hair. "No, time to go to sleep again. We're just going to bed. Good-night, Jewel." He stooped to kiss her, and her arms met around his neck.

"It was an April fool, wasn't it?" she murmured sleepily, and was unconscious again.

The mother hid her face for a moment on her husband's shoulder. "Help me to feel that we're doing right," she whispered, with a catch in her breath.

"As if I could help *you*, Julia!" he returned humbly.

"Oh, yes, you can, dear." She withdrew from his embrace, and going to the dresser, took down her hair. The smiling face of a doll looked up at her from the neighboring chair, where it was sitting bolt upright. Her costume was fresh from the modiste, and her feet, though hopelessly pigeon-toed, were encased in bronze boots of a freshness which caught the dim gaslight with a golden sheen.

Mrs. Evringham smiled through her moist eyes.

"Well, Jewel *was* sleepy. She forgot to undress Anna Belle," she said.

Letting her hair fall about her like a veil, she caught up the doll and pressed it to her heart impulsively. "You are going to stay with her, Anna Belle! I envy you, I envy you!" she whispered. An irrepressible tear fell on the sumptuous trimming of the little hat. "Be good to her; comfort her, comfort her, little dolly." Hastily wiping her eyes, she turned to her husband, still holding the doll. "We shall have to be very careful, Harry, in the morning. If we are harboring one wrong or fearful thought, we must not let Jewel know it."

"Oh, I wish it were over! I wish the next month were over!" he replied restively.

CHAPTER V
BON VOYAGE

At the dock next morning the scene was one of the usual confusion. The sailing time was drawing near and Mr. Evringham had not appeared.

Harry, with his little girl's hand in his, stood at the foot of the gang plank, peering at every newcomer and growing more anxious every moment. Jewel occupied herself in throwing kisses to her mother, who stood at the rail far above, never taking her eyes from the little figure in the blue sailor suit.

The child noted her father's set lips and the concentrated expression of his eyes.

"If grandpa doesn't come what shall I do?" she asked without anxiety.

"You'll go to England," was the prompt response.

"Without my trunk!" returned the child in protest.

Her father looked again at the watch he held in his hand. The order to go ashore was sending all visitors down the gang plank. "By George, I guess you're going, too," he muttered between his teeth, when suddenly his father's tall form came striding through the crowd. Mr. Evringham was carrying a long pasteboard box, and seemed breathless.

"Horse fell down. Devil of a time! Roses for your wife."

Harry grasped the box, touched his father's hand, kissed the child, and strode up the plank amid the frowns of officials.

Jewel's eager eyes followed him, then, as he disappeared, lifted again to her mother, who smiled and waved her hand to Mr. Evringham. The latter raised his hat and took the occasion to wipe his heated brow. He was irritated through and through. The morning had been a chapter of accidents. Even the roses, which he had ordered the night before, had proved to be the wrong sort.

The suspense of the last fifteen minutes had been a distressing wrong to put upon any man. He had now before him the prospect of caring for a strange child, of taking her out of town at an hour when he should have been coming into it. She would probably cry. Very well; if she did he determined on the instant to ride out to Bel-Air in the smoking car, although he detested its odors and uncleanness. The whole situation was enormous. What a fool he had been, and what an intelligent woman was Mrs. Forbes! She had seen from the first the inappropriateness, the impossibility, of the whole proposition. His attention was attracted to the fact that the small figure at his side was hopping up and down with excitement.

"There's father, there's father!" she cried, as Harry joined his wife at the rail and they lifted the wealth of roses from the box and waved them.

"We've wronged him, Harry!" exclaimed Julia, trying to see the little face below through her misty eyes. "How I love him for bringing me these sweet things! It gives me such a different feeling about him."

"Oh, father would as soon forget his breakfast as roses for a woman he was seeing off," returned Harry without enthusiasm, while he waved his hat energetically.

The steamer pulled out. The faces in the crowd mingled and changed places.

"I've lost them, I've lost them!" cried Julia. "Oh, where are they, Harry."

"Over there near the corner. I can see father. It's all right, dear," choking a little. "Jewel was skipping and laughing a minute ago. It will only be a few weeks, but confound it," violently, "next time we'll take her!"

Julia buried her face in the roses, on which twinkled a sudden dew, and tried to gather promise from their sweet breath.

Jewel strained her eyes to follow the now indistinguishable forms on the lofty deck, and her grandfather looked down at the small figure in the sailor suit, the short thick pigtails of flaxen hair tied with large bows of ribbon, and the doll clasped in one arm. At last the child turned her head and looked up, and their eyes met for the first time.

"Jove, she does look like Harry!" muttered Mr. Evringham, and even as he spoke the plain little face was illumined with the smile he knew, that surpassingly sweet smile which promised so much and performed nothing.

The child studied him with open, innocent curiosity.

"I can't believe it's you," she said at last, in a voice light and winning, a voice as sweet as the smile.

"I don't wonder. I don't quite know myself this morning," he replied brusquely.

"We have a picture of you, but it's a long-ago one, and I thought by this time you would be old, and—and bent over, you know, the way grandpas are."

Even in that place of drays and at eight o'clock A.M. these words fell not disagreeably upon irritated ears.

"I think myself Nature did not intend me to be a grandpa," he replied.

"Oh, yes, you're just the right kind," returned the child hastily and confidently. "Strong and—and handsome."

Mr. Evringham looked at her in amazement. "The little rascal!" he thought. "Has she been coached?"

"I suppose we may get away from here now," he said aloud. "There's nothing more to wait for."

"Didn't the roses make mother happy?" asked the little girl, trotting along beside his long strides. "I think it was wonderful for you to bring them so early in the morning."

Mr. Evringham summoned a cab.

"Oh, are we gong in a carriage?" cried Jewel, highly pleased. "But I mustn't forget, grandpa, there's something father told me I must give you the first thing. Will you take Anna Belle a minute, please?" and Mr. Evringham found himself holding the doll fiercely by one leg while small hands worked at the catch of a very new little leather side-bag.

At last Jewel produced a brass square.

"Oh, your trunk check." Mr. Evringham exchanged the doll for it with alacrity. "Get in." He held open the cab door.

Jewel obeyed, but not without some misgivings when her guardian so coolly pocketed the check.

"Yes, it's for my trunk," she replied when her grandfather was beside her and they began rattling over the stones. "I have a checked silk dress," she added softly, after a pause. It were well to let him know the value of her baggage.

"Have you indeed? How old are you, Julia? Your name is Julia, I believe?"

"Yes, sir, my *name's* Julia, but so is mother's, and they call me Jewel. I'm nearly nine, grandpa."

"H'm. Time flies," was the brief response.

Jewel looked out of the cab window in the noisy silence that followed. At last her voice was raised to sound through the clatter. "I suppose my trunk is somewhere else," she said suggestively.

"Yes, your trunk will reach home all right, plaid silk and all."

Jewel smiled, and lifting the doll she let her look out the window upon the uninviting prospect. "Anna Belle's clothes are in the trunk, too," she added, turning and speaking confidentially.

"Whose?" asked Mr. Evringham, startled. "There's no one else coming, I suppose?"

"Why, this is Anna Belle," returned the child, laughing and lifting the bisque beauty so that the full radiance of her smile beamed upon her companion. "That's your great-grandfather, dearie, that I've told you about," she said patronizingly. "We've been so *excited* the last few days since we knew we were coming," looking again at Mr. Evringham. "I've told Anna Belle all about beautiful Bel-Air Park, and the big house, and the big trees, and the ravine, and the brook. Isn't it nice," joyfully, "that it doesn't rain to-day, and we shall see it in the sunshine?"

"Rain would have made it more disagreeable certainly," returned Mr. Evringham, congratulating himself that he was escaping that further rain of tears which he had dreaded. "It is a good day for your father and mother to set out on their trip," he added.

"Yes, and they're only to be gone six little weeks," returned Jewel, smoothing her doll's boa; "and I'm to have this lovely visit, and I'm to write them very often, and they'll write to me, and we shall all be so happy!" Jewel trotted Anna Belle on her short-skirted knee and hummed a tune, which was lost in the rattle of wheels.

"You can read and write, eh?"

"Oh ye—es!" replied the child with amused scorn. "How would I get my lessons if I couldn't read? Of course—big words," she added conscientiously.

"Precisely," agreed Mr. Evringham dryly. "Big words, I dare say."

A sudden thought occurring to his companion, she looked up again.

"You pretty nearly didn't come," she said, "and just think, if you hadn't I was going to England. Father said so."

At the sweet inflections of the child's voice Mr. Evringham's brows contracted with remembrance of his wrongs. "I should have come. Your father might have known that!"

"I suppose he wouldn't have liked to leave me sitting on the dock alone, but I should have known you'd come. The funny part is I shouldn't have known *you*." Jewel laughed. "I should have kept looking for an old man with white hair and a cane like Grandpa Morris. He's a grandpa in Chicago that I know. He's just as kind as he can be, but he has the *queerest* back. He goes to our church, but says he came in at the eleventh hour. I think he used to have rheumatism. And while I was sitting there you could have walked right by me."

"Humph!"

"But then you'd have known *me*," went on Jewel, straightening Anna Belle's hat, "so it would have been all right. You'd have known there would be only one little girl waiting there, and you would have said, 'Oh, here you are, Jewel. I've come. I'm your grandpa.'" The child unconsciously mimicked the short, brusque speech.

Mr. Evringham regarded her rather darkly. "Eh? I hope you're not impudent?"

"What's that?" asked Jewel doubtfully.

Her companion's brow grew darker.

"Impudent I say."

"And what is impudent?"

"Don't you know?" suspiciously.

"No, sir," replied the child, some anxiety clouding her bright look. "Is it error?"

Mr. Evringham regarded her rather blankly. "It's something you mustn't be," he replied at last.

Jewel's face cleared. "Oh no, I won't then," she replied earnestly. "You tell me when I'm—it, because I want to make you happy."

Mr. Evringham cleared his throat. He felt somewhat embarrassed and was glad they had reached the ferry.

"We're going on a boat, aren't we?" she asked when they had passed through the gate.

"Yes, and we can make this boat if we hurry." Mr. Evringham suddenly felt a little hand slide into his. Jewel was skipping along beside him to keep up with his long strides, and he glanced down at the bobbing flaxen head with its large ribbon bows, while the impulse to withdraw his hand was thwarted by the closer clinging of the small fingers.

"Father told me about the ferry," said Jewel with satisfaction, "and you'll show me the statue of Liberty won't you, grandpa? Isn't it a splendid boat? Oh, can we go out close to the water?"

Mr. Evringham sighed heavily. He did not wish to go out close to the water. He wished to sit down in comfort in the cabin and read the paper which he had just taken from a newsboy. It seemed to him a very long time since he had done anything he wished to; but a little hand was pulling eagerly at his, and mechanically he followed out to where the brisk spring wind ruffled the river and assaulted his hat. He jerked his hand from Jewel's to hold it in place.

"Isn't this beautiful!" cried the child joyfully, as the boat steamed on. "Can you do this every day, grandpa?"

"What? Oh yes, yes."

Something in the tone caused the little girl to look up from her view of the wide water spaces to the grim face above.

"Is there something that makes you sorry, grandpa?" she asked softly.

His eyes were fixed on a ferry boat, black with its human freight, about to pass them on its way to the city.

"I was wishing I were on that boat. That's all."

The little girl lifted her shoulders. "I don't believe there's room," she said, looking smilingly for a response from her companion. "I don't believe even Anna Belle could squeeze on. Do you think so?"

Mr. Evringham, holding his hat with one hand, was endeavoring to fetter the lively corners of his newspaper in such shape that he could at least get a glimpse of headlines.

"Oh, I see a statue. Is that it, grandpa? Is that it?"

"What?" vaguely. "Oh yes. The statue of Liberty. Yes, that's it. As if there was any liberty for anybody!" muttered Mr. Evringham into his mustache.

"It isn't so very big," objected Jewel.

"We're not so very near it."

"Just think," gayly, "father and mother are sailing away just the way we are."

"H'm," returned Mr. Evringham, trying to read the report of the stock market, and becoming more impatient each instant with the sportive breeze.

"Julia," he said at last, "I am going into the cabin to read the paper. Will you go in, or do you wish to stay here?"

"May I stay here?"

"Yes," doubtfully, "I suppose so, if you won't climb on the rail, or—or anything."

Jewel laughed in gleeful appreciation of the joke. Her grandfather met her blue eyes unsmilingly and vanished.

"I wish grandpa didn't look so sorry," she thought regretfully. "He is a very important man, grandpa is, and perhaps he has a lot of error to meet and doesn't know how to meet it."

Watching the dancing waves and constantly calling Anna Belle's attention to some point of interest on the water front or a passing craft, she nevertheless pursued a train of thought concerning her important relative, with the result that when the gong sounded for landing, and Mr. Evringham's impassive countenance reappeared, she met him with concern.

"Doesn't it make you sorry to read the morning paper, grandpa?"

"Sometimes. Depends on the record of the Exchange." There was somewhat less of the irritation of a newsless man in the morning in the speaker's tone.

"Mother calls the paper the Daily Saddener," pursued Jewel, again slipping her hand into her grandfather's as a matter of course as they moved slowly off the boat. "I've been thinking that perhaps you're in a hurry to get to business, grandpa."

The child did not quote his words about the ingoing ferry boat lest he should feel regret at having spoken them.

"Well, there's no use in my being in a hurry this morning," he returned.

"I was going to ask, couldn't you show me how to go to Bel-Air, so you wouldn't have to take so much time?"

A gleam of hope came into Mr. Evringham's cold eyes and he looked down on his companion doubtfully.

"We have to go out on the train," he said.

"Yes," returned the child, "but you could put me on it, and every time it stops I would ask somebody if that was Bel-Air."

The prospect this offered was very pleasing to the broker.

"You wouldn't be afraid, eh?"

"Be what?" asked Jewel, looking up at him with a certain reproachful surprise.

"You wouldn't, eh?"

"Why, grandpa!"

"Well, I believe it would do well enough, since you don't mind. Zeke is going to meet this train. I'll tell the conductor to see that you get off at Bel-Air, and when you do, ask for Mr. Evringham's coachman. You'll see Zeke, a light-haired man driving a brown horse in a brougham. He'll take you home to his mother, Mrs. Forbes. She is my housekeeper. Now, do you think you'll understand?"

"It sounds very easy," returned Jewel.

Mr. Evringham's long legs and her short skipping ones lost no time in boarding the train, which they found made up. The relieved man saw the conductor, paid the child's fare, and settled her on the plush seat.

She sat there, contentedly swinging her feet.

"Now I can just catch a boat if I leave you immediately," said Mr. Evringham consulting his watch. "You've only a little more than five minutes to wait before the train starts."

"Then hurry, grandpa, I'm all right."

"Very well. Your fare is paid, and the conductor understands. You might ask somebody, though. Bel-Air, you know. Good-by."

Hastily he strode down the aisle and left the train. Having to pass the window beside which Jewel sat, he glanced up with a half uneasy memory of how far short of the floor her feet had swung.

She was watching for him. On her lips was the sweet gay smile and— yes, there was no mistake—Anna Belle's countenance was beaming through the glass, and she was wafting kisses to Mr. Evringham from a stiff and chubby hand. The stockbroker grew warm, cleared his throat, lifted his hat, and hurried his pace.

CHAPTER VI
JEWEL'S ARRIVAL

When her grandfather had disappeared, Jewel placed Anna Belle on the seat beside her, where she toed in, in a state of the utmost complacence.

"I have my work to do, Anna Belle," she said, "and this will be a good time, so don't disturb me till the train starts." She put her hand over her eyes, and sat motionless as the people met and jostled in the aisle.

Minutes passed, and then some one brushed the child's arm in taking the seat beside her. "Oh, please don't sit on Anna Belle!" she cried suddenly, and looked up into a pair of clear eyes that were regarding her with curiosity.

They belonged to a man with a brown mustache and dark, short, pointed beard, who carried a small square black case and had altogether a very clean, fresh, agreeable appearance.

"Do I look like a person who would sit on Anna Belle?" he asked gravely.

The doll was enthroned upon his knee as he set down his case, and the train started.

"If she annoys you I'll take her," said Jewel, with a little air of motherliness not lost upon her companion.

"Thank you," he replied, "but I'm used to children. She looks like a fine, healthy little girl," keeping his eyes fixed on the doll's rosy cheeks.

"Yes indeed. She's very healthy."

"Not had measles, or chicken pox, or mumps, or any of those things yet?" pursued the pleasant voice.

"Oh dear!" gasped Jewel. "Please let me take Anna Belle." She caught her doll into her arms and met her companion's surprised gaze.

"I haven't any of them," he returned, amused. "Don't be afraid."

"I'm not afraid," answered the child promptly. "There is nothing to be afraid of."

"I was only going to say," said the young man, "that if she was ailing I could prescribe for her. I have my case right here."

Jewel's startled look fell to the black case. "What's that! Medicine?" she asked softly.

"It certainly is. So you see you have a doctor handy if anything ails the baby."

The child gazed at him with grave scrutiny. "Do you believe in materia medica?" she asked.

The young doctor threw back his head and laughed heartily. "Well, yes," he answered at last. "I am supposed to."

To his surprise his neighbor returned to the attitude in which he had found her, with one hand over her eyes.

He ceased laughing and looked at her in some discomfiture. Her mouth was set seriously. There was no quiver of the rosy lips.

To his relief, in a minute she dropped her hand and began to hum and arrange her doll's hat.

The conductor approached, and as the doctor presented his ticket, he said, "This little girl's fare is paid, I believe." The conductor nodded and passed on.

"I'm to get off at Bel-Air," said Jewel. "I hope he doesn't forget."

"If he does, I shan't," said the doctor, "for I'm going to get off there myself."

The child's eyes brightened. "Isn't that nice!" she returned. Then she lifted Anna Belle and whispered something into her ear.

"No secrets," said the doctor.

"I was just reminding Anna belle how we are always taken care of," returned Jewel.

The young man regarded her with increasing interest and curiosity.

"Don't you wonder how I knew that your fare was paid?" he asked.

"How did you?"

"I met Mr. Evringham hurrying through the station. He said his granddaughter was on this train and asked me to look out for a little girl with a doll."

"Oh," returned the child, pleased, "then you know grandpa."

"I've known him ever since I was no bigger than you are. But even then," added the doctor mentally, "I hadn't supposed him capable of sending this baby out from the city alone."

Jewel watched the kind eyes attentively. "So you see," he went on, "all I had to do was to look for Anna Belle."

"And you nearly sat on her," declared the child.

"I deny it," returned the doctor gravely. "I deny it. You weren't looking. For one second I was afraid you were crying."

"Crying! What would I be crying for, coming to have a lovely visit at grandpa's!"

"I suppose you are in a hurry to see your aunt and cousin?" remarked the doctor.

"Yes, but I don't know them. You see," explanatorily, "they aren't my real relations."

"Indeed?"

"No, aunt Madge is my uncle's wife and cousin Eloise is her little girl, but not uncle Lawrence's."

The doctor thought a minute.

"Really? She is a very charming little girl, is your cousin Eloise. Aren't you going to tell me your name?"

"My name is Jewel."

"And I am Dr. Ballard, so now we are properly introduced." He smiled upon her with merry eyes, and she responded politely:—

"I'm very glad you found us."

Arrived at Bel-Air, the doctor picked up his case and Jewel followed him from the train. He looked about expectantly for Mrs. Evringham or her daughter. They were not there.

The little girl's quick eyes discerned a light-haired driver and a brown horse coming around a curve of the pretty landscape gardening which beautified the station. At the same moment Dr. Ballard recognized the equipage with relief.

"They've sent for you. That is all right," he said, and 'Zekiel, with one side glance at the little stranger, drew up by the platform.

"Good-morning, Zeke. Here is your passenger." He lifted Jewel to her place beside the driver, whose smooth, stolid face did not change expression.

"Do I wait for Mr. Evringham?" he asked, without turning his head in its stiff collar.

"No, Mr. Evringham remained in town."

"Is there a trunk?" pursued Zeke immovably.

"How about your trunk, little one?" asked the doctor.

Jewel produced a paper check. "A man gave grandpa this for it at the boat place."

"I'll see to having it sent up then." The doctor looked along the platform. "It didn't come this trip." He took the child's hand in his. "I shall see you again before long. Good-by."

Jewel looked after his retreating figure with some regret. Her present companion seemed carved out of wood. His plum-colored livery fitted without a wrinkle. His smooth, solemn face appeared incapable of speech.

The swift horse trotted through the village street at a great pace, and the visitor enjoyed the novel experience so intensely that she could not forbear stealing a look up at the driver's face.

He caught it. "Ain't afraid, are you?" he asked.

She looked doubtful. "Is it error for the horse to go so fast?" she returned.

"Error?" 'Zekiel regarded the child curiously. "Well, I guess it's considered one o' the biggest virtues a horse can have."

"Then why did you ask me if I was afraid? You're the third person who's asked me that this morning," returned Jewel, with wondering inflections in her soft voice. "Are New York people afraid of things?"

"Well, not so's you'd notice it as a rule," returned Zeke. "I'm glad if she ain't one o' the scared kind," he pursued, as if to himself.

"Oh, this is splendid," declared Jewel, relieved by her companion's smile; "I don't know as Anna Belle ever had such a good ride. See the trees, dearie! How the leaves are coming out! They aren't nearly so far out in Chicago; but oh," as the horse turned, "there's a big storm coming! What a black cloud! We're just in time."

"I don't see any cloud," said Zeke, staring about.

"Why, right there in front of us," excitedly, pointing at the long opaque mass against the sky.

"That? Why, that's hills." Zeke laughed. "The mountain they call it here. Pretty sickly mountain we'd think it was up Berkshire way."

"Oh, it's a mountain, Anna Belle," joyfully, "we're really seeing a mountain!"

"No you ain't," remarked Zeke emphatically. "Not by a large majority. Guess Chicago's some flat, ain't it?"

"We don't have hills, no. So now we're going to see grandpa's park, and the ravine, and the brook, and—and everything!"

Zeke stole a furtive look at the owner of the joyous voice. The voluminous ribbon bows behind her ears were mostly in evidence, as she bent her face over her doll in congratulation.

"Left Mr. Evringham in town, did you?" he asked.

"Yes, he was busy, and in a hurry to get to his office. Grandpa's such an important man."

"Is he?" asked Zeke.

"Why ye—es! Didn't you know it?"

"I surmised something of the kind. So Dr. Ballard looked after you."

"Yes,—and I do hope my trunk will come."

Jewel looked wistfully at the driver. In spite of his stiff and elegant appearance he had been surprisingly affable. "I have a checked silk dress," she added modestly.

"You don't say so!" ejaculated Zeke, wholly won by the smile bent upon him. "Well, now, if that trunk don't show up by noon, I'll have to do something about it."

"Oh, thank you!" exclaimed the child.

They now sped through the gates of the park and by the porter's lodge, and began the ascent of a winding road. Handsome residences were set among the fine trees, and at sight of each one Jewel looked expectant and eager.

"I expect mother'll be kind of looking out for us," continued Zeke. "Poor kid!" he added mentally.

"Grandpa said something about your mother."

"His housekeeper, Mrs. Forbes."

"Oh yes, of course I know about Mrs. Forbes," returned Jewel hastily and politely. "He told me your name too," she added suggestively.

"Yes, I'm Zeke. And you just remember," emphatically, "that I come when I'm called. Will you?"

"Yes," replied the child, laughing a little. "Do you know my name?"

"It's Julia, isn't it?"

"Yes, but if you called me by it perhaps I shouldn't come, for I'm used to the name of Jewel."

"Pretty name, all right," returned Zeke sententiously. "Now you can see your grandpa's house. The one with the long porch."

Jewel jumped up and down a little in the seat and held Anna Belle to get a good view. The brown horse trotted with a will, and in a minute more they had passed up the driveway and paused beneath the *porte-cochere*.

Mrs. Forbes threw open the door and stood unsmiling.

"Where is Mr. Evringham?" she asked, addressing her son.

"Stayed in town."

The housekeeper stepped forward and helped down the little girl, who had risen and was looking brightly expectant.

"How do you do, Julia," she said. "Did you come out alone on the cars?"

"No. Dr. Ballard came with me."

"Oh, that was the way of it. Zeke, hitch up the brougham. The ladies are going out to lunch."

"Why didn't they let me know?" grumbled Zeke. "Could have hitched up the brougham just as well in the first place."

"Don't ask *me*," returned his mother acidly. "Where is your bag, Julia? I hope you haven't left it in the train?"

"No, I didn't have any. I used mother's. She knew I'd have my trunk to-night."

"Then come in and I'll show you where your room is."

The child looked eagerly and admiringly from side to side as she followed Mrs. Forbes up two flights of broad shallow stairs and into an apartment which to her eyes seemed luxurious.

"Was this ever my father's room?" she asked.

"Why yes, I believe it was," returned Mrs. Forbes, to whom that circumstance had not before occurred.

"How kind of grandpa to let me have it!" said Jewel, highly pleased.

"He wasn't in it much, your father wasn't. Away at school or some other place mostly. Where's your trunk?"

"It's coming. Zeke said he'd attend to it." Jewel looked up happily. "I have a"—she was intending to communicate to Mrs. Forbes the exciting detail of her wardrobe when the housekeeper interrupted her.

"My son's name is Ezekiel," she said impressively.

"Oh," returned Jewel abashed. "He told me Zeke." She still stood in the middle of the large white room, Anna Belle in her arms, and with the surprised look in her serious face drew upon herself an unflattering mental comment.

"The image of Harry," thought Mrs. Forbes.

"Can I see aunt Madge and cousin Eloise?" asked the child, beginning to feel some awe of the large woman regarding her.

"They're getting ready to go out to lunch. They can't be disturbed now. You can sit here, or walk around until lunch time. You'll know when that is ready, because the gong will sound in the hall. Now when you go downstairs be careful not to touch the tall clock on the landing. That is a very valuable chiming clock, and you mustn't open its doors, for fear you would break something. Then if you go into the parlor you must never play on the piano unless you ask somebody, for fear Mr. Evringham might be trying to take a nap just at that time; then you mustn't go into the barn without permission, for it's dangerous where the horses are, and you might get kicked. If you're tired from your journey you can lie down now till lunch time; but whenever you do lie down, be sure to turn off this white spread, for fear you might soil it. Now I'm very busy, and I shan't see you again till lunch."

Mrs. Forbes departed and Jewel stood for half a minute motionless, feeling rather dazed by a novel sensation of resentment.

"As if we were babies!" she whispered to her doll. "She's the most afraid woman I ever saw, and she looks so *sorry*! She isn't our relation, so no matter, dearie, what she says. This is father's room, and we can think how he used to run around here when he was a little boy."

Tiptoeing to the door, Jewel closed it and began to inspect her new apartment.

The sweet smelling soap on the marble stand, the silver mountings of the faucets, the large fine towels, the empty closet and drawers, all looked inviting. Throughout her examination the little girl kept pausing to listen.

Surely aunt Madge and cousin Eloise would look in before they went out to their engagement. Mother had so often said how nice it was that they were there. Surely they didn't know that she had arrived. That was it, of course; and Mrs. Forbes was so sorry and anxious she would probably forget to tell them.

Some altercation was just then going on in the apartments of those ladies.

"We ought to speak to her before we go," said Mrs. Evringham persuasively. "Father would probably resent it if we didn't."

"I have told you already," returned Eloise, "that I do not intend doing one thing henceforward that grandfather could interpret as being done to please him."

"But that is carrying it ridiculously far, not to greet your cousin, who has come from a journey and is your guest."

"My guest!" returned the girl derisively. "We are hers more likely. I will not go to her. The sooner grandfather sends us away the better."

Mrs. Evringham looked worried.

"This is mania, Eloise!" she returned coaxingly. "Very well, I shall go and speak to the child. She shan't be able to tell her grandfather of any rudeness."

In a few minutes Jewel, sitting by her window, Anna Belle in her lap, heard the *frou-frou* of skirts in the hall, and with a knock at the door, a lady entered. She was arrayed in a thin black gown and wore a large black hat, that was very becoming.

Jewel's admiration went out to her on the instant and she started up.

The lady swept toward her, and bending, a delicate perfume wafted about Jewel as she felt a light touch of lips on her cheek.

"So this is Julia Evringham," said the newcomer.

"And you are aunt Madge," returned the child gladly, clinging to the gloved hand, which endured for a moment, and then firmly disengaged itself.

"Your father and mother got off all right I hope?" went on the airy voice. "I'm always afraid of winds at this season myself, but they may not have them. Your cousin Eloise and I are hurrying away to a luncheon, but we shall see you at dinner. You're very comfortable here? That's right. Good-bye."

She swept away, and the light again faded from Jewel's face as she went slowly back to her seat.

"Aunt Madge is afraid, too," she said to the doll. "We know there won't be winds, don't we, dearie? God will take care of father and mother."

An uncomfortable lump rose towards the child's throat.

Mrs. Evringham followed Eloise into the brougham, smiling.

"It couldn't be better," she announced with much satisfaction as they drove away.

"What?"

"She is plain—oh, plain as possible. Small eyes, large mouth, insignificant nose. She will never get on with father. He never could endure ugliness in a girl or woman. I have heard him say it was unpardonable. If it hadn't been that we were what we are, Eloise, I should never have dreamed of doing as I have done. Now if only some good fairy would open your eyes to see which side your bread is buttered on! You could do marvels with such a foil for contrast."

CHAPTER VII
THE FIRST EVENING

In the excitement of the early morning start, Jewel had eaten little breakfast, but the soft resonance of the Japanese gong, when it sounded in the hall below, found her unready for food.

However, she judged the mellow sound to be her summons and obediently left her seat by the window. As she went down she looked askance at the tall dark clock which, even as she passed, chimed the half hour melodiously. Certainly her important grandfather lived in a wonderful house. She paused to hear the last notes of the bells, but catching sight of the figure of Mrs. Forbes waiting below, she started and moved on.

"That's right. Come along," said the housekeeper. "Mr. Evringham likes everybody to be punctual in his house."

"Oh, has grandpa come home?" inquired Jewel eagerly.

"No, he won't be home for hours yet. Come this way."

The little girl followed to the dining-room, which she thought quite as wonderful as the clock; but her admiration of all she saw was no longer unmixed. Mrs. Forbes seemed to cast a shadow.

One place was laid at the table, one handsome chair was drawn up to it. Jewel longed to call Anna Belle's attention to the glittering array on the sideboard and behind the crystal doors of cabinets, but something withheld her.

She looked questioningly at the housekeeper. "I think I'll draw up another chair for Anna Belle," she said.

Mrs. Forbes had already decided, from small signs of assurance, that this Western child was bold. "Give her an inch, and she'll take an ell," she had said to herself. "I know her sort."

"Do you mean the doll?" she returned. "Put it down anywhere. You must never bring it to the table. Mr. Evringham wouldn't like it."

In silence Jewel seated the doll in the nearest chair against the wall, and as she slid up into her own, a neat maid appeared with a puffy and appetizing omelet.

Mrs. Forbes filled the child's glass with water, and the maid set down the omelet and departed.

Jewel's heart sank while Mrs. Forbes presented the souffle.

"I'm sorry," she began hesitatingly, "I never—I can't"—then she swallowed hard in her desperate plight. "Isn't it pretty?" she said rather breathlessly.

"It's very good," returned the housekeeper briefly, misconstruing the child's hesitation. "Shall I help you?"

"I—could I have a drink of milk? I don't—I don't eat eggs."

"Don't eat eggs?" repeated the housekeeper severely. "I'm sorry you have been allowed to be notional. Children should eat what is set before them. Taste of it."

"I—I couldn't, please." Jewel's face was averted.

Mrs. Forbes touched an electric bell. The maid reappeared. "Remove the omelet, Sarah, and bring Miss Julia a glass of milk."

That was the order, but oh, the tone of it! Jewel's heart beat a little faster as she took some bread and butter and drank the milk, Mrs. Forbes standing by, a portentous, solemn, black-robed figure, awful in its silence.

When the child set down the glass empty, she started to push back her chair.

"Wait," said Mrs. Forbes laconically. She again touched an electric bell. The maid reappeared, removed the bread and milk and served a dainty dessert of preserved peaches, cream, and cake.

"I've really had enough," said Jewel politely.

"Don't you eat peaches and cream, or cake either?" asked Mrs. Forbes accusingly.

"Yes'm," returned the child, and ate them without further ado.

"Your trunk has come," said Mrs. Forbes when at last Jewel slipped down from the table. "I will come up and help you unpack it."

"If only she wouldn't!" thought the child as she lifted Anna Belle, but the housekeeper preceded her up the stairs, breathing rather heavily.

Sure enough, when they reached the white room, there stood the new trunk that had been packed with so much anticipation. The bright black letters on the side, J. E., had power even now to send a little glow of pride through its possessor. She stole a glance at Mrs. Forbes, but, strange as it may appear, the housekeeper gave no evidence of admiration.

"I don't need to trouble you, Mrs. Forbes. I can unpack it," said the child.

"I'm up here now, and anyway, I'd better show you where to keep your things. Where's your key?"

Jewel laid down the doll and opened her leather side-bag, producing the key tied with a little ribbon.

Mrs. Forbes unlocked the trunk, lifted out the tray, and began in a business-like manner to dispose of the small belongings that had last been handled so tenderly.

"Mrs. Harry certainly knows how to pack," ran her thoughts, "and she'd naturally know how to sew. These things are as neat as wax, and the child's well fixed." In the tray, among other things, were a number of doll's clothes, some writing materials, a box of different colored hair ribbons, and a few books.

"Glad to see a Bible," thought Mrs. Forbes. "Shows Mrs. Harry is respectable." She glanced at the three other books. One was a copy of "Heidi," one was "Alice in Wonderland," and the third a small black book with the design of a cross and crown in gilt on the cover. Mrs. Forbes looked from this up at the child.

"What's this? Some kind of a daily book, Julia?"

"I—yes, I read it every day."

"Well, I hope you'll be faithful now your mother's gone. She's taken the trouble to put it in."

Jewel's eyes had caught a glimpse of green color. Eagerly she reached down into the trunk and drew out carefully a dress in tiny checks of green and white.

"That's my silk dress," she said, regarding it fondly.

"It is very neatly made," returned Mrs. Forbes repressively. "It doesn't matter at all what little girls have on if they are clean and neat. It only matters that they shall be obedient and good."

Jewel regarded her with the patience which children exercise toward the inevitable. "I'd like to fix Anna Belle's drawer myself," she said modestly.

"Very well, you may. Now here are your shoes and slippers, but I don't find any rubbers."

"No, I never wear rubbers."

"What? Doesn't it rain in Chicago?"

"Oh yes indeed, it rains."

"Then you must get your feet wet. I think you better have had rubbers than a silk dress! What was your mother thinking of?"

Jewel sighed vaguely. She wondered how soon Mrs. Forbes would go away.

This happy event occurred before long, and the little girl amused herself for a while with rearranging somewhat the closet and drawers. Then putting on her hat and taking her doll with her, she stole quietly down the thickly carpeted stairs, and opening the heavy hall door, went out upon the piazza. It was sheltered from the wind, and wicker chairs were scattered about. Jewel looked off curiously amid the trees to where she knew, by her father's description, she should find, after a few minutes' ramble, the ravine and brook. Pretty soon she would wander out there. Just now the sun was warm here, and the roomy chairs held out inviting arms. The child climbed into one of them. Father would come back here some happy day and find her. The thought brought a smile, and with the smile on her lips, her head fell back against a yielding cushion, and in a minute she had fallen asleep. Anna Belle toppled over backward. Her plumed hat was pushed rakishly askew, but little she cared. Her eyelids had fallen, too.

Mrs. Evringham and Eloise, returning late from their luncheon, came upon the little sleeping figure as they walked around the long piazza.

"There she is!" exclaimed Mrs. Evringham softly, putting up her lorgnette. "Behold your rival!"

Eloise regarded the sleeper without curiosity.

"At least she has not come uninvited," was her only comment.

"But she has come unwelcome, my dear," returned Mrs. Evringham with relish. "Just wait until our gracious host realizes what he has let himself in for. Oh, there's a good time coming, you may be sure. Hush, don't waken her! It would be a blessed dispensation if she were always to sleep while her grandfather is absent," and Mrs. Evringham led the way into the house, her laces fluttering.

On the first landing the ladies met Mrs. Forbes, troubled of countenance.

"I am looking for the child Julia," she said. "I can't think where she can have disappeared."

"You've not far to seek," returned Mrs. Evringham airily. "She is asleep on the piazza."

"Thank you." Mrs. Forbes hastened downstairs and out of doors. Glancing about she quickly perceived the short legs stretched in a reclining chair, and advanced toward the relaxed little figure.

"Julia, wake up!" she said, touching her.

The child stirred and opened her eyes. Her movement made the doll slip to the floor, and this caused her to come to herself suddenly.

"Why, I fell asleep, didn't I?" she said drowsily, reaching for the doll.

"Yes, and in Mr. Evringham's own chair!" responded Mrs. Forbes.

"They're all his, aren't they?" asked the child.

"Yes, but this is his special favorite, where he always lies to rest. Remember!" returned Mrs. Forbes. "Come right upstairs now and change your dress for dinner. He will be home in a few minutes."

"Oh, good!" exclaimed Jewel with satisfaction, and passed into the house. Mrs. Forbes was following ponderously. "Oh, you don't need to come with me," protested the child earnestly. "I can do it all myself."

"Are you sure?" doubtfully.

"Oh, ye—es!" replied the little girl, running lightly up the stairs.

"I ought to put her on the second floor," mused Mrs. Forbes, "if I've got to be running up and down; but I suppose she has done for herself a great deal. I suppose the mother hadn't time to be bothered. I'd like to make Mamzell change rooms with her."

Jewel hummed a tune as she took off her sailor suit, performed her ablutions, and then went to her closet to choose a frock for dinner. She decided on a blue dress with white dots chiefly because she would not have to change her hair ribbons. She had never herself tied those voluminous bows.

At last she was ready and danced toward the door, but some novel timidity made her hesitate and go back sedately to the chair by the window. Mrs. Forbes's impressive figure seemed to loom up with an order to her to wait the summons of the gong.

She sat there for what seemed a very long time, and at last a knock sounded at the door. Perhaps grandpa had come up. Jewel flew to open to him—and saw the white capped maid who had appeared at luncheon.

"They are all at table, and Mr. Evringham wishes you to come down," she said.

"But I was waiting for the gong."

"We only have that at noon."

Jewel's feet flew down the stairs. Her grandfather had sent for her. She was eager to reach him, yet when she entered the dining-room, her little face all alight, it was not so easy to run to him as she had fancied.

He sat stiffly at the foot of the table. Opposite him was aunt Madge, and at her left sat the prettiest young lady the child had ever seen.

Mrs. Forbes stood near Mr. Evringham, looking very serious.

Jewel took in all this at a glance, and contenting herself with greeting her grandfather's lifted eyes with a smile, she ran to Mrs. Evringham and turned her back.

"There's just one button in the middle, aunt Madge, that I can't reach," she explained softly.

Every eye at the table was regarding the child curiously, but she took no note of any one but her grandfather, and her dress buttoned, she ran to her chair and slid up on its smooth morocco. Eloise observed the little girl's loving expression.

"I am sorry you are late, Julia," said Mr. Evringham.

"Yes, so am I, grandpa," was the prompt response. "I wanted to be down here as soon as you came home, but I thought I ought to wait for the gong, and then it didn't ring."

Her eyes roved to where, directly opposite, the beautiful young lady was regarding her soberly.

Mrs. Evringham spoke. "That is your cousin Eloise, Julia."

Eloise inclined her graceful head, but made no further recognition of the child's admiring look.

"They haven't met before?" said Mr. Evringham, looking from one to the other.

"No," returned Mrs. Evringham with her most gracious manner. "It just happened that Eloise and I were engaged at luncheon to-day, and when we returned the little girl was taking a nap."

By this time Mrs. Forbes had brought Jewel's soup and she was eating. She looked up brightly at Mr. Evringham.

"Yes, grandpa, I went to sleep in your big chair on the piazza. I didn't know it was your special chair until Mrs. Forbes waked me up."

Her grandfather regarded her from under his heavy brows. He was resenting the fact that Eloise had made no effort to welcome the child. "Indeed?" he returned. "What did she wake you up for?"

"Because it was time to get ready for dinner," returned Jewel. "It reminded me of the story of Golden Hair, when she had gone to sleep on the bear's bed, the way Mrs. Forbes said, 'This is your grandfather's chair!'"

She looked around the table, expectant of sympathy. Only Mrs. Evringham seemed to wish to laugh, and she was making heroic efforts not to do so. Lovely Eloise kept her serious eyes downcast.

"Ha!" ejaculated Mr. Evringham, after a lightning glance of suspicion at his daughter-in-law. "I think I remember something about that. But Golden Hair tried three beds, I believe."

"Yes, she did, but you see there wasn't any little bear's chair on the piazza."

"Very true. Very true."

"Golden Hair was a great beauty, I believe," suggested Mrs. Evringham, looking at the child oddly. "She had yellow hair like yours."

Jewel put up a quick hand to the short tight braid which ended behind her ear. "Oh no, long, lovely, floating hair. Don't you remember?"

"It's a good while since I read it," returned Mrs. Evringham, laughing low and glancing at Eloise. Her father-in-law sent her a look of displeasure and turned back to Jewel.

"Dr. Ballard found you on the train, I suppose?"

"Yes, grandpa. We had a nice time. He is a very kind man." The child glanced across at her cousin again. She wished cousin Eloise would lift her eyes and not look so sorry. "I wonder," she added aloud, "why Dr. Ballard called cousin Eloise a little girl."

No one spoke, so Mrs. Evringham broke the momentary silence. "Did he?" she asked.

"Yes, he said that my cousin Eloise was a very charming little girl."

Jewel wondered why Eloise flushed and looked still sorrier, and why aunt Madge raised her napkin and turned her laugh into a cough. Perhaps it teased young ladies to be called little girls. Jewel regretted having mentioned it.

"I guess he was just April-fooling me," she suggested comfortingly, and the insistence of her soft gaze was such that Eloise looked up and met a smile so irresistible, that in spite of herself, her expression relaxed.

The softened look was a relief to the child. "I've heard about you, of course, cousin Eloise," she said, "and I couldn't forget, because your name is so nice and—and slippery. Eloise Evringham. Eloise Evringham. It sounds just like—like—oh, like sliding down the banisters. Don't you think so?"

Eloise smiled a little. "I hadn't thought of it," she returned, then relapsed into quiet.

Mrs. Forbes's countenance was stony. "Children should be seen and not heard," was her doctrine, and this dressmaker's child had an assurance beyond belief. She seemed to feel no awe whatever in her grandfather's presence.

The housekeeper caught Jewel's eye and gave her such a quenching look that thenceforward the little girl succumbed to the silence which the others seemed to prefer.

After dinner she would have a good visit with grandpa and talk about when father was a little boy. Her hopes were dashed, for just as they were rising from the table, a man was announced, with whom Mr. Evringham closeted himself in the library.

In the drawing-room aunt Madge and cousin Eloise both set themselves at letter-writing, and entirely ignored Jewel. The child looked listlessly at a book with pictures, which she found on the table, until half-past eight, when Mrs. Forbes came to say it was time for her to go to bed.

She rose and stood a moment, turning hesitatingly from her aunt to her cousin.

"Oh, is it bedtime?" asked aunt Madge, looking up from her letter. "Good-night, Julia. I hope you'll sleep well." Then she returned to her writing.

Eloise bit her lip as she regarded the little girl with a moment's hesitation, but no, she had decided on her plan of action. Mrs. Forbes was observing her. Eloise knew the housekeeper's attitude toward them was defensive, if not offensive. "Good-night," she said briefly, and looked down again.

"Good-night," returned Jewel quietly, and went out.

In the hall she hesitated. "I want to say good-night to grandpa," she said.

"Well, you can't," returned Mrs. Forbes decidedly. "He is talking business and mustn't be disturbed."

She followed the child up the staircase.

"I could go to bed alone, if I only knew where the matches are."

"You said you could dress alone, but you had to ask Mrs. Evringham to button your frock. Remember after this that I am the one to ask. She and Miss Eloise don't want to be bothered."

"Is it a bother to do a kindness?" asked Jewel in a subdued tone.

"To some folks it is," was the response. They had reached the door of the child's room; "but some folks can see their duty and do it," she added virtuously.

Jewel realized regretfully that her present companion belonged to the latter class.

"Now here, right inside the door," proceeded Mrs. Forbes, "is the switch. There's electricity all over this house, and you don't need any matches. See?" Mrs. Forbes turned the switch and the white room was flooded with light.

A few hours ago this magic would have evoked much enthusiasm. Even now Jewel was pleased to turn the light on and off several times, as Mrs. Forbes told her to do.

"Now I'll see if you can undress yourself," said the housekeeper. Jewel's deft fingers flew over the buttons in her eagerness to prove her independence. When at last she stood in her little white nightgown, so neat and fine in its small decorations, Mrs. Forbes said, "Do you want me to hear you say your prayers?"

"No, I thank you." With her hasty response Jewel promptly jumped into the bed, from which the white spread had been removed.

"I hope you always say them," said Mrs. Forbes, regarding her undecidedly.

"Yes'm, I always do."

The child cuddled down under the covers with her face to the wall, lest Mrs. Forbes should see a further duty and do it.

"You ought to say them on your knees," continued the housekeeper.

"I'd just as lief," replied Jewel, "but I don't believe God cares."

"Well," returned Mrs. Forbes solemnly, "it is a matter for your own conscience, Julia, if your mother didn't train you to it. Good-night."

"Good-night," came faintly from beneath the bedclothes.

Mrs. Forbes turned off the light and went out, closing the door behind her.

"If she'd always speak when she's spoken to, and be quiet and modest as she is with me, she'd be a very well-behaved child," she soliloquized. "I could train her. I shouldn't wonder at all if her mother should see a great difference in her when she comes back."

The housekeeper went heavily downstairs. Jewel, pushing off the bedclothes, listened attentively to the retiring steps, and when they could no longer be heard, she jumped out of bed nimbly, and feeling for the electric switch, turned on the light. Her breath was coming rather unevenly, and she ran over the soft carpet to where her doll lay. Catching her up, she pressed her to her breast, then sitting down in the big chair, she began to undress her, crossing one little bare foot over the other knee to make a lap.

"Darling Anna Belle, did you think I'd forgotten you?" she asked breathlessly. "Did you think you weren't going to have any one to kiss you good-night? It's hard not to have any one you love kiss you good-night." Jewel dashed her hand across her eyes quickly, then went swiftly on with her work. "You might have known that I was only waiting until that—that giantess went away. She wouldn't let me bring you down to dinner, dearie, but you didn't miss anything. Poor grandpa, I don't wonder any longer that he doesn't look happy. He has the sorriest people all around him that you ever saw. He lives in a big, beautiful castle, but it's Castle Discord. I named it that at dinner. Nobody loves one another. Of course grandpa loves me, because I'm his own little grandchild, but he's too sorry to show it. The beautiful enchanted maiden, and the Error fairy, and the giantess, are all making discord around him. A little flat is better than a big castle, isn't it? We know a flat—let's call it Harmony Flat, Anna Belle. Perhaps if we're very, very, good, we'll get back there some time." Jewel suddenly pressed the doll's nightdress against her wet eyes. "Don't, don't, dearie! I know it does seem a year since—since the boat this morning. If all the days were as long as this, we'd be very, very old when father and mother come home." The soft voice broke in a sob. "I don't know what I should do if you weren't a Christian Scientist, Anna Belle. We'll help each other all we can. Now come—come into bed and say your prayers."

"Say your—your prayer first, dearie," she whispered, sobbing:—

"'Father, Mother, God,
Loving me,—
Guard me when I sleep;
Guide my little feet
Up to Thee.'

"Now you'll feel—better, dearie. In a minute you won't be so—homesick for—for—father and mother. Hush, while I say mine."

Jewel repeated the Lord's Prayer. When she had finished, her breath still caught convulsively, so she continued:—

"Dear Father, Mother, God, loving me, help me to know that I am close to Thee. Help me to remember that things that are unhappy aren't real things. Help me to know that everything is good and harmonious, and that the people in this castle are Thy children, even if they do seem to have eyes like fishes. Help me to love one another, even the giantess, and please show grandpa how to meet error. Please let Dr. Ballard come to see me soon, because he has kind eyes, and I'm sure he doesn't know it's wrong to believe in materia medica. Please take more care of father and mother than anything, and say 'Peace be still' if the wind blows the sea. I know, dear Father in Heaven, that Thou dost not forget anything, but I say it to make me feel better. I am Thy little Jewel, and Anna Belle loves Thee, too. Take us into the everlasting arms of Love while we go to sleep. Amen."

Jewel brushed away the tears as she ceased, and with her usual quickness of motion, jumped out of bed to get a handkerchief. Turning on the electric light, she went to the chair over which hung the dotted dress. She remembered having slipped a clean handkerchief into its pocket before going to dinner.

In reaching for it her fingers encountered a scrap of paper in the depths of the pocket. She drew it forth. It was folded. She opened it and found it written over in a clear round hand.

"Is my little darling loving every one around her? People do not always seem lovely at first, but remember that every one is lovable because he is a thought of God. Those who seem unlovely are always unhappy, too, in their hearts. We must help them, and the best way to help is to love. Mother is thinking about her little Jewel, and no seas can divide us."

A slow smile gladdened the child's tear-stained face. She read the message again, then turned out the light for the last time and cuddled down in bed, her warm cheek pressing the scrap of paper in her hand, her breath still catching.

"Mother has spoken to us, Anna Belle," she whispered, clasping the doll close. "Wasn't it just like God to let her!" Then she fell asleep smiling.

CHAPTER VIII
A HAPPY BREAKFAST

Mrs. Forbes was on the porch next morning when Mr. Evringham returned from his canter.

"Fine morning, Mrs. Forbes," he said, as he gave Essex Maid into Zeke's hands.

"Very fine. A regular weather breeder. It'll most probably rain to-morrow, and what I wanted to speak to you about, Mr. Evringham, is, that the child hasn't any rubbers."

"Indeed? What else does she need?"

"Well, nothing that I can see. Her things are all good, and she's got enough of them. The trouble is she says she has never worn rubbers and doesn't want to, and if she gets sick I shall have to take care of her; so I hope, sir, you'll say that she must have them."

"Not wear them? Of course she must wear them," returned Mr. Evringham brusquely. "Get them to-day, if convenient, Mrs. Forbes."

The housekeeper looked relieved.

"I hope she's not making you any trouble, eh?" added Mr. Evringham.

"Not any more than she can help, I suppose," was the grudging reply. "She's a smart child, and being an only one, she's some notional. She won't eat this and that, and doesn't want to wear rubbers, but she's handy and neat, and is used to doing for herself; her mother hasn't had time to fuss with her, of course, and that's lucky for me. She seems very well behaved, considering."

Jewel had made heroic efforts while Mrs. Forbes assisted at her morning toilet, and this was her reward.

"Well, we mustn't have you imposed upon," returned Mr. Evringham, feeling guilty of the situation. "The child must obey you implicitly, implicitly."

So saying he passed into the house, and after making a change in his toilet, entered the dining-room. There he was seated, deep in his newspaper and waiting for his coffee, when the door opened, light feet ran to him, and an arm was thrown around his neck. He looked up to meet a happy smile, and before he could realize who had captured him, Jewel pressed a fervent kiss upon his cheek.

"Oh, grandpa, how nice and cold your cheek feels! Have you been out doors already?"

Mr. Evringham could feel the said cheek grow hot in surprise at this onslaught. He held himself stiffly and uncomfortably in the encircling arm.

"Yes, I've been out on horseback," he returned shortly. "I go every morning."

Jewel's eyes sparkled. "Oh, I'm so glad. Then I can watch you. I love to see anybody ride. When I see a beautiful horse something inside me gets warm. Father says I like just the same things he does. I must let you read your paper, grandpa, but may I say one thing more?"

"Yes."

"I didn't come last evening to kiss you good-night because you had somebody with you in the library, and, the giant—and Mrs. Forbes wouldn't let me; but I wanted to. You know I wanted to, don't you? I felt all sorry inside because I couldn't. You know you're the only real relation I have in the castle"—Here Mrs. Forbes's entrance with the coffee interrupted the confidence, and Jewel, with a last surreptitious squeeze of Mr. Evringham's neck, intended to finish her sentence eloquently, left him and went to her chair.

"You're to sit here this morning," said Mrs. Forbes, indicating the place opposite her employer. "Mrs. Evringham and her daughter don't come down to breakfast."

Jewel looked up eagerly. "Not ever?" she asked.

"Never."

The child shot a radiant glance across at her grandfather which he caught, the thread of his business calculations having been hopelessly broken. "Oh, grandpa, we're always going to have breakfast alone together!" she said joyously. Noting Mrs. Forbes's set countenance, she added apologetically, "They're so pretty, cousin Eloise and aunt Madge, I love to look at them, but they aren't my real relations, and," her face gladdening again, "to think of having breakfast alone with you, grandpa, makes me feel as if—as if I had a birthday!"

Mr. Evringham cleared his throat. The situation might have been a little easier if Mrs. Forbes had not been present, but as it was, he had never felt so embarrassed in his life.

"Now eat your oatmeal, Julia," said the housekeeper repressively. "Mr. Evringham always reads his paper at breakfast."

"Yes," replied the child with docility. She poured the cream from a small silver pitcher with a neatness that won Mrs. Forbes's approval; and Mr. Evringham read over headlines in the paper, while he sipped his coffee, without understanding in the least the meaning of the words. Mrs. Forbes was right. Discipline must be maintained. This was the time during which he wished to read his paper, and it was most astonishing to be so vigorously taken possession of by an utter stranger. Now was the time to repress her if she were to be repressed. Mrs. Forbes was right. After a while he glanced across at the child. She looked very small and clean, and she was ready with a quick smile for him; but she put a little forefinger against her lips jocosely. He cleared his throat again and averted his eyes, rumpling the paper as he turned a leaf.

Mrs. Forbes left the room with the oatmeal dishes.

Jewel leaned forward quickly. "Grandpa," she said earnestly, "if you would declare every day, over and over, that no error could come near your house, I think she would go away of her own accord."

Mr. Evringham stared, open paper in hand. "What? Who?"

"Mrs. Forbes."

"Go away? Mrs. Forbes? What are you thinking of! I couldn't get on without Mrs. Forbes."

"Oh!" Jewel leaned back with the long-drawn exclamation. "I thought she was what made you look sorry."

"No indeed. I have enough things to make me sorry, but she isn't one of them."

"Do you like her?" wonderingly.

"I—why—I respect her profoundly."

"Oh! It must be lots easier to respect her pro—the way you do, than to like her; but," with firm lips, "I've got to love her. I told Anna Belle so this morning, and especially if you want her to stay."

"Bless my soul!" Mr. Evringham looked in dismay as his *vis-à-vis*. "You must be very careful, Julia, not to offend or trouble her in any way," he said.

"All right, grandpa, I will, and then will you do me a favor too?"

"I must hear it first."

"Would you mind calling me Jewel? You know it isn't any matter about the rest, because they're not my real relations, but Julia is mother's name, and Jewel is mine; and when I love people very much, I like them to call me Jewel."

Mrs. Forbes here entered with a tray, and Mr. Evringham merely said, "Very well," twice over, and retreated into his newspaper.

On the tray were boiled eggs. Jewel glanced quickly up at Mrs. Forbes's impassive face. She might have remembered. Probably she did remember.

Life had not taught the child to be shy, as has been evidenced; so although Mrs. Forbes was an awing experience, she felt strong in the presence of her important grandfather, and only kept silence now in order not to interrupt his reading.

When at last he laid down his paper and began to chip an egg, Jewel glanced at those which Mrs. Forbes had set before her. Her little face had grown very serious.

"Grandpa, do you think it's error for me not to like eggs?" she asked. "Mother never said it was. She was willing I should eat something else."

"Of course, eat whatever you like," responded Mr. Evringham quickly.

Mrs. Forbes seemed to swell and grow pink. "You always have eggs, sir, and if there's two breakfasts to be got, will you kindly tell me what the other shall be?"

Mr. Evringham glanced up in some surprise at the unfamiliar tone.

"Oh, the oatmeal is a plenty," said Jewel, looking at the housekeeper, eager to mollify her.

"Try an egg. Perhaps you'll like them by this time," suggested Mr. Evringham.

"Do you like everything to eat, grandpa?"

Mr. Evringham, being most arbitrary and peculiar in his tastes, could only gain time by clearing his throat again, and taking a drink of coffee.

"Mrs. Forbes will bring you a glass of milk, I dare say," he returned at last, without looking up; and the housekeeper turned with ponderous obedience and left the room.

Nimbly Jewel slid down from her chair, and running around the table to her grandfather's place, put both her arms around his neck and whispered to him eagerly and swiftly, "If you have such a pro—something respect for

Mrs. Forbes, and it makes her sorry because I won't eat eggs, perhaps I ought to. If it offends thy brother to have you eat meat, you mustn't, the Bible says, so I suppose, if it makes Mrs. Forbes turn red and perhaps get the stomach ache to have me not eat eggs, I ought to; but grandpa, if you decide I must, please let me wait till to-morrow morning, so I can say the Scientific Statement of Being all day—"

Here Mrs. Forbes entered with a glass of milk on a little tray. She stood transfixed at the sight that met her.

"That child hasn't the fear of man before her eyes!" she ejaculated mentally, then she marched forward and deposited the milk beside Jewel's empty plate, while the child ran back and took her seat.

Mr. Evringham, gazing at his visitor in mute astonishment, was much disconcerted to receive a confiding gesture of raised shoulders and eyebrows, which, combined with a little smile, plainly signified that they had been caught. He took up his newspaper mechanically.

He had never had a daughter, and caresses had seldom passed between him and his children. His duties as a family man had always been perfunctory. He was tingling now from the surprise of Jewel's action, the feeling of the little gingham clad arms about his neck, the touch of the rose-leaf skin as she swept his cheek and ear in her emphatic half-whisper.

His mental processes were stiff when the subject related to things apart from the stock market, his horses, and golf, but he was finally understanding that his granddaughter had come to Bel-Air, prepared by accounts which had cast a glamour over everything and everybody in it. She had evidently found Mrs. Forbes fall below her expectations. He had been disillusioned concerning Mrs. Evringham and Eloise. As yet the halo with which he himself had been invested was intact. Was it to remain so? He still saw how foolish he had been to send for the child. He still wished, of course, that she was in Chicago now, instead of sitting across there from him in crisp short skirts, her head and shoulders only showing above the high table, and a little smile of good understanding waiting for him each time he looked up.

He had done very well during a lifetime without being hugged, yet the innocent incense, which had been rising spontaneously before him ever since the child entered the dining-room, had a strangely sweet savor. Such was the joy of breakfast alone with him that it made her feel as if she had a birthday! Perfectly absurd! Quite the most absurd thing that he had ever heard in his life.

Mrs. Forbes spoke. "Perhaps it is to be the same way about the rubbers, Mr. Evringham!" she said, much flushed. "Perhaps you will not insist upon Julia wearing rubbers!"

"Oh yes, yes, certainly," returned Mr. Evringham hastily, anxious to reinstate himself. "I wish you to have a pair of rubbers at once, Julia—Jewel. You surely don't mean that your mother has allowed you to wet your feet."

"I—I never noticed, grandpa, but," hopefully, "she lets me wet my hands, so why not my feet?"

"Bless me, what ignorance! Because the soles of your feet have large pores through which to catch cold. Hasn't any one ever told you that?"

Jewel smiled. "That would be a queer arrangement for God to make, don't you think?" she asked softly. "Just as if He expected us to walk on our hands."

Mrs. Forbes's eyes widened, and an irrepressible "Well!" escaped from her lips. "Has that young one reverence for anything in heaven above or earth beneath?" she queried mentally.

Mr. Evringham managed to recover himself sufficiently to say, "You shouldn't speak so, Jewel."

"But you know how it was about the tree of knowledge, grandpa," replied the child earnestly. "God told Adam not to eat of it, because then he'd believe in good *and* evil, and that always makes such lots and *lots* of trouble. The Indians don't have to wear rubbers."

"Drink your milk, Jewel," returned Mr. Evringham uncomfortably, not having the temerity to lift his eyes as high as his housekeeper's countenance. "No matter about the Indians. You are a civilized little girl, and you must wear rubbers while you live with me. Mrs. Forbes will very kindly buy them for you."

"Oh, I have money," returned Jewel brightly. "I have three dollars," she added, trying not to say it boastfully. "Fifty cents for every week father and mother are going to be away."

Mr. Evringham wiped his mustache. "You need not spend any of it for the rubbers," he returned. "You are buying those to please me."

"I shall love to wear them to please you, grandpa," she returned affectionately. "I'll put them on every time I can think of it."

"Only when it is wet, of course," he said. "When it is rainy."

"Oh yes," she returned, "when it's rainy."

"Harry looked like my father, and she does, by Jove," mused Mr. Evringham. "She's like me. Knows what she wants to eat, and cares for a horse, if she is a strange little being."

"You say you like horses?" he remarked suddenly.

"I just love them," answered Jewel, "and I came real close to them once. Father took me to the horse show."

"He did, eh?"

"Yes, he told mother he was going to blow me to it." The child laughed. "Father's the greatest joker; he says the funniest things. He didn't blow me to it at all. He took me in the cable car, and we had more *fun*! It was the most be—eautiful place you ever saw."

"It was, eh?"

"Yes. The music was playing, and there were coaches and four-in-hands and horns and men in red coats and beautiful little shiny carriages—and the horses! Oh, they all looked so proud and glad, and they trotted and ran and jumped over high fences, and the harness jingled and the people cheered!" The child's cheeks were glowing.

Mr. Evringham gave an exclamation that was almost a laugh. "You didn't sleep much that night, I'll wager!"

"No, I didn't want to. I stayed awake a long time to realize that God doesn't love one of His children any better than another, so of course some time I'll wear a tall shiny hat and ride over fences just like flying. I'll have a horse," Jewel added slowly, looking off with a rapt expression as at a long-cherished vision, "with a white star in his forehead!"

"H'm! Very good taste," returned Mr. Evringham, scarcely knowing what he was saying, so dazed was he by the extraordinary mixture of ideas.

After breakfast he had his usual interview with Mrs. Forbes concerning the important event of dinner. Jewel had run upstairs to dress Anna Belle.

The menu decided upon, Mr. Evringham still lingered.

"Mrs. Forbes, I have never had any experience with little girls. You have, no doubt," he said. "Am I right in thinking that my granddaughter is—is a rather unusual specimen?"

"She's older than Dick's hatband, sir," rejoined the housekeeper promptly.

"Are they, perhaps, teaching differently in the schools from what they used to?"

"Not that I know of, Mr. Evringham."

"She uses very unusual expressions. I can't make it out. You are an intelligent woman, Mrs. Forbes. Did you ever happen to hear of such a thing as the—a—a—Scientific Statement of Being!"

"Never in my life, sir," returned the housekeeper virtuously.

"Extraordinary language that, from a—a child of her years. She seems to have been peculiarly brought up. You heard her reference to—in fact to—the Creator."

"I did, sir. At the breakfast table, too! I was as shocked as you were, sir. Her mother put a Bible into her trunk, but it's plain she never taught her any reverence. The Almighty give her a jumping horse indeed! If you'll excuse me, Mr. Evringham, I think you should have said something right there."

The broker pulled his mustache. "I've listened to more unreasonable views of heaven," he returned.

"Do you think it was heaven she was talking about!"

Mr. Evringham shrugged his shoulders. "You can't prove anything by me. She's the most extraordinary child I ever listened to."

Mrs. Forbes pursed her lips. "You'd not believe, sir, how differently she behaves when she is alone with me. As mild-mannered and quiet as you'd wish to see anywhere. She scarcely speaks a word."

Mr. Evringham bit his lip and nodded. It gave him some amusement in the midst of his perplexity to remember the manner in which he had been advised to exorcise this tower of strength altogether.

"It's my opinion, sir, that children should be made to eat what is set before them," went on Mrs. Forbes, reverting to her principal grievance.

"It would save you a lot of trouble if I had been trained that way—eh, Mrs. Forbes?" returned the other, with extraordinary lightness.

"You are a very different thing, I should hope!" exclaimed Mrs. Forbes solemnly.

"Yes, about fifty years different. Hard to teach an old dog new tricks, eh? You might have some chops for her luncheon, perhaps, and an extra one for her breakfast. She hasn't eaten anything this morning."

For the first time an order from Mr. Evringham evoked no reply from his housekeeper. He felt the weight of her disapproval. "But get the overshoes by all means, as soon as convenient," he made haste to add. "Ring for Zeke, if you please, Mrs. Forbes. I must be off."

CHAPTER IX
A SHOPPING EXPEDITION

The housekeeper warned Jewel not to run out of doors that morning as she wished to accompany her to the shoe store.

"I'm not going to take you, Anna Belle," Jewel said to her doll. "I don't like to ask the giantess if I may, and of course, it won't be a very good time anyway, so you be patient and we'll go out together this afternoon."

Mrs. Forbes's long widow's veil, a decoration she never had discarded hung low over her black gown as she stepped deliberately down the stairs from her barn chamber.

"I am going with the little girl, Zeke, to buy her a pair of rubbers," she announced to her son.

"Going foot-back? Why don't you have out the 'broom'? One granddaughter's got as good a right to it as the other, hasn't she?"

"I should say so, but that child, Zeke, in addition to her wonderful boldness this morning with Mr. Evringham, that I told you about, is perfectly crazy over horses."

"H'm. That don't surprise me. A young one that can stand up to the governor wouldn't be afraid of anything in the way of horseflesh."

"So I decided," continued Mrs. Forbes, pulling on her roomy black gloves, "that it would be better for her to go this morning in the trolley."

"You *did*? Well if that ain't a regular step-mother act!" returned Zeke in protest. "The kid had a bully time coming home from the depot yesterday. Dick felt good, and he just lit out. I tell you her eyes shone."

"I like to do what's best for folks in the end," declared Mrs. Forbes virtuously. "Julia's parents are poor, and likely to be. She's only going to be here six weeks, and what is the sense of encouraging a taste she can't ever indulge? No, I'll take her in the trolley. It's a nice morning, and I shan't mind the walk down to the gate." The speaker marched with the dignity which was always inseparable from the veil toward the back door of the house to give some last orders, and Zeke lounged out with his rake toward the grounds at the front. There he caught sight of a small figure in hat and jacket waiting on the piazza. He turned toward it, and Jewel advanced with a smile of recognition. She had had to look twice to identify her fine plum-colored companion of yesterday's drive with this youth in shirt sleeves and a soft old hat.

"Well, little girl, how are you getting on?" he asked.

"Pretty well, thank you." Her beaming expression left no doubt that she was very glad to see him.

"Not particularly flattering if she is," he mused. "Fine ladies not out of their rooms yet, and ma doin' her duty by her to beat the band."

"Where's your doll?" he asked.

"I didn't bring her. I thought perhaps the—Mrs. Forbes would—would just as lief she didn't come."

"Ma *hasn't* played with dolls for quite a spell," agreed Zeke, with a smile that was sunshine to the child.

"You live out in the barn with the horses, don't you?" she asked eagerly. "Will you give me permission to go out there some time?"

"Sure. Come any time."

"Mrs. Forbes said I must ask permission," responded the child with an apprehensive glance behind her to see if her escort were arriving. "What—what is your name?"

"Forgotten this soon? I told you Zeke."

"I thought you did, but your mother said it was something very different."

"Ezekiel, perhaps."

"Yes, that's it. I won't forget again. How many horses has grandpa?"

"Two here, but I guess he's got more in the country. You come out to the barn any time you feel like it. You've heard of a bell cow, haven't you? Well, we've got the belle horse out there. She beats all creation."

"The one I saw yesterday," eagerly, "the one that runs away all the time?"

"No. This is Mr. Evringham's riding horse."

Jewel hopped and clapped her hands. "I'll see grandpa ride. Goody! I'll watch him."

"Go to your paths, Zeke," said a voice, and the veil appeared around the corner of the house.

Jewel quietly joined her stately companion, and walked away sedately beside her.

They did not exchange many words on their way to the park gates, for Mrs. Forbes needed her breath for the rather long promenade, and Jewel was busy looking at the trees and trim swards and crocus beds beside the winding road.

Outside the gate they had to wait but a minute before the car came, and after they had boarded it, the little girl was entertained by looking out of the window, and often wished for Anna Belle's sympathy in some novel sight or sound.

A ride of fifteen minutes brought them to the shoe store. Mrs. Forbes seemed to know the clerk, and Jewel was finally fitted to her guardian's satisfaction, but scarcely to her own, the housekeeper having selected the species known as storm rubbers, and chose them as large as would stay on.

"They're quite warm, aren't they?" said Jewel, looking down at her shiny feet and trying to speak cheerfully.

"When you wear them you want to be warm," was Mrs. Forbes's rejoinder.

"I brought my money," said the child, in a low voice.

"No. Your grandfather wishes to make you a present of these." The housekeeper's tone was final, and she paid for the overshoes, which were wrapped up, and then she led Jewel out of the store.

Next door was a candy shop with alluring windows.

"I'd like to go in here," said the little girl. "Would you mind?"

"Do you spend your money for candy, Julia?"

"Yes'm. Don't you like it?" Jewel lingered, looking at the pretty display. Easter had recently passed, and there were bright-eyed little yellow chickens that especially took her fancy.

"It isn't a question of liking it when people are poor," returned Mrs. Forbes. "I'm astonished that your mother encourages you to spend money for candy."

Jewel looked up quickly. "Did you think we were poor?" she asked, with disconcerting suddenness.

Mrs. Forbes hesitated. "Your mother is a dressmaker, isn't she?"

"Yes, she's just a splendid one. Everybody says so. We couldn't be poor, you know. She found out about God before I was old enough to talk, so you see all her poor time came before I can remember."

The housekeeper glanced about her furtively. "Julia, don't you know you shouldn't use your Creator's name on the street!" she exclaimed, when she had made certain that no one was listening.

"Why not?" asked the child.

"Why—why—it isn't a proper place. Some one might hear you."

"Well, won't you let me get some candy now? If I knew what kind you liked, Mrs. Forbes, I'd get it."

"I don't eat candy as a rule. It's not only extravagant, it's very unhealthy."

The little girl smiled. "How do you suppose your stomach knows what you put into it?" she asked. "I guess you're just a little—bit—afraid, aren't you?"

"Odder than Dick's hatband!" quoth Mrs. Forbes again, mentally. "I take horehound drops sometimes," she said aloud, "for a cold."

"Can't you sneeze a little now?" asked Jewel, amusement twinkling in her blue eyes. "I do want so much to go in here."

"Don't tempt Providence by making fun of sickness, Julia, or you'll live to regret it," returned Mrs. Forbes. "I don't mind getting some horehound drops, but be careful now and don't spend too much. A little girl's money always burns in her pocket."

"Yes'm," returned the child dutifully, skipping up to the door of the shop and opening it.

Mrs. Forbes followed slowly, and once inside, fell into conversation with the girl of whom she bought the cough candy. This gave Jewel opportunity to buy beside her caramels one of the lovely yellow chickens, which she designed for a special purpose.

"Now don't you eat that candy before lunch. It will take away your appetite. It is nearly lunch time now," said Mrs. Forbes as they left the store.

"And won't you either?" asked the child, offering the open caramel bag with a spontaneous politeness which somehow made the housekeeper feel at a disadvantage.

"No, thank you. Stop that car, Julia, and make them wait for me," she said, making haste slowly.

Once within, it took Mrs. Forbes a minute or two to get her breath, but she soon noticed that her companion's eyes were fixed upon a man seated a little way from them across the car. A smile kept coming to the child's lips, and at last the gentleman himself recognized that he was an object of interest. He looked at the strange little girl kindly. Her hand went unconsciously to the small gold pin she wore. The man smiled and touched one of similar pattern which was fastening his tie. In a minute more his street was reached, and as he passed Jewel on his way out of the car, he stooped and gave her ready hand a little pressure.

She colored with pleasure, and Mrs. Forbes swelled with curiosity and disapproval. She knew the man by sight as a highly respectable citizen. What was this wild Western child doing now? The car made too much noise to permit of investigation, so she waited until they had left it and entered the park gates.

"Julia," she said then, "where did you ever see that gentleman before?"

"I never did," replied the child.

"What do you mean by such bold actions, then? What will he think of you?"

"He'll think it's all right," returned Jewel. "We have the same—the same friends."

The housekeeper looked at her. It was beneath her dignity to ask further questions at present, but some time she meant to renew the subject.

"It's very wrong for a little girl to take any notice of strangers," she said.

"Yes'm," replied Jewel, "but he was—different."

Mrs. Forbes maintained silence henceforth until they reached home. "You may hang your hat and jacket in the closet under the stairs whenever you don't wish to go to your room," she said when she parted with her companion at the piazza, "but don't wander away anywhere before lunch."

"No'm. Thank you for taking me, Mrs. Forbes."

"You're welcome," returned that lady, and the long black veil swept majestically toward the barn.

Sweet and rippling music was proceeding from the house. Jewel tiptoed across the piazza to a long window, from whence she could see the interior of the drawing-room.

"It is the enchanted maiden," she said to herself, and sank down softly by the window, listening eagerly to the melodious strains and smooth runs which flowed from beneath the slender fingers. One piece followed another in quick succession, now gay, now grave, and the listener scarcely stirred in her enjoyment.

At last, suddenly, in the midst of a Grieg melody, the player ceased, and crossing her arms upon the empty music rack, bowed her head upon them in such an attitude of abandon that Jewel's heart leaped in sympathy.

"Oh cousin Eloise! What makes her so sorry?" she thought. The child's intuition had been strong to perceive the nature of her aunt Madge. "It must be such an awful thing to have your own mother an error fairy. That must be the reason. I wish I could tell her"—Jewel jumped to her feet, but just as she was determining to go to her cousin, the soft-tohed gong pealed its mellow summons, and she saw Eloise rise from the piano in time to meet her mother, who at that moment entered the room.

Jewel went into the house, hung up her hat and jacket, and deposited her packages. By the time she reached the dining-room her aunt and cousin were already seated. Mrs. Evringham put up her lorgnette as she greeted the child. Eloise nodded a grave good-morning, and Mrs. Forbes began to serve the luncheon.

Jewel looked in vain for any trace of excitement or tears on her cousin's lovely face. Eloise did not address her or any one. Mrs. Evringham did the talking. After a question as to how Jewel had spent the morning, and without listening to the child's reply, she began to talk to her daughter of a drive she wished to take that afternoon.

Jewel discerned that Mrs. Forbes was not kindly disposed toward the mother and daughter, and that they ignored the housekeeper; that Eloise was languid and out of sympathy with her mother, and that Mrs. Evringham was impatient with her, often to the verge of sharpness. The child was glad when luncheon was over; but before going upstairs she brought her small bag of caramels and offered them to the ladies.

Mrs. Evringham gave a little laugh of surprise and looked at Eloise, who took one with a sober "Thank you."

"I don't believe I could, child," said aunt Madge, glancing with amusement at the striped bag. "Keep them for yourself."

"You'll have some, won't you, Mrs. Forbes?" asked Jewel, and the housekeeper so strongly disapproved of Mrs. Evringham's manner that she accepted.

"Perhaps you would like to try some of our candy, Julia," said Mrs. Evringham, as the child followed her aunt and cousin upstairs.

Jewel paused while aunt Madge brought from her room into the hall a large box, beribboned and laced, full of a variety of confections.

"How pretty!" exclaimed the child.

"This is from your friend, Dr. Ballard," said her aunt. "He sent it to the charming little girl, Eloise."

Jewel, running on up to her room eating the creamy chocolate, wondered still more why her cousin should seem so sorry, with so much to make her happy.

"Now, Anna Belle, the time has really come," she said happily to her doll, as she took her in her arms and began putting on her jacket and hat. "We're going away from Castle Discord to seek our fortunes. We're going to leave the giantess, and leave the impolite error fairy, and leave the poor enchanted maiden, and go to find the ravine and the brook. Wait till I put on my oldest shoes, for we shall have to climb deep, deep down to get near to father."

At last she was ready, and when she had closed the heavy house door behind her, and had run down the driveway to the park road, a delicious sense of freedom possessed her.

"There goes the little Westerner," observed Mrs. Evringham, looking from her window. "It's a good thing she knows how to amuse herself."

"A good thing, indeed," returned Eloise. "There is no one here to do anything for her."

"She has wonderful assurance for such a plain little monkey," went on Mrs. Evringham.

"She has extremely good breeding," returned her daughter, coming to the window and following Jewel's retreating figure with her eyes, "and a charming face when she smiles."

"Very well. Look out for yourself, then. I thought last night, once or twice, at dinner, that she was rather entertaining to her grandfather."

"She has her doll," said Eloise wistfully. "Where can she be going? I wish I were going with her."

Mrs. Evringham laughed. "Well, you *are* bored. Pshaw, my dear! Lie down and get a little beauty sleep. Then we will go driving and see that charming spot Dr. Ballard told us about. I'm sure he will call to-night."

CHAPTER X
THE RAVINE

Outside the well-kept roads of Bel-Air Park, Nature had been encouraged to work her sweet will. The drive wound along the edge of a picturesque gorge, and it was not long before Jewel found the scene of her father's favorite stories.

The sides of the ravine were studded with tall trees, and in its depths flowed a brook, unusually full now from the spring rains.

The child lost no time in creeping beneath the slender wire fence at the roadside, and scrambling down the incline. The brook whispered and gurgled, wild flowers sprang amid the ferns in the shelter and moisture. The child was enraptured.

"Oh, Anna Belle!" She exclaimed, hugging the doll for pure joy. "Castle Discord is far away. There's nobody down here but God!"

For hours she played happily in the enchanting spot, all unconscious of time. Anna Belle lay on a bed of moss, while Jewel became acquainted with her wonderful new playmate, the brook. The only body of water with which she had been familiar hitherto was Lake Michigan. Now she drew stones out of the bank and made dams and waterfalls. She sailed boats of chips and watched them shoot the tiny rapids. She lay down on the bank beside Anna Belle and gazed up through the leafy treetops. Many times this programme had been varied, when at last equipages began to pass on the road above. She could see twinkling wheels and smart liveries.

With a start of recollection, she considered that she might have been a long time in the ravine.

"I wish somebody would let me bring a watch the next time," she said to her doll, as she took her up. "Haven't we had a beautiful afternoon, Anna Belle? Let's call it the Ravine of Happiness, and we'll come here every day— just every day; but perhaps it's time for grandpa to be home, dearie, so we must go back to the castle." She sighed unconsciously as she began climbing up the steep bank and crept under the wire. "I hope we haven't stayed very long, because the giantess might not like it," she continued uneasily; but as she set her feet in the homeward road, every sensation of anxiety fled before an approaching vision. She saw a handsome man in riding dress mounted on a shining horse with arched neck, that lifted its feet daintily as it pranced along the tree-lined avenue.

"Grandpa!" ejaculated Jewel, stepping to the roadside and pausing, her hands clasped beneath her chin and her eyes shining with admiration.

Mr. Evringham drew rein, not displeased by the encounter. The child apparently could not speak. She eyed the horse rather than its rider, a fact which the latter observed and enjoyed.

"Remind you of the horse show?" he inquired.

"It *is* the horse show," rejoined the child.

"This is Essex Maid, Jewel," said Mr. Evringham. He patted the mare's shining neck. "You shall go out to the barn with me some time and visit her." His eyes wandered over the ruffled hair, the hat on the back of the child's head, and the wet spots on her dress. "Run home now," he added. "I heard Mrs. Forbes asking for you as I came out."

He rode on, and Jewel, her face radiant, followed him with her eyes. In a minute he turned, and she threw rapid kisses after him. He raised his hat, and then a curve in the road hid him from view.

Jewel sighed rapturously and hurried along the road. The giantess had asked for her. Ah, what a happy world it would be if there were nothing at Bel-Air Park but grandpa, his horses, and the ravine!

Mrs. Forbes espied the child in the distance, and was at the door when she came in.

"After this, Julia, you must never go away without telling me where"— she began, when her eyes recognized the condition of the gingham frock, and the child's feet. "Look at how you've drabbled your dress!" she ejaculated.

"It's clean water," returned Julia.

"But your feet! Why, Julia Evringham, they are as wet as sop! Where have you been?"

"Playing by the brook in the ravine."

Mrs. Forbes groaned. "Nothing will satisfy a child but finding the place where they can get the dirtiest and make the most trouble. Why didn't you wear your rubbers, you naughty girl?"

"Why—why—it wasn't raining."

"Raining! Those rubbers are to keep your feet dry. Haven't you got any sense?"

Jewel looked a little pale. "I didn't know I should get wet in the brook," she answered.

"Well, go right upstairs now, up the backstairs, and take off every one of those wet things. Let me feel your petticoat. Yes, that's wet, too. You undress and get into a hot bath, and then you put on your nightgown and go right to bed."

"Go to bed!" echoed the child, bewildered.

"Yes, to bed. You won't come down to dinner. Perhaps that will teach you to wear your rubbers next time and be more careful."

Jewel found the backstairs and ascended them, her little heart hot within her.

"She's the impolitest woman in the whole world, Anna Belle!" she whispered. "I'm going to not cry. Mother didn't know what impoliteness there was at grandpa's or she wouldn't have let us come."

The child's eyes were bright as she found her room and began undressing. "But you mustn't be angry, dearie," she continued excitedly to her doll. "It's the worst error to be angry, because it means hating. You treat me, Anna Belle, and I'll treat you," she went on, unfastening her clothes with unsteady hands.

With many a pause to work at a refractory elastic or button, and many interruptions from catches in her breath, she murmured aloud during the process of her undressing: "Dear Father in Heaven, I seem to feel sorry all over, and full of error. Help me to know that I'm not a mortal mind little girl, hating and angry, but I am Thy child, and the only things I know are good, happy things. Error has no power and Love has all power. I love Mrs. Forbes, and she loves me. Thou art here even in this house, and please help me to know that one of Thy children cannot hurt another." Here Jewel slipped into the new wrapper her mother had made, and hurried into the white tiled bathroom near by. While she let the water run into the tub she put her hand into her pocket mechanically, in search of a handkerchief, and when she felt the crisp touch of paper she drew it out eagerly. It was covered, and she read the words written in her mother's distinct hand.

"Love to my Jewel. Is she making a stepping-stone of every trial, and learning to think less and less about herself, and more and more about other people? And does she remember that little girls cannot always understand the error that grown-up people have to meet, especially those who have not

Science to help them? They must be treated very gently, and I hope my little Jewel will be always kind and patient, and make her new friends glad she is there."

The child folded the paper and put it carefully back in her pocket. Then she took her bath, and returning to her room undressed her doll in silence. Finally, changing her wrapper for her nightdress, she climbed into bed, where she lay thinking and looking at the sunlight on the wall.

At dinner time the maid Sarah appeared with a tray. "Here's your dinner, Miss Julia," she said, looking at the heavy-eyed little girl. "It's too bad you're not well."

"I am well, thank you," replied Jewel. "I'm sorry you had to carry that heavy tray up so many stairs."

"Oh, I don't mind that," returned the girl good-naturedly. "I'll set it right here by the bed."

"Is grandpa down there?" asked Jewel wistfully.

"Yes, Miss Julia. They're all eating their dinner. I hope you'll enjoy yours."

Sarah went away, and the little girl spread some bread and butter and ate it slowly.

Meanwhile, when the family had gathered at the dinner table, Mr. Evringham looked up at his housekeeper.

"Where is Jewel?" he asked shortly. "I object to her being unpunctual."

"Yes, sir. She is having dinner in her room. She was very naughty and got wet in the brook."

"Ah, indeed!" Mr. Evringham frowned and looked down. He had been a little disappointed that the bright face was not watching to see him come home from his ride, but of course discipline must be maintained. "I'm sorry to hear this," he added.

Mrs. Evringham and Eloise found him a shade less taciturn than usual to-night. He felt vaguely that he now had an ally of his own flesh and blood in the house, a spirit sufficiently kindred to prefer his society to theirs, and this made him unusually lenient.

He meant to go upstairs after dinner, and warn Jewel to be more careful in future to conform to all Mrs. Forbes's rules; but the meal was scarcely over when a friend called to get him to attend some business meeting held that evening in the interests of the town, and he became interested in his statements and went away with him.

"Wasn't father quite agreeable this evening?" asked Mrs. Evringham of Eloise. "What did I tell you? I could see that he felt relief because that plain little creature was not in evidence. Father always was so fastidious. Of course it is selfish in a way, but it is no use to blame men for caring for beauty. They will do it."

"It was a shame to make that little girl stay upstairs," returned Eloise. "I judge she managed to amuse herself this afternoon, and so she gets punished for it. I should like to go up and sit with her."

"It would not be worth while," returned Mrs. Evringham quickly. "I'm sure Dr. Ballard will be here soon. You would have to come right down again."

"That is not the reason I don't go," returned the girl. "It is because I am not an Evringham, and I have determined not to arrive at friendly relations with any one of the name. When I once escape from here, they will have seen the last of me."

"The way of escape lies open," returned her mother soothingly. "I'm glad you have on that gown. If a man cares for a woman, he always loves to see her in white."

As soon as dinner was over, Mrs. Forbes ascended the stairs to see her prisoner. Jewel was lying quietly in bed, the tray, apparently untouched, beside her. The latter circumstance Mrs. Forbes observed at once.

"Why haven't you eaten your dinner, Julia?" she asked. "I hope you are not sulking."

"No'm. I don't believe I am. I don't know what that means."

"You don't know what sulky means?" suspiciously. "It is very naughty for a little girl to refuse to eat her dinner because she is angry at being punished for her own good."

"Did you send me to bed because you loved me?" asked Jewel. Her cheeks were very red, but even the disconcerted housekeeper could see that she was not excited or angry.

"Everybody loves good little girls," returned Mrs. Forbes. "Now eat your dinner, Julia, so I can carry down the tray."

"I did eat the bread. It was all I wanted. It was very nice."

The polite addition made the housekeeper uncertain. While she paused Jewel added, "I wish I could see grandpa."

"He's gone out on business. He won't be back until after you are asleep. And if you were thinking of complaining to him, Julia, I tell you it won't do any good. He will trust everything to me."

"Do you think I would trouble grandpa?" returned the child.

The housekeeper looked at her in silent perplexity. The blue eyes were direct and innocent, but there was a heaviness about them that stirred Mrs. Forbes uncomfortably.

"You must have got too tired playing this afternoon, Julia," she said decisively, "or you would be hungry for your dinner. You took that hot bath I told you to?"

"Yes'm."

"Where have you put your wet things? Oh, I see, you've spread them out very nicely; but those shoes—I shall have to have them cleaned and polished for you. Now go to sleep as quick as you can and have a long night's rest. I'm sure the next time you go out you won't be so careless."

Jewel's eyes followed the speaker as she bustled about and at last took up the tray.

"Will you kiss me good-night, Mrs. Forbes?" asked the child.

The surprised housekeeper set down her burden, stooped over the bed and kissed her.

"There now, I see you're sorry," she said, somewhat touched.

Jewel gave her a little smile. "No'm, I've stopped being sorry," she replied.

"She'd puzzle a Philadelphia lawyer," soliloquized the housekeeper as she descended the stairs with the tray. "I suppose her mother is uneducated and uses queer English. As the old ones croak, the young ones learn. The child uses words nobody ever heard of, and is ignorant of the commonest ones. I'm glad she's so fond of me if I've got to take care of her."

CHAPTER XI
DR. BALLARD

Mr. Evringham looked about, half in apprehension, half in anticipation, as he entered the dining-room the following morning. Jewel had not arrived, so he settled himself to read his paper. Each time there was a sound he glanced up, bracing himself for the approach of light feet, beaming face, and an ardent embrace. His interest in the news gradually lessened, and his expectancy increased. She did not come. At last he began to suspect that the unprecedented had happened, and that Mrs. Forbes herself was late.

He looked at his watch with suddenly rising amazement. It was ten minutes past the appointed time. He began feeling around with his foot for the electric bell. It was an unaccustomed movement, for his wishes were usually anticipated. By the time he found it, he had become a seriously injured man, and the peal he rang summoned Sarah suddenly.

"Bring me my coffee at once, if you please. What is the matter?"

The maid did not know. He was drinking his first cup when the housekeeper entered the room, flushed of countenance.

"You'll have to excuse me, Mr. Evringham. I couldn't come a minute sooner. Julia is sick."

"Sick! I should like to know why?"

"Why, she got sopping wet in that brook yesterday, and here, just as I knew it would be, she's got a fever."

"A fever, eh?" repeated Mr. Evringham in a startled tone.

"Yes, sir, and what's more, when I told her you would send for the doctor, it was worse than about the rubbers. She talked all the rubbish you can think of. I'm sure she's flighty—said she never had a doctor, that she always got well, and even cried when I told her that that was nonsense."

"Was she ill all night, do you think?"

"I don't know. I found her trying to get up when I went to her room, and I saw at once that she wasn't able to.

"Well, Mrs. Forbes, all I can do is to ask your pardon for adding so much to your cares. Let Sarah bring me my eggs, and then, if you please, telephone for Dr. Ballard to come over before his office hour."

"I will, sir, but I'll ask you to see the child before you go to town and make her promise to behave about the doctor. You'd have thought I was asking to let in a roaring lion."

"Shy, probably."

"Shy! That child shy!" thought Mrs. Forbes.

"She knows Dr. Ballard," continued the broker, "and if you had thought to mention him, she wouldn't have made any fuss."

"If you'll excuse me differing with you, Mr. Evringham, I don't think that child's got a shy bone in her body. In the trolley car yesterday, didn't she make up to a perfect stranger! She eyed him and fingered that little gold pin she wears, till he smiled and touched one of the same pattern in his own cravat. Young as she is, she's some kind of a free mason or secret society, you may be sure. I actually saw him take her hand and give her the grip as he got out of the car. Why you know who it is, it was Mr. Reeves of Highland Street."

"H'm. You are imaginative, Mrs. Forbes. Mr. Reeves is fond of children, and Jewel has a friendly way of looking at people."

The housekeeper bridled. "Well, all is, I guess, you'll find I ain't imaginative when you come to talk with her about the doctor," was the firm response. "When I said medicine she looked as scared as if I'd said poison."

"H'm. Been dosed then. Mother an allopath probably. Burnt child dreads the fire. I think homeopathy is the thing for children. Guy will do very well. Call him up at once, please. He might go out."

When Mr. Evringham had finished his breakfast, he climbed to the white room, planning as he went a short and peremptory speech to the rebellious one; for he had less time left than usual for his daily talk with his housekeeper before catching the train.

The curtains in the room were half drawn as he entered, and the child's figure looked small in the big white bed. She exclaimed as he drew near, and seizing his hand, kissed it.

"You'd better not kiss me, grandpa, because I'm so hot and uncomfortable," she said thickly. "Oh, how I wanted to see you all night!"

The little hands clinging to his were burning. He sat down on the edge of the bed.

"I'm very sorry for this, Jewel. It's your own fault, I understand, my girl."

"Yes, I know it is. When I first called the house Castle Discord and talked to Anna Belle about the error fairy, and the enchanted maiden, and the giantess, I didn't see it was hate creeping in and making me not careful to deny it all. I know it is all my fault."

Mr. Evringham gazed at the flushed face with startled eyes. "Dear me, this is really very bad!" he thought. "Delirious so early in the morning. I wish Guy would come!"

"Well, we'll soon have Dr. Ballard here," he said aloud, trying to speak soothingly. "He'll set you all right very soon."

"Oh, grandpa, dear grandpa," with the utmost earnestness, "would you please not send for the doctor? I won't be any trouble. I don't want anything to eat, only a drink of water, and I'll soon be well."

Her beseeching tone and her helplessness touched some unsuspected chord in her listener's breast.

"Jewel, don't you want to go out to the stable with me and feed Essex Maid with sugar?" he asked.

"Yes, grandpa," with a half sob.

"You don't want me to be unhappy and worried about you when I get into my office?"

"No, grandpa."

"And you liked Dr. Ballard, I'm sure, when you came out with him on the train day before yesterday."

"Day before yesterday! Oh, *was* it? It seems a year ago! But I wanted to come and see you so much I was willing to let father and mother go away, and I never thought that I wouldn't know when error was getting hold of me.

"Well, never mind now, Jewel. Dr. Ballard will help you, and as soon as you get well I'll take you for a fine long drive, if you'll be good. I'm sure you don't want to trouble me."

"No." Another half sob caught the child's throat. "Here is something I bought for you yesterday, grandpa." She drew from under the further pillow the yellow chicken, somewhat disheveled, and put it in his hand. "I meant to give it to you last night, but Mrs. Forbes kept me upstairs because she thought she ought to make me sorry, and so I couldn't."

The stockbroker cleared his throat as he regarded his new possession. "It was kind of you, Jewel," he returned. "I shall stand it on my desk. Now— ahem"—looking around the big empty room, "you won't be lonely, I hope, until the doctor comes?"

"No, I'd like to be alone, I have so much work to do."

"Dear me, dear me!" thought Mr. Evringham, "this is very distressing. She seems to have lucid intervals, and then so quickly gets flighty again."

"Besides, I like to think of the Ravine of Happiness," continued the child, "and the brook. Supposing I could lay my cheek down in the brook now. The water is so cool, and it laughs and whispers such pretty things."

"Now if you would try to go to sleep, Jewel," said Mr. Evringham, "it would please me very much. Good-by. I shall come to see you again to-night." He stooped his tall form and kissed the child's forehead, and her hot lips pressed his hand, then he went out.

At the foot of the stairs he encountered Mrs. Forbes waiting, and hastily put behind him the hand that held the chicken.

"Well, sir?"

"She's very badly off, very badly off, I'm afraid."

"I hope not, sir. Children are always flighty if they have a little fever. What about dinner, sir?"

"Have anything you please," returned Mr. Evringham briefly. "I wish to see Dr. Ballard as soon as he arrives. Tell Zeke I shall not go until the next train." With these words the broker entered his study, and his housekeeper looked after him in amazement. It was the first time she had ever seen him indifferent concerning his dinner.

"I wonder if he thinks she's got something catching," she soliloquized. Then a sudden thought occurred to her. "No great loss without some small gain," she thought grimly. "'T would clear the house."

She watched at the window until she saw Dr. Ballard's buggy approaching. Then she opened the door and met him.

"Your little visitor do you say?" asked the young doctor as he greeted her and entered. "What mischief has she been up to so soon?"

"Oh, the usual sort," returned Mrs. Forbes, and recounted her grievances. "She's the oddest child in the world," she finished, "and her last freak is that she doesn't want to have a doctor."

"Dear me, what heresy!" The young man smiled. "Which room, Mrs. Forbes?"

"Please go into the library first, Dr. Ballard. Mr. Evringham is waiting to see you."

The broker was sitting before his desk as the doctor entered, and he turned with a brief greeting.

"I'm glad you've come, Ballard. I'm very much troubled about the child. Her father and mother abroad you understand, and I feel the responsibility. She seems very flighty, quite wild in her talk at moments. I wished to warn you that one of her feverish ideas is that she doesn't want a doctor. You will have to use some tact."

The physician's face lost its careless smile. "Delirious, you say?"

"Yes, go right up, Guy. I'll wait for you here. It's so sudden. She was quite well, to all appearances, yesterday."

"Children are sensitive little mortals," remarked Dr. Ballard, and then Mrs. Forbes ushered him up to the white room. He asked her to remain within call, and entered alone.

The child's eyes were open as he approached the bed, the black case she remembered in his hand. By her expression he saw that her mind was clear.

"Well, well, Jewel, this isn't the way I meant you to receive me the first time I called," he said pleasantly, drawing up a chair beside the bed. The child put out her hand to his offered one and tried to smile. As he held the hand he felt her pulse. "This isn't the way to behave when you go visiting," he added.

"I know it isn't," returned Jewel contritely.

"The next time you go wading in the brook, take off your shoes and stockings, little one, and I think you would better wait until later in the season, anyway. You've made quick work of this business." As he talked the doctor took his little thermometer out of its case. "Now then, let me slip this under your tongue."

"What is it?" asked Jewel, shrinking.

"What! Haven't you ever had your temperature tried? Well, you have been a healthy little girl! All the better. Just take it under your tongue, and don't speak for a minute, please."

"Please don't ask me to. I can't."

"There's nothing to be afraid of. It won't hurt you." The doctor smiled.

"I know what that is now," said Jewell, regarding the little tube. "A man was cured of paralysis once by having a thing like that stuck in his mouth. He thought it was meant to cure him. I haven't paralysis."

The doctor began to consider that perhaps Mr. Evringham had not exaggerated. "Come, Jewel," he said kindly. "I thought we were such good friends. You are wasting my time."

A moment more of hesitation, and then the child suddenly opened her mouth and accepted the thermometer. She kept her eyes closed during the process of waiting, and at last Dr. Ballard took out the little instrument and examined it.

"Let me see your tongue."

The child stared in surprise.

"Put out your tongue, Jewel," he repeated kindly.

"But that is impolite," she protested.

He changed his position. The poor little thing was flighty, and no wonder, with such a temperature. He took her hand again. "I'll overlook the impoliteness. Run out your tongue now. Far as you can, dear."

The child obeyed.

Presently she said, "I feel very uncomfortable, Dr. Ballard. I don't feel a bit like visiting, so if you wouldn't *mind* going away until I feel better. You interrupted me when you came in. I have lots of work to do yet. When I get well I'd just love to see you. I'd rather see you than almost anybody in Bel-Air."

"Yes, yes, dear. I'll go away very soon. Where does your throat feel sore? Put your finger on the place."

Jewel looked up with all the rebuke she could convey. "You ought not to ask me that," she returned.

Dr. Ballard rose and went to the door. "Get me a glass of water, please, Mrs. Forbes."

"Not a glass. I want a whole pitcher full right side of me," said Jewel.

"Yes, a pitcher full also, if you please, Mrs. Forbes. Just let the maid bring them up."

The doctor returned to the bedside. "Now we'll soon forget that you wet those little feet," he said.

"That didn't do me any harm, that clean sweet brook. Mrs. Forbes didn't know what was the real matter."

"What was it, then?"

"My own fault," said Jewel, speaking with feverish quickness and squeezing the doctor's hand. "When I came here I found that nobody loved one another and everybody was afraid and sorry, and instead of denying it and helping them, I began voicing error and calling them names. I didn't keep remembering that God was here, and I called it Castle Discord and called Mrs. Forbes the giantess, and aunt Madge the error fairy, and cousin Eloise the enchanted maiden, and of course how could I help getting sick?"

Dr. Ballard leaned toward her. Was this an impromptu tale, or was it a fact that this child had been coldly treated and unhappy? "You have a sensitive conscience, Jewel," he returned.

Here Sarah entered, set down the tray with pitcher, glasses, and spoon, and departed. The doctor loosed the little hand he had been holding, took up his case, and opened it.

Jewel watched him with apprehension. "That's—medicine isn't it?" she asked with bated breath.

"Yes." The doctor carefully selected a bottle of liquid and set it on the table. "I think this one will do us."

Jewel's remark on the train about materia medica recurred to him, and he smiled.

"Dr. Ballard, aren't you a Christian?" she asked suddenly.

He glanced up. "I hope so."

"Then you'll forgive me if I won't take medicine. I put out my tongue, and I sucked the little glass thing because I didn't want to trouble you; but I have too much faith in God to take medicine." The child looked at the doctor appealingly.

He began to see light, and in his surprise, for a moment he did not reply.

"Jesus Christ would have used drugs if they had been right," she added.

"But He isn't here now," returned the astonished young man.

"Why, Dr. Ballard," in gentle reproach, "Christ is the Truth of God. Isn't He here now, healing us and helping us just the same as ever? Didn't He say He would be? You will see how much better I shall be to-night."

Dr. Ballard met the heavy eyes with his own kind, clear ones. "I see you have been taught in new ways, Jewel," he said seriously, "but you are only a little girl, and while you are in your grandfather's house you ought to do as he wishes. He wishes you to let me prescribe for you. No one who is ill can help making trouble. You have no right not to try to get well in the way Mr. Evringham and Mrs. Forbes wish you to."

Jewel felt herself in a desperate position. The corners of her lips twitched down. Dr. Ballard thought he saw his advantage, and leaned his fine head toward her. She impulsively threw her arms around his neck.

"You don't want to hurt my feelings, Jewel," he said. She was crying softly.

"No—it would make me—very—sorry, but it would be—worse—to hurt—God's. Please don't make me, please, please don't make me, Dr. Ballard!"

She was increasingly excited, and he feared the effect.

"Very well then, Jewel," he returned. "I don't want to do you more harm than good."

"Oh, thank you!" she exclaimed fervently, through her tears.

"But Mrs. Forbes must think you have the medicine. You haven't told her that you are—ahem—a Christian Scientist. I suppose that is what you call yourself."

"Yes, sir. A Christian Scientist. Oh, you're the kindest man," pursued the relieved child. "I realized in my prayer that you didn't know it was wrong to believe in material medica, for you reflect love all the time."

While she was talking and wiping her eyes the doctor took the pitcher and one of the glasses to the window, and stood with his back to her.

"Now then," he said, returning, "we'll put this half glass of water on the table. I put the spoon across it so, and when Mrs. Forbes is next in the room you take a couple of spoonfuls and that will satisfy her. You may tell her that I wanted you only to take it about four times during the day. If you are better when I come back this evening, I will not insist upon your taking any pellets on your tongue. Here is the other glass for you to drink from."

With a few more kind words Dr. Ballard took his departure, and going downstairs met Mrs. Forbes. "The little girl has a heavy feverish cold. She understands how to take her medicine. She will probably sleep a good deal. Let her be quiet."

He went on to the study, where Mr. Evringham was waiting, sitting at the desk, his head on his hand, frowning at the yellow chicken. He looked up expectantly as the doctor entered.

"Well?" he asked.

Dr. Ballard came forward and seated himself in a neighboring chair.

"Do you know what you have upstairs there?" he asked in a low tone.

"For heaven's sake, Guy, don't tell me it's something serious—something infectious!" Mr. Evringham turned pale.

The doctor's sudden smile was reassuring. "It does seem to be infectious to some degree," he returned, "but I don't believe you'll catch it."

"What are you grinning at, boy?" asked the broker sharply.

"Don't be alarmed, Mr. Evringham, but the fact is, that you have in your house a small and young but perfectly formed and well-developed specimen of a Christian Scientist."

"What, man!" The broker grew red again.

Dr. Ballard nodded deliberately. "Your little granddaughter belongs to the new cult; and I can assure you she is dyed in the wool, and moreover is all wool and a yard wide."

"The devil you say!" ejaculated Mr. Evringham. "But," he added with a sudden thought, "that may be a part of the poor child's feverish nonsense. She was full of talk of castles and giantesses and fairies and what not when I was up there."

"Yes. She is no flightier than you are this minute. All these titles are those she has given to your house and household in the last two days, and according to her diagnosis, it is that indulgence from which she is suffering now, and not from too much brook. She says she has 'voiced error.'"

The doctor looked quizzically at his friend, who returned his gaze, nonplussed.

"That's it—'error,'" rejoined Mr. Evringham, "that's what she is often saying. This explains her vocabulary, in all probability. She has sometimes the strangest talk you ever listened to. Well, that's the mother's doing, of course, and not the child's fault. I maintain it is not the child's fault. With it all, Ballard, I tell you she's a very well meaning child—a rather winning child, in fact. Good natured disposition. I hope she's not very ill. I do, indeed. Ha! That, then, is why she was so excited at the thought of having a doctor. Tomfoolery!"

"Yes, that was it. We've had some argument." The young doctor smiled. "She doesn't consider me hopeless, however. She told me that she had mentioned to the Lord that she was sure I didn't know it was wrong to believe in materia medica."

No one for years had heard Mr. Evringham laugh as he laughed at this. The doctor joined him.

"I'm not surprised," said the broker at last. "If there is anything she does not mention to her Creator, I have yet to learn what it is. How did you get around her, Ballard?"

"Oh, I used a little justifiable hocus-pocus about the medicine. That's all."

"And you think it's not anything very serious, then?"

"I think not. Where there's so much temperature it is a little hard to tell at first with a child. This evening I shall make a more thorough examination. The ice is broken now, and it will be easier. She will be less excited. I see," glancing at the yellow chicken, whose beady eyes appeared to be following the conversation, "the little girl has found her way even into this sanctum."

Mr. Evringham cleared his throat as he followed the doctor's glance. "No," he responded shortly. "She has not found her way in here yet. That is—my chicken. She bought it for me."

Dr. Ballard lifted his eyebrows and smiled as he arose.

"Come back before dinner if possible, Ballard. I shall be uneasy."

CHAPTER XII
THE TELEGRAM

Mrs. Forbes entered Jewel's room after speaking with the doctor. The little girl looked at her eagerly. A plan had formed in her mind which depended for its success largely on the housekeeper's complaisance, and she wished to propitiate her.

"I want to fix it so you can call me when you need anything, Julia," she said. "The doctor has told you about taking the medicine, and here is a little clock I'm going to put on your table right by the bed, and I've brought up a bell. I shall leave the farther door open so the sound of this bell will go right down the backstairs, and one of us will come up whenever you ring. Dr. Ballard says it's best for you to be quiet."

"Yes'm," replied Jewel. "Do you think, Mrs. Forbes—would it be too much trouble—would he have time—could I see Jeremiah just a few minutes?"

"See who?"

"Jeremiah—the gentleman who lives with the horses."

"Do you mean my son Ezekiel?"

"Oh, yes'm. Ezekiel. I knew it was a prophet. He always speaks very kindly to me, and I like him. I wish I could see him just a few minutes."

Mrs. Forbes was very much astonished and somewhat flattered. "It's wonderful, the fancy that child has taken to me and mine," she thought.

"Well, folks must be humored when they're sick," she replied. "Let me see," looking at the little clock, "yes, Mr. Evringham's missed the second train. There'll be five or ten minutes yet, and 'Zekiel's got to wait anyway. I guess he can come up and see you."

"Oh, thank you, Mrs. Forbes!" returned Jewel.

The housekeeper made her way out to the barn, where her son in his livery was waiting and reading the paper.

"The doctor's gone, Zeke, and the child wants to see you."

"Me?" returned the coachman in surprise. "Why the bully little kid!"

"Yes, come and be quick. There won't be much time. You watch the clock that's side of her bed, and don't you be late."

'Zekiel followed with alacrity. His mother, starting him up the backstairs, gave him directions how to go, and remained below.

Jewel, her eyes fixed on the open back door of her room, felt a leap of the heart as Zeke, fine in his handsome livery, came blushing and tiptoeing into the room.

"I'm so glad, I'm so glad!" she exclaimed in her soft, thick voice. "Shut the door, please."

"I told you to remember you'd only got to say 'Zeke' and I'd come," he said, approaching the bed. "I'm awful sorry you're sick, little kid."

"Did you ever hear of Christian Science, Zeke?" she asked hurriedly.

"Yes, I did. Woman I knew in Boston cured of half a dozen things. She held that Christian Science did it."

"Oh, good, good. I'm a Christian Scientist, and nobody here is, and I want to send a telegram to Chicago, to a lady to treat me. Nobody would do it for me but you. *Will* you?"

It would have taken a hard heart to resist the appeal, and Zeke's was soft.

"Of course I will," he answered. "Going right to the station now to take Mr. Evringham. I can send it as well as not."

"Get some paper, Zeke, in the top bureau drawer. There's a pencil on the bureau."

He obeyed, and she gave him an address which he wrote down. "Now this: 'Please treat me for fever and sore throat. Jewel.'"

Zeke wrote the message and tucked it into a pocket.

"Now please get my leather bag in the drawer," said the child, "and take out money enough."

The young fellow hesitated. "If you haven't got plenty of money"—he began.

"I have. You'll see. Oh, Zeke, you've made me so happy!"

The coachman's clumsy hands fumbled with the clasp of the little bag.

"I can do it," said Jewel, and he brought it to her and watched her while she took out the money and gave it to him. He took a coin, returned the rest to the bag, and snapped it.

"Say, little girl," he said uneasily, "you look to me like a doctor'd do you a whole lot o' good."

Jewel gazed at him in patient wonder.

"Who made the doctor?" she asked.

Zeke stood on one foot and then on the other.

"God did, and you know it, Zeke. He's the one to go to in trouble."

"But you're going to that Chicago woman," objected Zeke.

"Yes, because she'll go to God for me. I'm being held down by something that pretends to have power, and though I know it's an old cheat, I haven't understanding enough to get rid of it as quickly as she will. You see, I wouldn't have been taken sick if I hadn't believed in a lie instead of denying it. We have to watch our thoughts every minute, and I tell you, Zeke, sometimes it seems real hard work."

"Should say so," returned 'Zekiel. "The less you think the better, I should suppose, if that's the case. I've got to be going now."

"And you'll send the telegram *surely*, and you won't speak of it to any one?"

"Mum's the word, and I'll send it if it's the last act; but don't put all your eggs in one basket, little kid. I know Dr. Ballard's been here, and now you do everything he said, like a good girl, and between the two of 'em they ought to fix you up. I'd pin more faith to a doctor in the hand than to one in the bush a thousand miles away, if 't was *me*."

Jewel smiled on him from heavy eyes. "Did you ever hear of God's needing any help?" she asked. "I'll never forget your being so kind to me, never, Zeke; and when error melts away I'm coming out to the stable with grandpa. He said I should. Good-by."

As soon as the plum-colored livery had disappeared Jewel drew herself up, took the water pitcher between her hot little hands, and drank long and deeply. Then with a sigh of satisfaction she turned over in bed and drew Anna Belle close to her.

"Just see, dearie," she murmured, "how we are always taken care of!"

Mrs. Evringham saw Dr. Ballard's buggy drive away and lost no time in discovering who had needed his services.

"It's the child," she announced, returning to Eloise's room.

"Poor little thing," returned the girl, rising.

"Where are you going? Stay right where you are. She has a high fever, and they're not sure yet what it may be. Mrs. Forbes is doing everything that is necessary. Father has waited over two trains. He hasn't gone to the city yet."

At the mention of Mr. Evringham Eloise sank back in her chair.

"Dr. Ballard is coming again toward evening," continued Mrs. Evringham, "and I shall talk with him and find out just the conditions. Mrs. Forbes is very unsatisfactory, but I can see that she thinks it may be something infectious."

Eloise lifted a suddenly hopeful face. "Then you would wish to leave at once?" she said.

"Not at all. Father would surely hear to reason and send the child to the hospital. They are models of comfort in these days, and it is the only proper place for people to be ill. I shall speak to Dr. Ballard about it to-night."

As soon as Eloise had seen her grandfather drive to the station she eluded her mother, and gathering her white negligee about her, went softly up to Jewel's room and stood at the closed door. All was still. She opened the door stealthily. With all her care it creaked a little. Still no sound from within. She looked toward the bed, saw the flushed face of the child and that she was asleep, so she withdrew as quietly.

During the day she inquired of Mrs. Forbes if she could be of any service, but the housekeeper received the suggestion with curt respect, assuring her that Dr. Ballard had said Jewel would sleep a good deal, and should not be disturbed.

Mrs. Evringham overheard the question and welcomed the reply with relief.

Jewel ate the bread and fruit and milk that Mrs. Forbes gave her for her late lunch, and said that she felt better.

"You look so," returned the housekeeper. The child had not once called her upstairs during the morning. She certainly was as little trouble as a sick child could be.

"If 't was anybody else," mused Mrs. Forbes, regarding her, "I should say that she sensed the situation and knew she'd brought it on herself and me, and was trying to make up for it; but nobody can tell what she thinks. Her eyes do look more natural. I guess Dr. Ballard's a good one."

"It don't seem to hurt you to swallow now," remarked Mrs. Forbes.

"No'm, it doesn't, she answered.

"Now then, you see how foolish and naughty it was the way you behaved about having the doctor this morning. Look how much better you are already!"

"Yes'm, I love Dr. Ballard."

"You well may. He's done well by you." Mrs. Forbes took the tray. "Now do you feel like going to sleep again? The doctor won't come till about six o'clock. Your fever'll rise toward evening, and that's the time he wants to see you. I shall sleep in the spare room next you to-night."

"Thank you, Mrs. Forbes. You are so kind; but you won't have to," replied the child earnestly. "Would you please draw up the curtains and put Anna Belle's clothes on the bed? Perhaps I'll dress her after a while. It doesn't seem fair to make her stay in bed when it wasn't her error."

"I don't think you'd better keep your arms out," returned Mrs. Forbes decidedly. "I'll put up the curtains, but when you come to try to do anything you'll find you are very weak. You can ring the bell when you want to, you know. And don't take your medicine again for an hour after eating. I'd take another nap right away if I was you."

When she had gone out, Jewel shook her head at the doll, whose face was smiling toward her own. "You denied it, didn't you, dearie, the minute she said it," she whispered. "Error is using Mrs. Forbes to hold me under mortal mind laws, but it can't be so, because God doesn't want it, and I'm not afraid any more."

Jewel put her hand under her pillow and drew out the two slips of paper that bore her mother's messages. These she read through several times. "Of course there are more, Anna Belle. I shouldn't wonder if there was one in every pocket, but I don't mean to hunt. Divine love will send them to me just when I need them, the way He did these. I'm sorry I can't dress you, dearie, because you've just reflected love all the time, and ought not to be in bed at all; but I must obey, you know, so there won't be discord. I'd love to just hop up and get your clothes, but you'll forgive me for not, I know."

Again Jewel put her hand under her pillow and drew forth her copy of "Science and Health." "I'll read to you a little, dearie." She opened the book and read, "Rise in the strength of Spirit to resist all that is unlike God." Jewel paused and thought for a minute. "You might think, Anna Belle, that that meant rise against Mrs. Forbes, but it doesn't. It means rise against all error, and one error is believing that Mrs. Forbes is cross or afraid." She went on reading for several minutes, passing glibly over familiar phrases and sticking at or skipping words which presented difficulties.

While she was thus employed Eloise again stole quietly to her cousin's door, and hearing the soft voice she grew pale. Her mother had exacted a promise from her that she would not enter the room until Dr. Ballard consented, so after a minute's hesitation she fled downstairs and found Mrs. Forbes.

"I think the little girl must be worse! She is talking to herself incessantly."

Mrs. Forbes regarded the pale face coldly. "I guess there's some mistake. She was better when I saw her half an hour ago. I'll go up in a minute."

The minute stretched to five; Jewel had slept scarcely at all the night before, and by the time the housekeeper had laboriously reached her door, her voice had grown fainter, then stopped, and she was sound asleep.

"I wish Mamzell would keep her finger out of this pie," soliloquized Mrs. Forbes as she retraced her steps.

When Mr. Evringham returned from the city, his first question, as Zeke met him, was concerning Jewel.

"Mother says she's slept the most of the day," replied the coachman, his head stiff in his high collar and his eyes looking straight ahead.

"H'm. A good sign does she think, or is it stupor?"

"I couldn't say, sir."

Reaching the house, a long pasteboard box in his hands, Mr. Evringham found that his grandchild was still asleep.

"I fear the worst, Mrs. Forbes," he said with nervous curtness. "When a stupor attacks children it is a very bad sign I am told. I'll just ring up Ballard."

He did so, but the doctor had gone out and was intending to call at the park before he returned.

"I really think it is all right, Mr. Evringham," said Mrs. Forbes, distressed by her employer's uneasiness. "Dr. Ballard expected she'd sleep a great deal. He told me not to disturb her."

"Oh, very well then, perhaps it is not to be regretted. Kindly put those roses in the deep vase, Mrs. Forbes."

"Yes, sir." She took up the box. "Besides, Mr. Evringham, if she does get worse, you know the hospital here is one of the very best, and you" —

Mr. Evringham wheeled and frowned upon the speaker fiercely. "Hospital!" he ejaculated. "An extraordinary suggestion, Mrs. Forbes! Most extraordinary! My granddaughter remains in my house."

Mrs. Forbes, crimson with surprise and mortification, retreated. "Very well, sir," she faltered. "Will you have the roses on the dinner table, Mr. Evringham?"

"No. Set them here on my desk if you please." With this Mr. Evringham began walking up and down the floor, pausing once to take up the yellow chicken. During the day the soft moan, "I wanted you so all night, grandpa," had been ringing in his ears.

"Mrs. Forbes has no understanding of the child," he muttered, "and of course I cannot expect anything from the cat and her kitten."

With this he began again his promenade. Mrs. Forbes returned with the roses, and simultaneously Mr. Evringham saw Essex Maid arching her neck as she picked her steps past the window.

"By the way," he said curtly, "let Zeke take the Maid back to the barn. I'll not ride to-day."

"It's very fine weather, sir," protested Mrs. Forbes.

"I'll not ride. I'll wait here for Dr. Ballard."

The housekeeper went forth to give the order.

"I never saw Mr. Evringham so upset in my life," she said in an awestruck tone.

"I saw the governor wasn't real comfortable," returned the boy. "Guess he's afraid he's goin' to catch the mumps or something. It would be real harrowin' if he got any worse case of big head than he's got already."

Mr. Evringham was little accustomed to waiting, and by the time Dr. Ballard appeared, his nervousness had become painful. "The child's slept too much, I'm sure of it, Ballard," was his greeting. "I don't know what we're going to find up there, I declare I don't."

"It depends on whether it's a good sleep," returned the doctor, and his composed face and manner acted at once beneficially upon Mr. Evringham.

"Well, you'll know, Guy, you'll know, my boy. Mrs. Forbes saw you coming, and she has gone upstairs to prepare the little girl. She'll be glad to see you this time, I'll wager."

The broker, roses in hand, ascended the staircase after the physician. Mrs. Forbes was standing at the foot of the bed, and the room was pleasantly light as they entered. Jewel, the flush of sleep on her cheeks, was looking expectantly toward the door. Dr. Ballard came in first and she smiled in welcome, then Mr. Evringham appeared, heavy roses nodding in all directions before him.

"Grandpa!" exclaimed the child. "Why, grandpa, did *you* come?"

There was no mistaking the joy in her tone. Dr. Ballard paused in surprise, while the stockbroker approached the bed.

"I brought you a few flowers, Jewel," he said, while she pressed his disengaged hand against her cheek.

"They're the most lovely ones I ever saw," she returned with conviction. "They make me happy just to look at them."

"Well, Jewel," said the doctor, "I hear you've been making up for lost sleep in great shape." His eyes, as he spoke, were taking in with concentrated interest the signs in her face. He came and sat beside the bed, while Mr. Evringham fell back and Mrs. Forbes regarded the child critically.

"Well, now, you're a good little patient," went on the doctor, as he noted the clear eyes.

"Yes, Dr. Ballard, I feel just as nice as can be," she answered.

"No thickness in the voice. I fancy that sore throat is better." The young doctor could not repress his smile of satisfaction. "I was certain that was the right attenuation," he thought. "Now let us see."

He took out the little thermometer, and Jewel submitted to having it slipped beneath her tongue.

As Dr. Ballard leaned back in his chair to wait, he looked up at Mr. Evringham. "It is very gratifying," he said, "to find these conditions at this hour of the day. I felt a little more uneasy this morning than I confessed." He nodded in satisfactory thought. "I grant you medicine is not an exact science, it is an art, an art. You can't prescribe by hard and fast rules. You must take into consideration the personal equation."

Presently he leaned forward and removed the thermometer. His eyes smiled as he read it, and he lifted it toward Mr. Evringham.

"I can't see it, boy."

"Well, there's nothing to see. She hasn't a particle of temperature. Look here, little one," frowning at Jewel, "if everybody recovered as quickly as you have, where would we doctors be?"

Turning again and addressing Mr. Evringham, he went on, "I'm particularly interested in this result because that is a remedy over which there has been some altercation. There's one man to whom I shall be glad to relate this experience." The doctor leaned toward his little patient. "Jewel, I'm not so surprised as I might be at your improvement," he said kindly. "You will have to excuse me for a little righteous deception. I put medicine into that glass of water, and now you're glad I did, aren't you? I'd like you to tell me, little girl, as near as you can, how often you took it?"

"I didn't take it," replied the child.

Dr. Ballard drew back a little. "You mean," he said after a moment, "you took it only once?"

"No, sir, I didn't take it at all."

There was a silence, during which all could hear the ticking of the clock on the table, and the three pairs eyes were fixed on Jewel with such varying expressions of amazement and disapproval that the child's breath began to come faster.

"Didn't you drink any of the water?" asked Dr. Ballard at last.

"Yes, out of the pitcher."

"Why not out of the glass?"

"It didn't look enough. I was so thirsty."

They could not doubt her.

Mr. Evringham finally found his voice.

"Jewel, why didn't you obey the doctor?" His eyes and voice were so serious that she stretched out her arm.

"Oh, grandpa," she said, "please let me take hold of your hand."

"No, not till you answer me. Little girls should be obedient."

Jewel thought a minute.

"He said it wasn't medicine, so what was the use?" she asked.

Mr. Evringham, seeming to find an answer to this difficult, bit the end of his mustache.

Dr. Ballard was feeling his very ears grow red, while Mrs. Forbes's lips were set in a line of exasperation.

"Grandpa," said Jewel, and the child's voice was very earnest, "there's a Bible over there on the table. You look in there in the Gospels, and you'll find everywhere how Jesus tells us to do what I've done. He said he must go away, but he would send the Comforter to us, and this book tells about the Comforter." Jewel took the copy of "Science and Health" from under the sheet.

"God's creation couldn't get sick. It's just His own image and likeness, so how could it? And when you can get right into God's love, what do you want of medicine to swallow? God wouldn't be omnipotent if He needed any help. You see I'm well. Isn't that all you want, grandpa?"

The appeal of her eyes caused the broker to stir undecidedly. "I never did have any use for doctors," he thought, after the manner of many who, nevertheless, are eager to fly to the brotherhood for help at the first suggestion of pain. Moreover, the humor of the situation was beginning to dawn upon him, and he admired the fine temper and self-control with which the young physician pulled himself together and rose.

"*I* am glad you are well, Jewel, very," he said; "but the next time I am called to prescribe for a little Christian Scientist I shall put the pellets on her tongue." He smiled as he took up his case and said good-by.

Mr. Evringham followed him down the stairs, heroically resisting the impulse to laugh. Only one remark he allowed himself as he bade the doctor good-by.

"You're quite right, Ballard, in your theory. Jewel has been here only three days, but I could have told you that in doing anything whatever for her, it is always absolutely necessary to consider the personal equation."

CHAPTER XIII
IN THE LIBRARY

As Mr. Evringham turned from the closed door he met his daughter-in-law coming out into the hall.

"I've been watching for Dr. Ballard," she said with annoyance. "I don't see why I didn't hear him come down." At this juncture she paused, surprised to observe that her father-in-law was laughing. She attributed this unusual ebullition to ridicule of herself.

"I only wanted to ask if Julia's illness is infectious," she went on with dignity. "Eloise and I are naturally very anxious. We should like to do anything for her we can, if it is quite safe."

"Madam, don't, I pray, for all our sakes, run any risk," returned Mr. Evringham, his lips still twitching as he bowed mockingly.

"It would be very foolish," answered Mrs. Evringham, unabashed. "You wouldn't care to have more invalids on your hands. It has been all I could do to keep Eloise away from the sick room to-day."

"Is it possible!" commented Mr. Evringham, smoothing his mustache.

"Not only possible but true, and I wished to go to headquarters and find out the exact state of the case."

Again the broker's shoulders began to shake.

"Ballard isn't headquarters," he replied.

Mrs. Evringham regarded him, startled. She wondered if affairs were perhaps very serious, and her father-in-law's nerves overstrained. She knew that he had dispensed with the afternoon ride which was so important to him.

She grew a shade paler. "I wish you would tell me, father, just what the doctor said," she begged.

Mr. Evringham raised a protesting hand. "I couldn't think of it," he laughed. "It would give me apoplexy."

His daughter-in-law began to retreat, and the broker passed her and went into his study, still laughing.

Mrs. Evringham stood with lips parted, looking after him. Her heart beat fast. The doctor had called twice. He had come down the stairs in dead silence just now. She knew it, for she had been listening and waiting to intercept him. She had meant to say a number of pretty things to him concerning Eloise's anxiety about her little cousin. Her own anxiety redoubled, and she hurried to her daughter's room and narrated her experience.

"I really think we may have to go, Eloise," she finished nervously. "Even if it isn't infectious, it is so dreadfully dispiriting to be in a house where there is a dangerous illness, and possibly worse. I've been thinking perhaps we might go in town and take lodgings for a while. No one need know it. We could even stay there through the summer. None of our friends would be in town; then in autumn we could come back here."

Eloise's lip curled. "I doubt that," she returned. "Grandfather will be forearmed. I prophesy, mother, that you will never get our trunks up here again after you once take them out."

"Really, Eloise, you do put things most repulsively," returned Mrs. Evringham with vexation. "Besides, how do we know what the future is going to bring forth? Father behaves to me as if he might be on the verge of brain fever himself."

"Poor little Jewel!" exclaimed the girl. "I hope she will pull through, but if she is the cause of our leaving here, I shall always love her memory."

"I don't know whether father will even come to dinner," said Mrs. Evringham, pursuing her own thoughts, "but I suppose we shall see Mrs. Forbes. I do hope she has some sense about using disinfectants. It's outrageous for her to come near the dining-room when she is taking care of that child. Of course they'll have a nurse at once. Forbes doesn't like going out of her beaten track."

"I can't forget that poor little voice rambling on so monotonously this afternoon," said Eloise. "I strained my ears to listen, but I could make out only that she said something about 'love' and then about 'righteousness.' What a word for that little mouth."

"I've seen smaller," remarked Mrs. Evringham.

When finally they entered the dining-room punctually at the appointed hour,—even Mrs. Evringham dared take no liberties with that,—the host was there and greeted them as usual. Mrs. Forbes came in and took her position near him. Her employer gave her a side glance. His fears for Jewel allayed, his regard for his housekeeper's opinions had returned in full force.

He wished to ask for the little girl, to ask what she was doing now, and what she would like sent up for dinner, but he had not the courage. The aghast countenance which Mrs. Forbes had exhibited at the moment when the enormity of Jewel's conduct transpired remained in his memory. The housekeeper's appearance at present was noncommittal. Mrs. Evringham sent her piercing and questioning glances in vain.

The silence in the usually silent room had not had time to become noticeable when the portiere was pushed aside and Jewel, arrayed in the dotted dress and carefully bearing the tall vase of nodding roses, entered the room.

Mrs. Evringham uttered a little cry and dropped her spoon. Eloise stared wild-eyed. The housekeeper flushed.

"Good evening," said the child, glancing about as she approached, and sighing with relief as she set the heavy vase on the edge of the table. "I had to come down so carefully not to spill, grandpa, that it made me a little late. Mrs. Forbes said you brought me the roses under false—false pretends, so I thought perhaps you would like them on the table."

The housekeeper, hurrying forward, seized the vase from its precarious position and placed it in the centre of the board. "I didn't tell you you might come downstairs," she said, as she buttoned the middle button of Jewel's dress.

The little girl looked up in innocent surprise. "You said I might dress me, so why should anybody have to bring up my dinner?" she asked.

Mrs. Forbes's countenance looked so lowering that Mr. Evringham hastened to speak in his brusque and final fashion. "She is here now. Might as well let her stay."

Jewel jumped into her chair and turned toward him with an apologetic smile. "I couldn't make my hair look very nice," she said, with the lift of her shoulders which he had come to connect with her confidential moments. Remembering the feverish child of the morning, he looked at her in silent wonder. The appearance of her flaxen head he could see was in contrast to the trim and well-cared-for look it had worn when she arrived.

"Poor little thing!" he thought. "She looks motherless—motherless." Involuntarily he cast a glance of impatience at his other guests. The expression of blank amazement on their faces stirred him to amusement.

"If you are afraid of infection, Madge, don't hesitate to retire to your room," he said. "Your dinner will be sent to you."

"What does this mean!" ejaculated Mrs. Evringham. "Why is Dr. Ballard coming twice a day to see that child?"

"To cure her, of course," returned the broker, his lips breaking into smiles. "Why do doctors generally visit patients?"

"Then when he came the second time he found her well?"

"Ha, ha," laughed Mr. Evringham, "yes, that's it. He found her well."

Eloise and her mother gazed at him in astonishment. Mrs. Forbes's face was immovable. A sense of humor was not included in her mental equipment, and she considered the whole affair lamentable and unseemly in the extreme.

"Grandpa," said Jewel, looking at him with gentle reproach, "you're not laughing at Dr. Ballard, are you? He's the *kindest* man. I love him, next to you, best of anybody in Bel-Air"—then thinking this declaration might hurt her aunt and cousin, she added, "because I know him the best, you know. He tried to deceive me about the medicine, but it was only because he didn't know that there isn't any righteous deceiving. He meant to do me good."

Mrs. Evringham looked curiously from the child to her father-in-law. As she herself said later, she had never felt so "out of it" in her life. As the subject concerned Dr. Ballard, she wished to understand clearly what circumstance could possibly have induced Mr. Evringham to laugh repeatedly.

"I was passing your door this afternoon," said Eloise, addressing Jewel, "and I heard you talking. I knew there was no one with you, and I feared you were very ill."

The little girl was always pleased when her beautiful cousin looked at her.

"I guess I was reading. Of course I was in a hurry to get well, so as soon as the fever was gone and I felt comfortable, I began to read out loud from 'Science and Health' to Anna Belle. She's a Christian Scientist, too."

The faces of Mrs. Evringham and Eloise were studies as they gazed at the speaker.

Mr. Evringham glanced at them maliciously under his heavy brows as Sarah brought in the second course.

"Is Anna Belle your doll?" asked Eloise, for the moment sufficiently interested almost to lose her self-consciousness.

"Yes," eagerly. "Would you like to see her?" Jewel gave a fleeting glance at Mrs. Forbes. "She always comes to the table with me at home," she added.

"Sit still," murmured Mrs. Forbes in low, sepulchral warning.

"Now then, Jewel," said Mr. Evringham as he began to serve the filet, "you didn't take the doctor's medicine. What do you think made that high fever go away?"

The little girl looked up brightly. "Oh, I telegraphed to Mrs. Lewis, one of mother's friends in Chicago, to treat me."

"The dev—What do you mean, child?"

Mr. Evringham gazed at her, and his tone was so fierce, although he was only very much amazed, that Jewel's smile faded. The corners of her lips drew down pitifully, and suddenly she slipped from her chair, and running to him threw her arms around his neck and buried her averted face, revealing two forlorn little flaxen pigtails devoid of ribbons.

"What's this, Jewel?" he said quickly, fearfully embarrassed before his wondering audience. "This is very irregular, very irregular." He dropped his fork perforce, and his hand closed over the little arm across his cravat.

Jewel was trying to control a sob that struggled to escape, and saying over and over, as nearly as he could understand, something about God being Love.

"Go right back to your chair now, like a good girl."

"Do you—love me?" whispered Jewel.

"Yes—yes, I do."

"You spoke like" —a sob— "like hating."

"Not at all, not at all," rejoined Mr. Evringham quickly, "but I was very much surprised, very."

"Shall I take her upstairs, sir?" asked Mrs. Forbes, nearly bursting with the outrage of such an interruption to her employer's sacred dinner.

"No, she's going to sit right down in her chair and not make any trouble. Don't you like those roses I brought you, Jewel?" he added awkwardly, hoping to make a diversion. He was successful. She lowered her face, a fleeting April smile flitting over it.

"Did grandfather bring you those lovely roses?" asked Eloise.

Mr. Evringham flashed her his first glance of approval for so quickly taking the cue.

"Yes," replied the child, her breath catching as she went back to her chair. "I seemed so sick when he went away this morning was the reason; so now I'm well again—they belong to everybody, don't they, grandpa?"

Mr. Evringham paused to consider a reply. He desired to be careful in public not to draw upon himself that small catapult.

"They belong to you still, Jewel. I never take back my presents," he returned at last.

"And I think Mrs. Forbes was mistaken about the false pretends," said the child, swallowing and looking apologetically at the housekeeper, "because who would pretend such error as sickness, and of course you'd know I didn't pretend."

"Certainly not," said Mr. Evringham. "Mrs. Forbes didn't mean that. The whole thing seems like a dream now," he added.

"What else could it seem like?" returned Jewel, smiling faintly toward her grandfather with an air of having caught him napping.

"Like reality," he returned dryly.

She gazed at him, her smile fading.

He looked up apprehensively and cringed a little, not at all sure that the next instant would not find the rose-leaf cheek next his, and a close whisper driving cold chills down his back; but the child only paused a moment.

"Reality is so much different from sin, disease, and death," she said at last, in a matter-of-fact manner. It was too much for Mrs. Evringham's risibles. She laughed in spite of her daughter's reproachful glance.

"How wonderful if true!" she exclaimed.

"It is true," returned Jewel soberly. "Even Anna Belle knows that; but I'm sure that you haven't learned anything about Christian Science, aunt Madge," she added politely.

"What makes you so sure?" returned Mrs. Evringham banteringly.

Jewel flushed with embarrassment and glanced at her grandfather involuntarily, but he was busy eating and evidently would not help her.

"I'd rather not say," replied the child at last, and her rejoinder incited her aunt to further merriment.

"Aunt Madge doesn't laugh in a nice way," thought Jewel. "It's even pleasanter when she looks sorry."

"What is real then, Jewel?" asked Eloise gravely.

The child flashed upon her a sweet look.

"Everything good and glad," she answered.

Something rose in the girl's throat, and she pressed her lips together for an instant.

"You are happy to believe that," she returned.

"Oh, I don't believe it," replied Jewel. "It's one of the things I *know*. Mother says we only believe things when we aren't sure about them. Mother knows such a lot of beautiful truth."

The child looked at her cousin wistfully as she spoke. Eloise could scarcely retain her proud and nonchalant bearing beneath the blue eyes. They seemed to see through to her wretchedness.

She did not look at Jewel again during dinner. At the close Mr. Evringham pushed his chair back.

"I should like you to come with me into my study, Jewel, for a few minutes."

The child's face brightened, and she left the table with alacrity. Mr. Evringham stood back to allow his guests to pass out. They went on to the drawing-room, where Mrs. Evringham's self-restraint was loosed.

"The plot thickens, Eloise!" she said.

"And we are not going away," returned the girl.

"Decidedly not," declared her mother with emphasis.

"There is no hope of our catching anything that Jewel has now," went on Eloise.

Her mother glanced at her suspiciously. "What, for instance?"

"Oh," returned the girl, shrugging her shoulder, "faith, hope, and charity."

Mrs. Evringham laughed. "Indeed! Is the wind in that quarter? Then with the Christian Science microbe in the house, there's no telling what may happen to you. Something more serious than a fever, perhaps." She nodded knowingly. "This sudden recovery looks very queer to me. I'd keep the child in bed if I were in authority. Some diseases are so treacherous. There's walking typhoid fever, for instance. She may have it for all we know. I shall have a very serious talk with Dr. Ballard when he comes."

An ironical smile flitted over the girl's lips as she drifted toward the piano. "I judge from the remarks at the table, that the less you say to Dr. Ballard on the subject of to-day's experiences the better."

"I know it," indignantly. "I'm sure that child must have played some practical joke on him. I want to get to the bottom of it. What a strange little monkey she is! How long will father stand it? What did you think, Eloise, when she swooped upon him so suddenly?"

"I thought of just one sentence," returned the girl. "'Perfect love casteth out fear.'"

"Why in the world should she love him?" protested Mrs. Evringham.

"She would love us all if we would let her," returned Eloise, the phrases of "Vogel als Prophete" beginning to ripple softly from beneath her fingers. "I saw it from the first. I felt it that first evening, when we behaved toward her like a couple of boors. Any one can see she has never been snubbed, never neglected. She got out of the lap of love to come to this icebox. No wonder the change of temperature made her ill!"

"Why, Eloise, what has come over you? You never used to be disagreeable. It's a good thing the child is amiable. It's the only thing left for a plain girl to be."

"No one will ever remember that she is plain," remarked Eloise.

Her mother raised her eyebrows doubtingly. "Perhaps your perceptions are so keen that you can explain how Jewel managed to telegraph to Chicago to-day," she said. "It reminded me of Dooley's comments on Christian Science. Do you remember what he said about 'rejucin' a swellin' over a long distance tillyphone'?"

"I can't imagine how she managed it," admitted Eloise.

Neither could Mr. Evringham. He had taken Jewel into his study now with the intention of finding out, deeming a secluded apartment more desirable for catechism which might lay him liable to personal attack.

As they entered the library he turned on the light, and Jewel glanced about with her usual alert and ready admiration.

"Is this your own, own particular room, grandpa?" she asked.

"Yes, where I keep all my books and papers."

The child's eye suddenly lighted on the yellow chicken, and she looked up at Mr. Evringham with a pleased smile. He had forgotten the chicken, and took the seat before his desk, glancing vaguely about to see which chair would be least heavy and ponderous for his guest. She settled the matter without any hesitation by jumping upon his knee. Jewel had a subject on her mind which pressed heavily, and before her companion had had time to do more than wink once or twice in his surprise, she proceeded to it.

"Do you know, grandpa, I think it's hard for Mrs. Forbes to love people very much," she said in a lowered voice, as if perhaps the walls might have ears. "I wanted to ask her yesterday morning if she didn't love me whom she had seen, how could she love God whom she hadn't seen. Grandpa, would you be willing to tie my bows?"

"To tie"—repeated Mr. Evringham, and paused.

The child was gazing into his eyes earnestly. She put her hand into her pocket and took out two long pieces of blue ribbon.

"You see, you're my only real relation," she explained, "and so I don't like to ask anybody else."

The startled look in her grandfather's face moved her to proceed encouragingly.

"You tie your neckties just beautifully, grandpa; and Mrs. Forbes does her duty so *hard*, and she wants to have my hair cut off, to save trouble." Jewel put her hand up to one short pigtail protectingly.

"And you don't want it cut off, eh?"

"No; and mother wouldn't either. So it would be error, and I'm sure I could learn to fix it better than I did to-night, if you would tie the bows. Just try one right now, grandpa."

"With the house full of women!" gasped Mr. Evringham.

"But none of them my real relatives," replied Jewel, and she turned the back of her head to him, putting the ribbons in his hands.

His fingers fumbled at the task for a minute, and his breathing began to be heavy.

"Is it hard, grandpa?" she asked sympathetically. "You can do it. You reflect intelligence." Then in an instant, "Oh, I've thought of something." She whisked about, took the ribbons and tied one tightly around the end of each braid, then ducking her forehead into his shirt front, "Now put your arms around my neck and tie the bow just as if it was on yourself." Eureka! The thing was accomplished and Mrs. Forbes outwitted. The broker was rather pleased with himself, at the billowy appearance of the ribbon which covered such a multitude of sins in the way of bad parting and braiding. He took his handkerchief and wiped the beads of perspiration from his brow, while Jewel regarded him with admiring affection.

"I knew you could do just *anything*, grandpa!" she said. "You see," looking off at a mental vision of the housekeeper, "we could come in here every morning for a minute before breakfast, and she'd never know, would she?" The child lifted her shoulders and laughed softly with pleasure at the plot.

Mr. Evringham saw his opportunity to take the floor.

"Now Jewel, I would like to have you explain what you meant by saying that you telegraphed to Chicago to-day, when you didn't leave your bed."

She looked up at him attentively. "Ezekiel took it for me," she replied.

Mr. Evringham unconsciously heaved a sigh of relief at this commonplace information. His knowledge of the claims of Christian Science was extremely vague, and he had feared being obliged to listen to a declaration of the use of some means of communication which would make Marconi's discoveries appear like clumsy makeshifts.

"But I think, grandpa, perhaps you'd better not tell Mrs. Forbes."

"How did you manage to see Zeke?"

"I asked his mother if he might come to see me before he took you to the train."

Mr. Evringham pulled his mustache in amusement. "Did he pay for the telegram?"

"Why no, grandpa. I told you I had plenty of money."

"And you think that Mrs. Somebody in Chicago cured you?"

"Of course not. God did."

"But she asked Him, eh?"

Jewel's innocent eyes looked directly into the quizzical ones. "It's pretty hard for a little girl to teach you about it if you don't know," she said doubtfully.

"I *don't* know," he replied, his mood altered by her tone, "but I should like to know what you think about it. Your cure was a rather surprising one to us all."

"I can tell you some of the things I know."

"Do so then."

"Well" —a pause— "there wasn't anything to cure, you see."

"Ah! You weren't ill then!"

"No—o," scornfully, "of course not. I knew it all the time, but it seemed so real to me, and so hot, I knew I'd have to have some one else handle the claim for me."

"It certainly did seem rather real." Mr. Evringham smiled.

Jewel saw that he did not in the least comprehend.

"You know there isn't any devil, don't you, grandpa?" she asked patiently.

"Well, sometimes I have my doubts."

The little girl tried to discover by his eyes if he were in earnest.

"If you believe there is, then you could believe that I was really sick; but if you believe there isn't, and that God created everybody and everything, then it is so easy to understand that I wasn't. Think of God creating anything bad!"

Mr. Evringham nodded vaguely. "When mother comes home she'll tell you about it, if you want her to." She sighed a little and abruptly changed the subject. "Grandpa, are you going to be working at your desk?"

"Yes, for a while."

"Could I sit over at that table and write a letter while you're busy? I wouldn't speak." She slipped down from his knee.

"I don't know about your having ink. You're a rather small girl to be writing letters."

"Oh no, I'll take a pencil—because sometimes I move quickly and ink tips over."

"Quite so. I'm glad you realize that, else I should be afraid to have you come to my study."

"You'd better not be afraid," the child shook her head sagely, "because that makes things happen."

Her grandfather regarded her curiously. This small Bible student, who couldn't tie her own hair ribbons, was an increasing problem to him.

CHAPTER XIV
FAMILY AFFAIRS

He continued to watch the child furtively, while she made her arrangements for writing. Finding that no chair in the room would bring her to a proper height for the table, she looked all about, and finally skipped over to the morocco lounge and tugged from it a pillow almost too heavy for her to carry; but she arrived with it at the chair, much to the amusement of Mr. Evringham, who affected absorption in his papers, while he enjoyed the exhibition of the child's energy and independence.

"She's the kind that 'makes old shears cut,' as my mother used to say," he mused, and turning, the better to view the situation, he found Jewel mounted on her perch and watching him fixedly.

She looked relieved. "I didn't want to disturb you, grandpa, but may I ask one question?"

"Yes."

"Did I consult Dr. Ballard this afternoon?"

"Not that I noticed," returned Mr. Evringham; and Jewel suspected from his expression that she had said something amusing.

"Well, it was a word that sounded like consult that Mrs. Forbes said I did."

"Insult, perhaps," suggested Mr. Evringham.

"Oh yes. How do you spell it, grandpa?"

Mr. Evringham told her, and added dryly, "That was rather too strong language for Mrs. Forbes to apply to the fact."

"Yes," replied the child. "I knew it was a hating word." Then without further parley she squared her elbows on the table and bent over her sheet of paper.

"I wonder what version of it she'll give her mother," thought the broker, rummaging vaguely in the pigeon holes of his desk. His labors finally sifted down to the unearthing of a late novel from a drawer at his right hand, and lowering a convenient, green-shaded electric light, he lit his cigar, and was soon lost in the pages of the story.

At last he became conscious that the pencil at the table had ceased to move, and lowering his book he looked up. His granddaughter had been watching for this happy event, and she no sooner met his eyes than, with a smile of satisfaction, she jumped from her morocco perch and brought him a sheet of paper well and laboriously covered.

"I suppose it isn't all spelled right," she said. "I didn't want to disturb you to ask; but will you please direct this to Dr. Ballard?"

"To Dr. Ballard!" repeated Mr. Evringham. His curiosity impelled him. "Shall I see if it is spelled right?"

Jewel assenting, he read the following in a large and waving hand.

DEAR DOCTOR BALUD—Mrs. Forbs felt bad because I did not take your Medsin. She said it was an insult. I want to tell you I did not meen an Insult. We can't help loving God beter than any body, but I love you and if I took any medsin I would rather take yours than any boddy's. Mrs. Forbs says you will send a big Bill to Grandpa and that it was error to waist it. Please send the Bill to me because I have Plenty of munny, and I shall love to pay you. You were very kind and did not put any thing on my Tung.

Your loving JEWEL.

Mr. Evringham continued to look at the signature for a minute before he spoke. Jewel was leaning against his arm and reading with him. The last lines slanted deeply, there being barely room in the lower corner for the writer's name.

"I can't write very straight without lines," she said.

"You do very well indeed," he returned. "About that bill, Jewel," he added after a moment. "Perhaps you would better let me pay it. I believe you said you had three dollars, but even that won't last forever, you know. You've spent some of it, too. How much, now?"

"I've spent fifty cents." Jewel cast a furtive look around at the chicken, "And, oh yes, fifty cents more for the telegram. How much do you think Dr. Ballard's bill will be?"

"I think it will take every cent you have left," returned Mr. Evringham, gravely, curious to hear what his granddaughter would say in this dilemma.

Her reply came promptly and even eagerly. "Well, that's all right, because Divine Love will send me more if I need it."

"Indeed? How can you be sure?"

Jewel smiled at him affectionately. "Do you mean it grandpa?"

"Why yes. I really want to know."

"Even after God sent you Essex Maid?" she asked incredulously.

"You think the mare is the best thing in my possession, eh?"

"Ye—es! Don't you?"

"I believe I do." As Mr. Evringham spoke, this kinship of taste induced him to turn his face toward the one beside him. Instantly he found himself kissed full on the lips, and while he was recovering from the shock, Jewel proceeded:—

"God has given you so many things, grandpa, that's why it surprised me to have you look so sorry when I first came." The child examined his countenance critically. "I don't think you look so sorry as you used to. I know you must have lots of error to meet, and perhaps," lowering her voice to an extra gentleness, "perhaps you don't know how to remember every minute that God is a very present help in trouble. Mother says that even grown-up people are just finding out about it."

As she paused Mr. Evringham hesitated, somewhat embarrassed under the blue eyes. "We all have plenty to learn, I dare say," he returned vaguely.

He had more than once wished that he had taken more notice of Harry's wife during his opportunity at the hotel. He had looked upon the interview as a distasteful necessity to be disposed of as cursorily as possible.

His son had married beneath him, some working girl probably, whose ability to support herself had turned out to be a deliverance for her father-in-law when the ne'er-do-well husband shirked his responsibilities; and Mr. Evringham had gone to the hotel that evening intending to make it clear that although he performed a favor for his son, there were no results to follow.

His granddaughter's fearlessness, courtesy, and affection had forced him to wonder as to the mother who had fostered these qualities. He remembered the eloquence of his son's face when Harry expressed the wish that he might know Julia, and a vague admiration and respect were being born in the broker's heart for the deserted woman who had worked with hand and brain for her child—his grandchild was the way he put it—with such results as he saw.

Some perception of what Harry's sensations must have been during the last six months came to him as he sat there with the little girl's arm about him. Harry had come home and discovered his child, his Jewel. A frown gathered on the broker's brow as he realized the hours of vain regret his son must have suffered for those lost years of the child's life.

"Served him right, served him perfectly right!"

"What grandpa?"

The question made Mr. Evringham aware that the indignant words had been muttered above his breath.

"I was thinking of your father," he replied. "Has he learned these things that your mother has taught you?"

"Oh yes," with soft eagerness; "father is learning everything." Jewel saw her grandfather's frown and she lowered her voice almost to a whisper. "Don't feel sorry about father, grandpa. He says he's the happiest man in the world. Mother didn't find out about God till after father had gone to California, or he wouldn't have gone; and for a long time she didn't know where he was, and I was only beginning to walk around, so I couldn't help her; but when I got bigger I had father's picture, and we used to talk to it every day, and at last mother knew that Divine Love would bring father back; and pretty soon he began to write to her, and he said he couldn't come home because he felt so sorry, and he was going to the war. So then mother and I prayed a great deal every day, and we knew father would be taken care of. And then mother kept writing to him not to be sorry, because error was nothing and the child of God could always have his right place, and everything like that, and at last the war was over and he came home." Jewel paused.

Mr. Evringham wondered what she was seeing with that far-away look.

Presently she turned to him with the smile of irresistible sweetness— Harry's smile—and a surprising fullness came in the broker's throat. "Father's just splendid," she finished.

Her grandfather was not wholly pleased with the verdict. He had gained a taste for incense himself.

"He has been at home over six months, I believe," he returned.

"Yes, all winter; and we have more *fun!*"

"Your father is not a Christian Scientist, I presume," remarked Mr. Evringham.

"Oh yes, he's learning to be. Of course he goes to church—"

"He does, eh?" put in the broker, surprised.

"Of course; and he studies the lesson with us every day. He had been sorry so much and so long, you know, mother said he was all ready; and beside—beside"—Jewel hesitated and became silent.

"Beside what?"

She began very softly and half reluctantly. "Father had a sickness two or three times when he first came home, and he was healed, and so he was very grateful and wanted to know about God."

"H'm. I'm glad he was. I hope he will make your mother very happy after this."

"He does." The child lost her seriousness and laughed reminiscently. "Father and I have the *best* times. Mothers says he's younger than I am."

"You miss him, eh?" Mr. Evringham half frowned into the fresh little face.

"Oh yes, I do," with a sigh, "but it would be error to be sorry when I could come to see you, grandpa."

Mr. Evringham cogitated a minute on the probable loneliness of the last three days, and began to wonder what this philosophy could be which gave practical help to a child of eight years. He was still holding the letter to Dr. Ballard in his hand.

"I think I'll let you direct this yourself, Jewel," he said. He rose and brought the morocco cushion to his desk chair. "Sit up here and I will tell you the address."

She obeyed, and Mr. Evringham watched the little fingers clenched around the pen as she strove to resist its tendency to write down hill on the envelope.

"And you're quite sure that more money will be forthcoming when yours is gone, eh?" he asked when the feat was accomplished.

"Oh yes; if I need it."

"How will it come, for instance?"

She looked up quickly. "I don't need to know that," she replied.

Mr. Evringham bit his lip. "That's unanswerable," he thought, "and rather neat."

At this moment a knock sounded at the library door, and a moment afterward Mrs. Forbes presented herself.

"Excuse me, Mr. Evringham. I'm afraid Julia has been in your way, staying so long."

"No, Mrs. Forbes, thank you," he returned. "She had a letter to write, and I have been reading."

"Very well. It is her bedtime now." The housekeeper's tone was inexorable, and Jewel lifted her shoulders as she glanced up at her grandfather, and again he found himself taken into a confidence which excluded his excellent housekeeper. "It is better for us to yield," said Jewel's shoulders and mute lips. Before Mr. Evringham could suspect her intention, she had jumped up on the cushion nimbly as a squirrel, and hugging him in a business-like manner, kissed him twice.

"Good-night, grandpa."

"Good-night, Jewel," he returned, going to the length of patting her shoulder.

She jumped down and ran to Mrs. Forbes. "You needn't come with me, you know," she said, holding up her face. Mrs. Forbes hesitated a moment. She had not as yet recovered from this latest liberty taken with the head of the house.

"Let me feel of your hands, Julia." She took them in hers and touched the child's cheeks and forehead as well. "You seem to feel all right, do you?"

"Yes'm."

"No soreness or pain anywhere?"

"No'm. Good-night, Mrs. Forbes."

The housekeeper stooped from her height and accepted the offered kiss.

"Do you prefer to go alone, Jewel? Isn't it lonely for you?" asked Mr. Evringham.

"No—o, grandpa! Anna Belle is up there."

"You're not afraid of the dark then?"

Jewel looked at the speaker, uncertain of his seriousness. He seemed in earnest, however. "The dark is easy to drive away in this house," she replied. "It is so interesting, just like a treatment. The room seems full of darkness, error, and I just turn the switch," she illustrated with thumb and finger in the air, "and suddenly—there isn't any darkness! It's all bright and happy, just like me to-day!"

"Indeed!" returned Mr. Evringham, standing with his feet apart and his arms folded. "Is that what the lady in Chicago did for you to-day?"

"Yes, grandpa," Jewel nodded eagerly. She was so glad to have him understand. "She just turned the light, Truth, right into me."

"She prayed to the Creator to cure you, you mean."

Jewel looked off. "No, not that," she answered slowly, searching for words to make her meaning plain. "God doesn't have to be begged to do anything, because He can't change, He is always the same, and always perfect, and always giving us everything good, and it's only for us—not to believe—in the things that seem to get in the way. I was believing there was something in the way, and that lady knew there wasn't, and she knew it so *well* that the old dark fever couldn't stay. Nothing can stay that God doesn't make—not any longer than we let it cheat us."

"And she was a thousand miles away," remarked Mr. Evringham.

"Why, grandpa," returned Jewel, "there isn't any space in Spirit." She gave a little sigh. "I'm real sorry you're too big to be let into the Christian Science Sunday-School."

Mrs. Forbes lips fell apart.

"One moment more, Jewel," said Mr. Evringham. "Mrs. Forbes was telling me of the gentleman who spoke to you on the trolley car yesterday."

"Oh yes," returned the child, smiling at the pleasing memory. "The Christian Scientist!"

"What makes you think he is a Christian Scientist?" asked Mr. Evringham.

"I know he was. He had on the pin." Jewel showed the one she wore, and her grandfather examined the little cross and crown curiously.

"I wonder if it's possible," he soliloquized aloud.

"Oh yes, grandpa, he is one, and if he's a friend of yours he can explain to you so much better than a little girl can."

After the child had left the room Mr. Evringham and his housekeeper stood regarding one another. His usually unsmiling countenance was relaxed. Mrs. Forbes observed his novel expression, but did not suspect that the light twinkling in his deep-set eyes was partly due to the sight of her own pent-up emotion.

He hooked one thumb in his vest and balanced his eyeglasses in his other hand.

"Well, what do you think of her?" he inquired.

"I think, sir," returned the housekeeper emphatically, "that if anybody bought that child for a fool he wouldn't get his money's worth."

"Even though she is a Scientist?" added Mr. Evringham, his mustache curving in a smile.

"She's too smart for me. I don't like children to be so smart. The idea of her setting up to teach you Mr. Evringham!"

"That shouldn't be so surprising. I read a long time ago something about certain things being concealed from the wise and prudent and revealed unto babes."

"Babes!" repeated Mrs. Forbes. "We've been the babes. If that young one can lie in bed with a fever, and wind every one of us around her finger the way she's done to-day, what can we expect when she's up and around?"

The broker laughed. "She's an Evringham, an Evringham!" he said.

"You may laugh, sir, but what do you think of her wheedling me into sending Zeke up, and then getting him off on the sly with that telegram? I faced him down with it to-night, and Zeke isn't any good at fibbing."

"I'll be hanged if I don't think it was a pretty good thing for me," rejoined Mr. Evringham, "and money in my pocket. It looked as if I was in for Ballard for a matter of weeks."

"But the—the—the audacity of it!" protested Mrs. Forbes. "What do you think she said after you and Dr. Ballard had done downstairs? I tried to bring her to a sense of what she'd done, and all she answered was that she had known that God would deliver her out of the snare of the fowler. Now I should like to ask you, Mr. Evringham," added Mrs. Forbes in an access of outraged virtue, "which of us three do you think she called the fowler?"

"Give it up, I'm sure," returned the broker; "but I can imagine that we seemed three pretty determined giants for one small girl to outwit."

"She'd outwit a regiment, sir; and I don't see how you can permit it."

Mr. Evringham endeavored to compose his countenance. "We must allow her religious liberty, I suppose, Mrs. Forbes. It's a matter of religion with her—that is, we must allow it as long as she keeps well. If Ballard had found her worse to-night, I assure you I should have consigned all Christian Scientists to the bottom of the sea, and that little zealot would have taken her medicine from my own hand. All's well that ends well, eh?"

Mrs. Forbes had caught sight of the incongruous adornment of her employer's desk.

With majestic strides she advanced upon the yellow chicken and swept it into her apron. "Julia must be taught not to litter your room, sir."

"I beg your pardon," returned the broker firmly, also advancing and holding out his hand. "That is my chicken."

Slowly Mrs. Forbes restored the confiscated property, and Mr. Evringham examined it carefully to see that it was intact, and then set it carefully on his desk.

Mrs. Forbes recalled the confectioner's window. "She must have bought that chicken when my back was turned!" she thought. "That young one could have given points to Napoleon."

CHAPTER XV
A RAINY MORNING

The next morning it rained so heavily that Mr. Evringham was obliged to forego his ride. Wet weather was an unmixed ill to him. It not only made riding and golf miserable, but it reminded him that rheumatism was getting a grip on one of his shoulders.

"It is disgusting, perfectly disgusting to grow old," he muttered as he descended the broad staircase. On the lower landing Jewel rose up out of the dusk, where she had been sitting near the beautiful clock. Her bright little face shone up at him like a sunbeam.

"You didn't expect to see me, grandpa, did you?" she asked, and as it did not even occur to him to stoop his head to her, she seized his hand and kissed it as they went on down the stairs.

"I was so disappointed because it rained so hard. I was going to see you ride."

"Yes. Beastly weather," assented Mr. Evringham.

"But the flowers and trees want a drink, don't they?"

"'M. I suppose so."

"And the brook will be prettier than ever."

"'M. See that you keep out of it."

"Yes, I will, grandpa; and I thought the first thing this morning, I'll wear my rubbers all day. I was so afraid I might forget I put them right on to make sure."

They had reached the hall, and Jewel exhibited her feet encased in the roomy storm rubbers.

"Great Scott, child!" ejaculated Mr. Evringham, viewing the shiny overshoes. "What size are your feet?"

"I don't know," returned the little girl, "but I only have to scuff some, and then they'll stay on. Mrs. Forbes said I'd grow to them."

"So you will, I should think, if you're going to wear them in the house as well as out." It was against Mr. Evringham's principles to smile before breakfast, at all events at any one except Essex Maid; but the large, shiny overshoes that looked like overgrown beetles, and Jewel's optimistic determination to make him happy, even offset his painful arm.

"The house doesn't leak anywhere," he said. "I think it will be safe for you to take them off until after breakfast."

Jewel lifted her shoulders and looked up at him with the glance he knew.

"Unless we're going out to the stable," she said suggestively.

He hesitated a moment. "Very well," he returned. "Let us go to the stable."

"But first we must tie the ribbons," she said with a joyous chuckle. She would have skipped but for the rubbers. As it was, she proceeded circumspectly to the library, drawing the broker by the hand. "I want you to see, grandpa, if you don't think I made my parting real straight this morning," she said as she softly closed the door.

"Gently on my arm, Jewel," he remonstrated, wincing as she returned, flinging her energetic little body against him. "I have the rheumatism like the devil—pardon me."

She looked at him suddenly, wondering and wistful. "Oh, have you?" she returned sympathetically. "But it is only like the devil, grandpa," she added hopefully, "and you know there isn't any devil."

"I can't discuss theology before breakfast," he returned briefly.

"Dear grandpa, you shan't have a single pain!" She held her head back and looked at him lovingly.

"Very likely not, when I've begun playing the harp. Now where are those con—those ribbons?"

Jewel's eyes and lips grew suddenly serious and doubtful, and he observed the change.

"Yes, your hair ribbons, you know," he added hastily and with an attempt at geniality.

"Not if you don't like to, grandpa."

"I love to," he protested. "I've been looking forward to it all the morning. I thought 'never mind if I can't go riding, I can tie Jewel's hair ribbons.'"

The child laughed a little, even though her companion did not. "Oh grandpa, you're such a joker," she said; "just like father."

But he saw that she doubted his mood, and the toe of one of the overshoes was boring into the carpet as she stood where she had withdrawn from him.

"Let us see if you parted your hair better," he said in a different and gentler tone, and instantly the flaxen head was bent before him, and Jewel felt in her pocket for the ribbons. He had not the heart to say what he thought; namely, that her parting looked as though a saw had been substituted for a comb.

"Very well, very well," he said kindly.

When the ribbons were at last tied, the two proceeded to the dining-room. Here an open fire of logs furnished the cheerful light that was lacking outside. The morning paper hung over the back of a chair, warming before the blaze.

Mrs. Forbes entered from the butler's pantry and looked surprised. "I didn't expect you down for half an hour yet, sir. Shall I hurry breakfast?"

"No; I'm going to take Jewel to the stable." Mr. Evringham stopped and took a few lumps of sugar from the bowl.

"Julia, where are your rubbers?" asked the housekeeper.

"On," said the child, lifting her foot.

"I only hope they'll stay there," remarked her grandfather. "I think, Mrs. Forbes, you must buy shoes as I've heard that Chinamen do,—the largest they can get for the money."

He disappeared with his happy little companion, and the housekeeper looked after them disapprovingly.

"They're both going out bareheaded," she mused. "I'd like to bet—I would bet anything that she asked him to take her. He never even stopped to look at the paper. He's just putty in her hands, that's what he is, putty; and she's been here three days."

Mr. Evringham's apprehensions proved to have foundation. Halfway to the barn Jewel stepped in a bit of sticky mud and left one rubber. Her companion did not stop to let her get it, but picking her up under his well arm, strode on to the barn, where they appeared to the astonished Zeke.

Jewel was laughing in high glee. She was used to being caught up in a strong arm and run with.

Mr. Evringham shook the drops from his head. "Get Jewel's rubber please, Zeke," he said, pointing with his thumb over his shoulder.

"I was Cinderella," cried the child gayly. "That's my glass slipper out there in the mud."

Zeke would have liked to joke with her, but that was an impossibility in the august presence. He cast a curious glance at the little girl as he left the barn. He had received his mother's version of yesterday's experience. "Well, it looks to me as if there was something those Christian Science folks know that the rest of us don't," he soliloquized. "I saw her with my own eyes, and felt her with my own hands. Mother says children get up from anything twice as quick as grown folks, but I don't know."

"Don't you love a stable, grandpa?" exclaimed Jewel. "Oh, I'm too happy to scuff," and she kicked off the other rubber. Even while she spoke Essex Maid looked around and whinnied at sight of her master.

"She knows you, she knows you," cried the little girl joyously, hopping up and down.

"Of course," said Mr. Evringham, holding out his hand to the delighted child and leading her into the stall. The mare rubbed her nose against him. "We couldn't get out this morning, eh, girl?" said the broker, caressing her neck, while Jewel smoothed the bright coat as high as she could reach. Her grandfather lifted her in his arms. "Here, my maid, here's a new friend for you. In my pocket, Jewel."

The child took out the lumps of sugar one by one, and Essex Maid ate them from the little hand, touching it gently with her velvet lips. Zeke came in and whistled softly as he glanced at the group in the stall.

"Whew," he mused. "He's letting her feed the Maid. I guess she can put her shoes in *his* trunk all right."

Mr. Evringham set Jewel on the mare's back and she smoothed the bright mane and patted the beautiful creature.

"I'd like to gallop off now over the whole country," she said, her face glowing.

"I shouldn't be surprised either if you could do it bareback," returned Mr. Evringham; "but you must never come into either of the stalls without me. You understand, do you?"

"Yes, grandpa. I'm glad you told me though, because I guess I should have." The child gave a quick, unconscious sigh.

"Well we'd better go in now."

"How kind you are to me," said the child gratefully, as she slid off the horse's back with her arms around her grandfather's neck.

He had forgotten his rheumatic shoulder for the time.

"You can bring those rubbers in later," he said to Zeke, and so carried Jewel out of the barn, through the rain, and into the house.

Mrs. Forbes watched the entrance. "Breakfast is served, sir," she said with dignity. She thought her employer should have worn a hat.

Jewel was not offered eggs this morning. Instead she had, after her fruit and oatmeal, a slice of ham and a baked potato.

Her roses were fresh this morning and opening in the warmth of the fire, but Mr. Evringham's eyes were caught by a mass of American Beauties which stood in an alcove close to the window.

"Where did those come from?" he demanded.

"They belong to Miss Eloise," replied Mrs. Forbes. "She asked me to take care of them for her."

"Humph! Ballard again, I suppose," remarked the broker.

"I hope so," responded Mrs. Forbes devoutly.

Mr. Evringham had spoken to himself, and he glanced up from his paper, surprised by the prompt fervor of the reply. The housekeeper looked non-committal, but her meaning dawned upon him, and he smiled slightly as he returned to the news of the day.

"Dr. Ballard must love Cousin Eloise very much," said Jewel, mashing her potato. "He sent her a splendid box of candy, too."

She addressed her remark to Mrs. Forbes, and in a low tone, in order not to disturb her grandfather's reading.

"Any girl can get candy and flowers and love, if she's only pretty enough," returned Mrs. Forbes; "but she mustn't forget to be pretty."

The speaker's tone appealed to Jewel as signifying a grievance. She looked up.

"Why, somebody married you, Mrs. Forbes," she said kindly.

Mr. Evringham's paper hid a face which suddenly contorted, but the housekeeper's quick-glancing eyes could not see a telltale motion.

She gave a hard little laugh. "You think there's hope for you then, do you?" she returned.

"I guess I'm not going to be married," replied Jewel. "Father says I'm going to be his bachelor maid when I grow up."

"Shouldn't wonder if you were," said Mrs. Forbes dryly.

The owner of the American Beauties and the beribboned bonbon box was taking her coffee as usual in bed. This luxurious habit had never been hers until she came to Bel-Air; but it was her mother's custom, and rather than undergo a tete-a-tete breakfast with her host, she had adopted it.

Now she had made her toilet deliberately. There was nothing to hurry for. Her mother's voice came in detached sentences and questions from the next room.

"Dear me, this rain is too trying, Eloise! Didn't you have some engagement with Dr. Ballard to-day?"

"He thought he could get off for some golf this afternoon."

"What a disappointment for the dear fellow," feelingly. "He has so little time to himself!"

Eloise gave a most unsympathetic laugh. "More than he wishes he had, I fancy," she returned.

She came finally in her white negligee into her mother's room. Mrs. Evringham was still in bed. Her eyeglasses were on and she regarded her daughter critically as she came in sight. She had begun to look upon her as mistress of the fine old Ballard place on Mountain Avenue, and the setting was very much to her mind. The girl sauntered over to the window, and taking a low seat, leaned her head against the woodwork, embowered in the lace curtains.

"How it does come down!" said Mrs. Evringham fretfully. "And I lack just a little of that lace braid, or I could finish your yoke. I suppose Forbes would think it was a dreadful thing if I asked her to let Zeke get it for me."

"Don't ask anything," returned Eloise.

"When you are in your own home!" sighed Mrs. Evringham.

"Don't, mother. It's indecent!"

"If you would only reassure me, my child, so I wouldn't have to undergo such moments of anxiety as I do."

"Oh, you have no mercy!" exclaimed the girl; and when she used that tone her mother usually became tearful. She did now.

"You act as if you weren't a perfect treasure, Eloise—as if I didn't consider you a treasure for a prince of the realm!"

A knock at the door heralded Sarah's arrival for the tray, and Mrs. Evringham hastily wiped her eyes.

"Yes, you can take the things," she said as the maid approached. "I can't tip you as I should, Sarah. I'm going to get you something pretty the next time I go to New York."

Sarah had heard this before.

"And if you know of any one going to the village this morning, I want a piece of lace braid. Have you heard how Miss Julia is?"

"She was down at breakfast, ma'am, and Mr. Evringham had her out to the stable to see Essex Maid."

"He did? In the rain? How very imprudent!"

After Sarah had departed with her burden, Mrs. Evringham took off her eyeglasses.

"There, Eloise, you heard that? It's just as I thought. He is taking a fancy to her."

The girl smiled without turning her head. "Oh no, that wasn't your prophecy, mother. You said she was too plain to have a chance with our fastidious host."

"Well, didn't she look forlorn last night at the dinner table?" demanded Mrs. Evringham, a challenge in her voice.

"Indeed she did, the poor baby. She looked exactly as if she had two female relatives in the house, neither of whom would lift a finger to help her, even though she was just off a sick bed. The same relatives don't know this minute how or where she spent the evening."

"I felt very glad she was content somewhere away from the drawing-room," returned Mrs. Evringham practically. "You know we expected Dr. Ballard up to the moment the roses arrived, and from all I gathered at the dinner table, it would have been awkward enough for him to walk in upon that child. Besides, I don't see why you use that tone with me. It has been your own choice to let her paddle her own canoe, and you've had an object lesson now that I hope you won't forget. You wouldn't believe me when I begged you to exert yourself for your grandfather, and now you see even that plain little thing could get on with him just because she dared take him by storm. She has about everything in her disfavor. The child of a common working woman, with no beauty, and a little crank of a Christian Scientist into the bargain, and yet now see! He took her out to the stable to see Essex Maid! I never knew you contradictory and disagreeable until lately, Eloise. You even act like a stick with Dr. Ballard just to be perverse." Mrs. Evringham flounced over in bed, with her back to the white negligee.

Eloise had seen what she had been watching for. Her grandfather had driven away to the station, so she arose and came over to the foot of the bed.

"I know I'm irritable, mother," she said repentantly. "The idleness and uselessness of my life have grated on me until I know I'm not fit to live with.

If I had had any of the training of a society girl, I could bear it better; but papa kept my head full of school,—for which I bless him,—and now that the dream of college is hopeless, and that the only profession you wish for me is marriage, I dread to wake up in the mornings."

The young voice was unsteady.

Mrs. Evringham heaved a long sigh. "Give me patience!" she murmured, then added mentally, "It can't be many days, and she won't refuse him."

"Go down to the piano and play yourself good-natured," she returned. "Then come up and we'll go on with that charming story. It quite refreshed me to read of that coming-out ball. It was so like my own."

Eloise, her lips set in a sad curve, rose and left the room. Once in the hall, she paused for a minute. Then instead of descending the stairs, she ran noiselessly up the next flight. The rain was pelting steadily on the dome of golden glass through which light fell to the halls. She stole, as she had done yesterday, to the door of Jewel's room.

Again as yesterday she heard a voice, but this time it was singing. The tones were very sweet, surprisingly strong and firm to proceed from lips which always spoke so gently. The door was not quite closed, and Eloise pressed her ear to the crack. Thus she could easily hear the words of Jewel's song:—

> *"And o'er the earth's troubled, angry sea*
> *I see Christ walk;*
> *And come to me, and tenderly,*
> *Divinely, talk."*

The hymn stopped for a minute, and the child appeared to be conversing with some one.

Eloise waited, openly, eagerly listening, hoping the singer would resume. Something in those unexpected words in the sweet child voice stirred her. Presently Jewel sang on:—

> *"From tired joy, and grief afar,*
> *And nearer Thee,*
> *Father, where Thine own children are*
> *I love to be!"*

The lump that rose in the listener's throat forced a moisture into her eyes.

"I never could hear a child sing without crying," she said to herself in excuse, as she leaned her forehead on her hand against the jamb of the door and waited for the strange stir at her heart to quiet.

The house was still. The rain swept against the panes, and tears stole from under the girl's long lashes—tears for her empty, vapid life, for the hopelessness of the future, for the humiliations of the present, for the lack of a love that should be without self-interest.

"I like that verse, Anna Belle," said the voice within. "Let's sing that again," and the hymn welled forth:—

"From tired joy, and grief afar,
And nearer Thee,
Father, where Thine own children are
I love to be!"

"Is there a haven?" thought the swelling, listening heart outside. "Is there a place far alike from tired joy and grief?"

"'Father, where Thine own children are,'" quoted Jewel. "We know where a lot of them are, don't we, Anna Belle, and we do love to be with them." A pause, and a light sigh, which did not reach the listener. "But we're at grandpa's now," finished the child's voice.

Eloise's breaths came long and deep drawn, and she stood motionless, her eyes hidden.

CHAPTER XVI
THE FIRST LESSON

Jewel looked up as she heard a knock. Sarah had made the bed and gone. Who could this be?

At her "Come in," Eloise entered the room. The child's face brightened questioningly. She rose and gazed at the enchanted maiden, very lovely in the wrapper of white silk, open at the throat, and with little billows of lace cascading down to the toes of her white Turkish slippers.

"Good-morning, cousin Eloise," said the child, waiting for the message or order which she supposed to be forthcoming.

"Good-morning." The girl cast a comprehensive glance around the rather bare room. Her eyes bore no traces of the tears so recently shed, but her face was sad. "I heard you singing," she said.

"Yes. Did I disturb anybody?" asked the child quickly.

"No. It is nice to be like the birds that sing in the rain."

"Like the robin out there," returned Jewel, relieved. "Did you hear him?" She ran to the window and threw it open, listening a minute. "No, he has gone."

"You said you would show me your doll," went on Eloise when the window was closed again.

"Oh," returned Jewel pleased, "did you come to see Anna Belle? She's right here. We were just going to have the lesson." She took the doll from the depths of a big chair and held her up with motherly pride. "Would you—won't you sit down a minute?"

To her great satisfaction, her beautiful visitor condescended to take the chair Anna Belle had vacated, and held out her white, ringless hands for the doll.

"How neatly her clothes are made," said the girl, examining Anna Belle's garments.

"Yes, my mother made her all new ones when she knew she was going to Europe, so that she would be neat and not mortify me. Would you like to see her clothes?" eagerly.

"Yes, I should."

Jewel brought them, her quick little fingers turning them back and forth, exhibiting the tiny buttonholes and buttons, and chattering explanations of their good points.

"It was a great deal for your mother to do all this, when she is such a busy woman," said Eloise.

"Yes, she did it evenings, and then surprised me just when we were coming away. Wasn't it lovely?"

"Very."

"I love prettiness," said the child. As she spoke she regarded the grave face beside her. "When I first noticed that my nose wasn't nice, and neither were my eyes, I almost cried."

Eloise looked up at her, at a loss for a reply.

"But then I remembered that of course God never made anything that wasn't perfectly beautiful, so I knew that it would come right some time, and I asked mother when she thought it would."

"What did she say?" returned Eloise, wondering at this original optimism.

"She said we could never tell how soon anything would come right to our sense, but so long as we knew that Creation was perfect and beautiful, we could be patient about everything—big things and little things; and then I remember how she talked to me about being careful never to pity myself." Jewel gave her head a little serious shake. "You know it's very bad error to pity yourself, no matter what kind of a nose you have."

Eloise had sunk back in the large chair and was attentively watching the child standing beside her, while she still held Anna Belle. She had never before held converse with a Christian Scientist, but her state of mind precluded the perception of a humorous side to anything.

"Wrong to pity yourself no matter what happens?" she asked.

"Yes—because—because—" Jewel looked off. She knew that it was error, but it was hard to explain why to the lovely grown-up cousin who was so strangely sorry. "Well, you see," she added after the moment's thought, "it isn't having faith in God, it isn't knowing that you're His child, and that He takes care of you."

"No, I suppose not; but I have never learned how to know that, Jewel."

"I know you haven't," returned the little girl, and she slipped her hand toward her cousin's. The girl met it halfway and held it close. "Since I've seen you," Jewel went on slowly, "I know that prettiness isn't enough to make a person happy—nor all your lovely clothes—nor having people fond of you and sending you presents—nor making the sweetest music; but you can be happy, cousin Eloise, unless you're doing wrong."

"I am doing wrong, but I can't help it." The girl took her supporting hand from the doll and pressed it to her eyes a second before dropping it. "What were you doing when I came in?"

"I was just going to get the lesson."

"Oh, do you go on with your studies? Perhaps I can help you better than Anna Belle."

"Would you cousin Eloise?" Jewel flushed with pleasure. "Some of the words are so long. I thought I'd ask grandpa to-night."

"Why didn't you wish to come to me?" questioned Eloise, well knowing why.

The little girl looked a trifle embarrassed. "I didn't want to trouble you. Of course you aren't my real relations," she said modestly.

"Do you remember that, too!" exclaimed Eloise.

Jewel started at the hurt voice. "Would you like to be?" she asked earnestly. "I wish you were, because"—she hesitated and smiled with her head a little on the side, "because I might look more like you."

The gravity of Eloise's lips remained unbroken. "I want you to promise me something, Jewel. I want you to promise not to tell your grandfather that I have been with you to-day."

"Why? He'd be glad I was happy."

"I have a reason. I will help you with your studies every day if you won't tell him."

"I might without meaning to," rejoined the child, her alert little mind busy with the new problem suddenly presented to it.

"I will make a rainbow scarf for Anna Belle if you will never speak of me to your grandfather."

"Why do you say my grandfather? He's yours, too."

"Not at all. Didn't you just say I was not your real relation?"

"Oh but, cousin Eloise," Jewel was sure of the hurt now, though the why or wherefore was a mystery, "of course he wishes you were."

"Oh no he doesn't." The answer came quick and sharp, and the child reviewed mentally her own observations of the household. Her heart swelled with the desire to help.

"Now, cousin Eloise," her breath came a little faster with the thronging thoughts for which her vocabulary was insufficient, "error does try to cheat people so. Just think how kind you were inside all the time, though you wouldn't smile at me. You're willing to make Anna Belle a scarf. I called you the enchanted maiden, because you were too sorry to try to make people happy, and now grandpa's just like that; he's enchanted, too, if he doesn't make you happy, because he's just as *kind* inside, oh, just as *kind* as he can be."

"He likes you," returned Eloise.

Jewel regarded her for a silent moment. "I noticed when I came," she said at last, apologetically, "that nobody here seemed to love one another; and the house was so grand and the people were so beautiful that I couldn't understand; and I called it Castle Discord."

Eloise gave a little exclamation. "I call it the icebox," she returned.

Jewel's face lighted. "That's it, that's all it is," she said eagerly. "It's easy to melt ice. Love melts everything."

"It's pretty slow work sometimes," said Eloise.

"Then you have to put on more love. That's all. Have you"—the child asked the question a little timidly, "have you put on much love to grandpa?"

"Why should I love him?" asked Eloise. "He doesn't love me."

"Oh dear," said Jewel. After a minute's thought her face brightened. "I guess I'll show you my dotted letter."

She ran to the closet where hung her dotted challie dress and took from the pocket the message that had come to her the evening of her arrival. "My mother put a letter into all my pockets for a happy surprise; and this one came the first night, when I was feeling all sorry and alone, and it comforted me. Perhaps it will comfort you."

She put the paper into the girl's hand, and Eloise read it. She turned it over and read it a second time.

Jewel stood beside her chair watching, and seeing that her cousin seemed interested, she ran and brought her little wrapper. "Perhaps you'd like to see this one too," she said feeling in the pocket for the second message.

Eloise accepted and read it. Every word of the two notes came to the mind of the young girl as suggestions from another planet, so foreign were they to any instruction or advice that had ever fallen to her lot.

She gave a slight exclamation as she finished. "Is your mother a saint?" she asked, looking up suddenly.

"No," returned Jewel innocently. "She's a Christian Scientist."

Eloise suddenly put out her hand, and drawing Jewel to her, hid her forehead on the child's breast.

"I wish you were older," she said.

Jewel put her little hands on the shining waves of hair she had admired from afar. "I wish my mother was here," she answered. "Did you like those things mother said?"

"Oh yes; but they're from heaven, and I'm in the other place," replied Eloise disconsolately.

"Then let's look in another pocket!" exclaimed Jewel. "I'll look in my best dress. Perhaps she'd put the best one there."

The girl lifted her head, and the child went eagerly to the closet, coming back with a folded paper. "We'll read it together. You read it out loud, and I'll look over your shoulder."

The rain slanted against the window in gusts as the two heads bent above the paper. Eloise read:—

"Mother is thinking of you, little daughter, every day and every night, and the thing she hopes the most is, that you never let the day go by without studying the lesson. The words may be hard sometimes, but perhaps some one will read it with you, and if they do not, then you go on trying your best, and you will learn more and more all the time; for truth will shine into your thought and help you. Grandpa will give you plenty of bread and butter, but you must remember that Spirit, not matter, satisfieth. You would starve without the Bible and the text-book, and very soon the joy would go out of everything. Give my love to Anna Belle, and tell her not to go out to play any day until you have read the lesson."

"Your mother speaks as if you learned Christian Science out of the Bible," said Eloise.

"Of course," returned Jewel.

"I thought a woman got it up," said the girl. "I thought your church worshipped her."

The child smiled at the phrase. "You know Christ was the first one. That's why we call ourselves that. We couldn't be Christian Scientists if we worshipped any one but God," she answered. "Of course we love Mrs. Eddy. Just think how good and unselfish a person has to be before they can hear God's teaching. He showed her how to remind people of the things that Christ taught, and how to get rid of their sins and sickness. We love her dearly for helping people so much, and shouldn't you think everybody would? But they don't. Some people think hating thoughts about her, just as if she was teaching bad things instead of good ones. Mother says it reminds her of what the Saviour said, 'For which of these works do ye stone me?'"

"Ah, but you see," returned Eloise, "Christian Scientists let people die sometimes without a doctor."

"But lots of people they do cure are the ones doctors said would have to die."

"I know they claim that."

"And such a lot of people pass on while doctors are taking care of them I wonder why it makes everybody so angry when a Scientist goes without any."

Eloise smiled faintly as she shook her head. "It is more respectable to die with a doctor at your side," she returned.

"Are you really willing to help me with the lesson, cousin Eloise? If you are, it would be nice if you would get your Bible too."

The girl looked embarrassed. "I haven't any."

"Well, your mother's would do just as well," said Jewel politely.

"She hasn't any—here, I'm sure."

The little girl stood very still a moment. "No wonder they're sorry," she thought.

"All right. We can both look over one," she answered, and going to the dresser she brought her books.

"Was this the study you meant?" asked Eloise, looking at the three books curiously. "I thought I was offering to help you with something I knew about. I used to learn verses out of the Bible when I was a little girl in Sunday-school. I don't know anything about it now."

"But you can read everything, the big words and all," replied Jewel. "I wish I could."

Eloise saw that this reply was designed to minister to her self-respect. She took up the small black book lying with the Bible. "What is this?"

"That is 'Science and Health,' that Mrs. Eddy wrote to explain to us what the Bible means; and this other one is to tell us where to pick out the places for the day's lesson." Jewel pulled up a chair, and seating herself, turned over the leaves of the Quarterly briskly until she found the right date.

"Please find Zechariah, cousin Eloise."

"What's that?" asked the girl helplessly.

"It's in the Old Testament. Would you rather I'd find them? All right, then you can take 'Science and Health' and find that part."

"I hope it's easy, for I'm awfully stupid, Jewel."

"Oh, it's very easy. You'll see." The child found the chapter and verse in the Bible and read, with her finger on the line. Eloise looked over and read with her. Thus they went through all the verses for the day, then Jewel began to give the page and line to be read in the text-book.

This volume was small and agreeable to handle, the India paper pleasant to the girl's dainty touch. According to the child's request, she read aloud the lines which were called for.

"That's all," said Jewel at last. "Oh cousin Eloise, it's just lovely and easy to get the lesson with you," she added gratefully.

Eloise made no response. Her eye had been caught by a statement on the page before her, and she read on in silence.

Jewel waited a minute and then, seeing that her cousin was absorbed, she laid down the Quarterly and took up her doll and sat still, watching the pretty profile, undisturbed by doubts as to what her cousin might think of the book she held, and full of utter confidence that He who healeth all our diseases would minister to her through its pages.

At last Eloise again became conscious of her surroundings. She turned to her companion, a skeptical comment on her lips, but she suppressed the words at sight of the innocent, expectant face. She certainly had nothing to give this child better than what she already possessed.

"You can read it any time when you feel sorry, cousin Eloise, that and my Bible too. Mother always does."

"Does she ever feel sorry?"

"Sometimes; but it can't last where the Bible is."

"I never saw that the Bible had anything to do with us," said Eloise.

"Why—ee!" Jewel suddenly dropped Anna Belle and again took up the Bible.

"What do you think I opened to?" holding the verse with her finger as she looked up. Then she read, "'If ye love them that love you what thank have ye?' Now isn't that something to do with you and grandpa?"

"I don't see how I can love people who don't choose to be lovable," returned Eloise. "What's the use of pretending?"

"But then," said the child, "the trouble is that everything that isn't love is hate."

Her visitor raised her eyebrows. "Ah! I should have to think about that," she returned.

"Yes, you'd better," agreed Jewel. Then she turned to the Psalms and read the ninety-first.

When she had finished she looked up at her cousin, an earnest questioning in her eyes.

"That is very beautiful," said Eloise. "I never heard it before. How well you read it, Jewel."

"Yes," replied the child. "It's so much easier to read things when you know them by heart." Then she turned to the Twenty-third Psalm and read it.

"Yes, I've heard that one. It's beautiful of course, but I never thought of its having anything to do with us." Eloise was watching her cousin curiously. It seemed too strange for belief that a healthy child of her age should be taking a vital interest in the Bible and endeavoring to prove a position from its pages.

When the girl finally rose to go she turned at the door:—

"Remember your promise not to tell grandfather about this morning," she said.

Jewel, hovering about her, looked troubled.

"Would you just as lief tell me why?" she asked.

Eloise gave the ghost of a smile. "It would be a long story, and I scarcely think you would understand."

"I think I could obey you better if you would tell me."

"Very well. We, my mother and I, are not Mr. Evringham's real relations,—to put it as you do,—and we have come here because my poor father lost his money and we have nowhere else to go. We came without being invited, and it hurts to have to stay where we are not wanted. I don't wish grandfather to think that I am being kind to you, for fear he will believe that I am doing it to make him like me better and because I want to stay here."

The girl spoke slowly and with great clearness.

Jewel looked at her, speechless with surprise and perplexity.

Eloise went on: "I don't want to stay here, you understand. I wish to go away. I would go to-day if my mother were willing."

Her large eyes grew dark as she closed, and the child received a sense of the turbulence that underlay her words.

"Thank you for explaining," she returned in an awed tone. "I wish my mother was here; but God is, and He'll take care of you, cousin Eloise. Mother says we don't ever need to stay in the shadow. There's always the sunshine, only we must do our part, we must come into it."

"How Jewel? Supposing you don't know how."

"You can learn how," replied the child earnestly, "right in those books. Lots of sorry people grow glad studying them."

CHAPTER XVII
JEWEL'S CORRESPONDENCE

While Jewel still stood turning over in her mind what she had heard, charming strains of music began coming up through the hall. Cousin Eloise had gone to the piano.

"I almost which I hadn't made her tell me," thought the child, "for how can I help grandpa not to be sorry they are here? Wouldn't I be sorry to have aunt Madge come and live with me when I never asked her to?" She stood for some minutes wrestling with the problem, but suddenly her expression changed. "I was forgetting!" she exclaimed. "I mustn't get sorry too. God is All. Mortal mind can't do anything about it." She closed her eyes, and pressing her hand to her lips, stood for a minute in mute realization; then with a smile of relief, she took up Anna Belle.

"Let's go down, dearie, and hear the music," she said light heartedly.

When the summons to luncheon sounded and Mrs. Evringham entered the parlor, she found the child curled up in a big chair, her doll in her lap, listening absorbedly to the last strains of a Chopin Ballade.

"Do you like music, Julia?" she asked patronizingly, as her daughter finished and turned about.

"The child's name is Jewel," said Eloise.

"Yes, aunt Madge, I love it," replied the little girl; "and I didn't know people could play the piano the way cousin Eloise does."

Mrs. Evringham smiled. "I suppose you've not heard much good music."

"Yes'm, I've heard our organist in church."

"And Jewel can make good music herself," said Eloise. "She can sing like a little lark. I've been up in her room this morning."

Mrs. Evringham welcomed the look on her daughter's face as she made the statement. "Thank fortune Eloise has played herself into good humor," she thought.

"Indeed? I must hear her sing some time. You're playing unusually well this morning, my dear. I wish Dr. Ballard could have heard you. Come to luncheon."

The three repaired to the dining-room, where Mrs. Forbes's glance immediately noted the presence of Anna Belle. She took her from Jewel's arms and placed her on a remote corner of the sideboard, in the middle of which glowed the American Beauty roses.

Mrs. Evringham approached them with solicitude.

"They're looking finely, Mrs. Forbes," she said suavely. "You surely understand the care of roses." She lifted the silver scissors that hung from her chatelaine and succeeded in severing one of the long stems.

"Here, little girl," she added, advancing to Eloise, "you need this in your white gown to cheer us up this rainy day."

The girl shrank and opened her lips to decline, but restrained herself and submitted to have the flower pinned amid her laces.

Jewel gazed at her in open admiration. The glowing color lent a wonderful touch to the girl's beauty. Mrs. Evringham laughed low at the fascinated look in the plain little face, and luncheon began.

To Jewel it differed much from the ones that had preceded it. Mrs. Forbes might hover like a large black cloud, aunt Madge might rail at the weather which cut her off from her afternoon drive, but the morning's experience seemed to have put the child into new relations with all, and Eloise often gave her a friendly glance or smile as the meal progressed.

It was destined to a surprising interruption. In the midst of the discussion of lamb chops and Saratoga chips the door opened, and in walked Dr. Ballard. The shoulders of his becoming raincoat were spangled with drops, his hat was in his hand, a deprecatory smile brightened his face.

"Forgive me, won't you?" he said as he advanced to Mrs. Evringham and clasped the outstretched hand which eagerly welcomed him. "It was my one leisure half hour to-day."

He brought the freshness of the spring air with him, and he went on around the table shaking hands with the others, and finally drew up a chair beside Jewel.

"No, I can't eat anything," he declared in response to the urging of Mrs. Evringham and the housekeeper. "Can't stay long enough for that."

His eyes fastened on the graceful girl opposite him, who was trying to offset her blushes by a direct and nonchalant gaze. The rose on her breast seemed to be scorching her cheeks. She knew that her mother was exulting in the lucky inspiration which had made her set it there.

"How good of you to come and cheer us!" exclaimed Mrs. Evringham. "Do take off your coat and stay for a cosy hour. We will have some music."

"Don't tempt me. I have an office hour awaiting me. I came principally to see this little girl."

Jewel had leaned back in her chair and was watching his bright face expectantly.

"I'm glad of it," rejoined Mrs. Evringham devoutly. "I distrust these sudden recoveries, Dr. Ballard. Do make very sure that she hasn't one of those lingering, treacherous fevers. I've heard of such things."

Dr. Ballard's eyes laughed into those of his little neighbor. "She doesn't look the part," he returned.

Jewel gave a glance around the table. "Will you excuse me?" she said politely, then she reached up to the doctor's ear.

"Shall I go and get my money?" she whispered.

He shook his head. "No," he replied in a low tone. "I came to thank you very much for your note, and to tell you that you don't owe me anything. I'm not usually a 'no cure, no pay' doctor. I take the money anyway, but this time I'm going to make an exception."

"Why?" asked Jewel, speaking aloud as long as he did.

"Well, you see, you didn't take the medicine. That makes a difference. Most people take it."

"Ye—es," rejoined Jewel rather doubtfully. She was not sure of this logic.

"So now we're perfectly square," went on the doctor, "but don't you fall ill again." He shook his head at her. "I want us to remain friends."

"We'd always be friends, wouldn't we?" returned Jewel, smiling into his laughing eyes.

"When is our golf coming off, Miss Eloise?" he asked, looking across the table again.

"When the weather permits," she responded graciously.

"I guess that's going to be all right," commented Mrs. Forbes mentally. "She's as pretty as a painting with that rose on, and her mother looks as contented as a cat with her paw on a mouse. She don't mean to play with that mouse, either. She won't run any risks. She'll take it right in. You're pretty near done for, my young feller, and your eyes look willing, I must say."

The spring rain proved to be a protracted storm. Mr. Evringham made his hours long in the city. Eloise came up to Jewel's room each morning and read the lesson with her, always reading on to herself after it was finished. She made the child tell her of the circumstances of her recent illness and cure, and listened to Jewel's affectionate comments on Dr. Ballard's kindness with an inscrutable expression which did not satisfy the child.

"You love him, don't you?" asked the little girl.

Eloise gave a slight smile. "If everything that isn't love is hate, I suppose I ought to," she returned.

"Yes, indeed," agreed Jewel; "and he has been so kind to you I don't see how you can help it."

The girl sighed. "Don't grow up, Jewel," she said. "It makes lots of trouble."

On the second one of her visits to the child's room she put her hand on the flaxen head. "I'd like to fix your hair," she said. "Mrs. Forbes doesn't part it nicely."

"I do it myself," returned Jewel; "but I'd be glad to have you."

So Eloise washed the thick flaxen locks and dried them. Then she parted and brushed the hair, and when it was finally tied, Jewel regarded the reflection of her smooth head with satisfaction.

"It looks just the way mother makes it," she said. "I'm going to write to mother and father to-night, and I'm going to tell them how kind you are to me."

That evening, in Mr. Evringham's library, Jewel wrote the letter.

Her grandfather, after making some extremely uncomplimentary comments upon the weather, had lowered his green-shaded electric light and established himself beneath it with his book.

He looked across at the child, who was situated as before at the table, her crossed feet, in their spring-heeled shoes, dangling beneath.

"May I smoke, Jewel?" he asked, as he took a cigar from the case. He asked the question humorously, but the reply was serious.

"Oh yes, grandpa, of course; this is your room; but you know nobody likes tobacco naturally except a worm."

Mr. Evringham's deep-set eyes widened. "Is it possible? Well, we're all worms."

Jewel smiled fondly at him, her head a little on one side, in its characteristic attitude.

"You're such a joker," she returned.

"If you really dislike smoke," said the broker after a minute, "perhaps you'd better take your letter up to your room."

"I don't mind it," she returned. "Father used to smoke. It's only a little while since it gave him up."

"You mean since he gave it up."

"No. When people study Christian Science, the error habits that they have just go away."

"Indeed? I'm glad you warned me." Mr. Evringham blew a delicate ring of smoke toward the table, but Jewel had begun to think of her parents, and her pencil was moving. Her grandfather noted the trim appearance of the bowed head.

"I don't know but I was cut out for a man milliner after all," he mused complacently. "Those bows have really a very chic appearance."

His book interested him, and he soon became absorbed in its pages. Jewel occasionally coming to an orthographic problem looked up and waited, but he did not observe her, so she patiently kept silence and resumed her work. At last the letter was finished.

She looked again at her grandfather, and opened her cramped little hand with relief. The back of her neck was tired with her bending posture. She leaned back in the heavy chair to rest it while she waited. The eyelids, grown heavy with her labors, wavered and winked. The rain dripped down the panes, as if it had fallen into a monotonous habit. The sound was soothing. Jewel fell asleep.

When finally Mr. Evringham glanced at her he smiled. "Little thoroughbred," he mused; "she'd never disturb me." He rose and crossed to the child. There lay the finished letter. He took it up with some anticipation:—

DEAR MOTHER AND FATHER——It is most time to get a leter from you but I will not wait to tell you I am happy and well.

Grandpa is the kindest man and he has the most Beautiful horse, her name is Essecks made. He let me sit on her back and give her Sugar. Cosin Elloees is the prettiest one of all. She has things that make her sorry but she is very kind to me. She washed my hare today and she helps me get the lesson. There is a docter here he is lovly. He tried to cure me when I had a claim but Mrs. Lewis did. Cosin Elloees reads S. and H when we get throo the lesson and I think she will be glad Pretty soon and not afrade Grandpa doesn't want her and Ant maj. She won't let me tell grandpa she is kind to me, but I can Explane beter when you come home.

Grandpa's kindness is inside, and he Looks sorry but noboddy cood help loving him. I love you both every minnit and the leters in my pocket help me so much.

Your dear

JEWEL.

Mr. Evringham had scarcely finished reading this epistle when Jewel's head slipped on the polished woodwork against which she was leaning and bumped against the side of the chair with a jar which awoke her.

Seeing her grandfather standing near she smiled drowsily. "I fell asleep, didn't I?" she said, and rubbed her eyes; then noting the sheet of paper in Mr. Evringham's hand, memory returned to her. She sat up with a start.

"Oh, grandpa, you haven't read my letter!" she exclaimed, with an accent of dismay which brought the blood to the broker's face. He felt a culprit before the shocked blue eyes.

"To—to see if it was spelled right, you know," he said. "You had me do it before."

"Yes, I wanted you to then," returned the child; "but it is error to read people's letters unless they ask you to, isn't it?"

"Yes, it's confoundedly bad form, Jewel. I beg your pardon. You didn't mean me to see those sweet things you said about me, eh?"

"That was no matter. It was cousin Eloise's secret. She trusted me." The child's eyes filled with tears.

The broker cleared his throat. "No harm done, I'm sure. No harm done," he returned brusquely, to cover his discomfiture. For the first time he made an advance toward his granddaughter. "Come here a minute, Jewel." He took her hand and led her to his chair, and seating himself, lifted her into his lap. The corners of her lips were drawing down involuntarily, and as her head fell against his broad shoulder, he took out his handkerchief and dried her eyes. "I hope you'll forgive me," he said. "After this I will always wait for your permission. Now what is this about cousin Eloise?"

Jewel shook her head, not trusting herself to speak.

"You can't tell me?"

"No."

"Then don't you think perhaps it was a good thing I read your letter after all, if it is something I ought to know?"

The speaker was not so interested to discover the secrets of his beautiful guest as to set himself right with this admirer. He did not relish falling from his pedestal.

"Do you think perhaps Divine Love made you do it, grandpa?" asked the child tremulously, with returning hope.

Mr. Evringham was quite certain that it had been curiosity, but he was willing to accept a higher sounding hypothesis.

"Mother explained to me about God making 'the wrath of man to praise Him,'" added Jewel after the moment's pause. "If it makes you kind to cousin Eloise, perhaps we can be glad you read it."

"What is the matter with Eloise?" asked Mr. Evringham.

Jewel sat up, fixed him with her eyes, pressed her lips together, and shook her head.

"You won't tell me?"

The head went on firmly shaking.

"Then let me read the letter again."

"No, grandpa," decidedly.

He kept one arm around her as he smoothed his mustache. "Is there something you think I ought to do?"

A light seemed to illumine the eyes that the little girl kept fixed on his, but she did not speak.

"Do you think it discourteous for me to spend my evenings away from those two? They don't want me, child."

Still she did not speak. Mr. Evringham was divided between a desire to shake her and the wish to see the familiar fondness return to her face.

"You wrote that Eloise thinks I do not want her and her mother here. Her intelligence is of a higher order than I feared. Well, what can be done about it? I've been asking myself that for some time. How would it do to settle some money upon them and then say good-by?"

"If you did it with love," suggested Jewel.

"It's my impression that they could dispense with the love under those circumstances." The broker gave a slight smile.

The child put an impulsive little hand on his shoulder. "No indeed, grandpa. Nobody can do without love. It hurts cousin Eloise because she isn't your real relation. She doesn't know how kind you are inside." The child's lips closed suddenly.

"She fixed your hair very nicely," Mr. Evringham viewed the flaxen head critically. "That's one thing in her favor."

"She's full of things in her favor," returned Jewel warmly. "Error's using you, grandpa, not to love her. If we don't love people we can't be sure anything we do to them is right."

Mr. Evringham raised one hand and scratched his head slowly, regarding Jewel with what she felt was intended to be a humorous air.

"Couldn't you give me an easier one?" he asked.

"Oh grandpa," the flaxen head nestled against his breast and the child sighed. "I wish everybody knew how kind you are," and the broker patted her shoulder and enjoyed the clinging pressure of her cheek, for it assured him that again he stood firmly on the pedestal.

CHAPTER XVIII
ESSEX MAID

The rain and wind lasted for three days, clearing at last on an evening which proved eventful.

Mr. Evringham had taken a long ride into the country roundabout, and Jewel had been down at the gate to greet his return. He swung her up into the saddle with him, and in triumph she rode to the barn.

Mrs. Evringham observed this from the window and reported to Eloise.

"I didn't suppose father would be so indulgent to any living thing as he is to that child," she said rather dejectedly. "Do you know, Eloise, Mrs. Forbes says that Jewel spends every evening with him in his study."

"Indeed? I'm not surprised. He had to take pity on her since we would not."

Mrs. Evringham sighed. "I really believe nobody was ever so exasperating as you are," she returned. "When Jewel first came, if you remember, I wished to welcome her,—in fact I did,—but you refused to be decently civil. Now you speak as if we had made a mistake, and that it was my fault. I wish you would let Dr. Ballard prescribe for you. I don't think you are well."

"He does prescribe roses and chocolates, and I take them, don't I?"

"Yes, and after this you can have some golf. It will do you good."

To-day was the third during which Eloise had helped her cousin with the morning lesson and brushed and braided her hair. Jewel had had many minds about whether to tell Eloise of her escaped secret. An intuition bade her refrain, but the sense of dishonesty was more than the child could bear; so that morning, during the hair braiding, she had confessed. She began thus:—

"I wrote to my father and mother last night how good you were to me."

"Did you tell them how good you were to me?" asked the girl, so kindly that the child's heart leaped within her and she more than ever wished that she had nothing to confess.

"I wish I could be, cousin Eloise; I meant to be, but error crept in." The girl was learning something of the new phraseology, and she smiled at Jewel in the glass and was surprised to find what troubled eyes met hers. "I went to sleep that night waiting for grandpa to be through with his book, and when I waked up he had read my letter."

Eloise's smile faded. "Tell me again what you said in it," she returned.

Jewel's lips quivered. "I said how kind you were, and washed my hair, and asked me not to tell grandpa—"

"You put that in?" Eloise interrupted eagerly.

The child took courage from her changed tone. "Yes; I said you didn't want him to know you were kind to me."

The girl smiled slightly and went on with her brushing.

"He wished he hadn't read it when he saw how sorry I was. He asked my pardon and said he had done bad form. I don't know what that is."

"It's the worst thing that can happen to some people," returned Eloise. "Good form is said to be the New York conscience."

"Oh," responded Jewel, not understanding, but too relieved and grateful that her cousin was not unforgiving to press the matter.

Eloise fell into thought. Mr. Evringham had certainly been more genial at table, conversation had been more general and sustained last evening than ever before the advent of Jewel, and he had not sneered, either. Eloise searched her memory for some word or look that might have given hurt to her self-esteem, but she could find none.

On this evening Mr. Evringham was in unusual spirits at dinner time. He told of the pleasure of Essex Maid at finding herself free of the stable again, and of the gallop he had taken among the hills.

The meat course had just been removed when Sarah came in with a troubled face, saying that Zeke wanted to see Mr. Evringham. Something was the matter with Essex Maid. She seemed "very bad."

The master's face changed, and he moved back from the table. The countenances of the others showed consternation. Mrs. Forbes turned pale. Had Zeke done anything, or left something undone? She dropped her tray and hastened after Mr. Evringham. Eloise noticed that Jewel's eyes were closed. In a minute the child pushed back from the table, and without a word to the others she hurried to the scene of trouble. She met Mrs. Forbes rushing to the kitchen for hot water.

"Go straight into the house, Jewel," cried the housekeeper with an anger born of her excitement. "Don't you go near that barn and get in the way."

The child, scarcely hearing her, fled on. As she entered the barn she heard her grandfather's voice addressing Zeke, who was flinging a saddle on Dick.

"Dr. Busby'll leave anything when he knows it's the Maid." He didn't need to say "hurry." Zeke was as anxious as his master to get the veterinary surgeon.

Essex Maid had fallen in her stall and was making her misery apparent, tossing her head and rolling her eyes. Her master's teeth were set.

"Grandpa, may I try to help?" came Jewel's eager voice.

"Go away, child," sternly. "You'll get hurt."

"But may I treat her?"

"Do anything," brusquely; "but don't come near."

Jewel ran to the back of the barn, dropped on the floor, and buried her face in her hands.

Five minutes passed, ten, fifteen. Zeke rode up to the barn door, white and wild-eyed in the twilight.

"Dr. Busby was away!" he gasped. "They tried to get him on the telephone, and at last did. He'll be here in a few minutes."

"The Maid's better," said Mr. Evringham, wiping his forehead. "There hasn't been a repetition of the attack." Mrs. Forbes stood by, fanning herself with her apron. The mare was standing quietly.

"Great Scott, but I'm glad!" replied Zeke devoutly. "I've seen 'em keel up with that. You can go through me with a fine tooth comb, Mr. Evringham, and you won't find a thing I've neglected for that mare." Excitement had placed the young fellow beyond his awe for the master.

"I believe you, boy," returned the broker. In his relief he would have believed anything.

"See the poor kid," said Zeke, catching sight of the little figure sitting out of earshot, where the twilight touched her.

Mr. Evringham wheeled and strode back to the child. Her face was still hidden.

"Don't cry, Jewel," he said kindly, his voice unsteady. "She's better."

The child looked up radiantly. "I knew it!"

The unexpected look and exclamation startled her grandfather. "Zeke says the doctor can't get here for a little while," he went on, "but the mare is out of pain."

"It's all right," rejoined the child joyously. "The doctor ought not to come. We shall do better without him."

The first gleam of her meaning began to shine across the broker's mind. He stared down at the little figure, uncertain whether to laugh or cry, sufficiently shaken to do either.

"Why, you midget you," he said, picking the child up in his arms; "have you been trying your tricks over here in the corner?"

"That isn't the way to talk, grandpa, when God has helped us so," returned Jewel earnestly.

Zeke, following his employer, had heard this colloquy, and stared open mouthed.

When Dr. Busby arrived he was a much injured man. "The mare's perfectly fit," he grumbled. "You've made me leave an important case."

"Very sorry," returned Mr. Evringham, trying to look so. "The fact is the Maid has given us a scare in the last hour that I shouldn't like repeated. Look her over carefully, Busby, carefully."

"I have." The veterinary gave a cross look around the group, his glance resting a moment on the upturned face of a little flaxen-haired girl who stood with her hand in Mr. Evringham's.

"He's falling into his dotage, I guess," said the doctor privately to Zeke, as he prepared to ride away.

"Don't fool yourself," returned the young fellow. "The mare pretty near scared me into a fit. My knees ain't real steady yet."

He stood watching the disappearing figure of the veterinary. "That kid believes praying did it," he mused. "I ain't going to believe that, of course, but the whole thing was the queerest ever."

Mr. Evringham, after one more visit to the stall of Essex Maid, started back to the house, Jewel skipping beside him.

Mrs. Forbes remained in the barn, one hand still pressed to her ample bosom, a teakettle in the other.

"What'd you calc'late to do, ma?" inquired her son, approaching her.

"Wring out hot flannels. It's sense to treat colic the same, whether it's in a horse or a baby."

Zeke laughed. "Essex Maid didn't think so, did she?"

"Wouldn't let us do a thing. I saw the tears drip out of Mr. Evringham's eyes plain as I see you now. Zeke Forbes, you'll never know what it was to me to have you come in and speak the way you did. You couldn't have done it if you'd mistreated the horse any way."

"Thank you," returned the coachman emphatically. "I ain't monkeying with buzz saws this year."

"Not knowingly you wouldn't. But, child," —Mrs. Forbes set down the kettle and pressed the other hand tighter to her bosom as she came closer to him, "last night you'd been drinking when you came home."

"Ho!" laughed Zeke uncomfortably, "just a smile or two with the boys. By ginger, you've got a nose on you, mother."

"Can you think of your father and then laugh over it, Zeke? There hasn't a man ever come to be a sot that didn't laugh about it in the first place."

"Now, mother, now, now," said the young fellow in half-impatient tones of consolation, as he took the handkerchief from her apron pocket and wiped her eyes, where tears began to spring. "You must trust a chap to do what's right. I ain't a fool. Don't you think about this again. I can take care of myself. Come now, to change the subject, what's your opinion of Christian Science as applied to horses with the colic?"

"What do you mean?" returned the housekeeper in an unusually subdued tone.

"Why, didn't you catch on? The kid was over there in the corner treating the Maid. That's what they call it, treating 'em. Mr. Evringham laughed when he found out, and she jumped on him. Yes, she did; came right out and told him that wasn't the way to show his gratitude, or something like that. Think of the nerve!"

"I ain't surprised. That child can't surprise me."

"But what do you think of it, ma? I tell you 't was queer, the way that mare's pain stopped. Of course I ain't going to believe—but," firmly, "I can't get away from a notion that those Christian Science folks know something that we don't. Busby was madder'n a hornet. I didn't scarcely know what to say to him."

"Don't be soft, Zeke," returned his mother, picking up the kettle. "The time for superstition has gone by."

As Jewel and her grandfather entered the house they heard music.

"That's cousin Eloise playing. Have you heard her grandpa?"

"Yes, when they first came."

"Than you haven't sat with them in the evening for a long time?" suggested the child.

"No. I—I didn't wish to monopolize their society. I wanted to give Dr. Ballard a chance. He is a friend of theirs, you know."

"Yes, but I think cousin Eloise would be glad if she thought you liked her playing. It's very beautiful, isn't it, grandpa?"

"Yes, I dare say. Then, besides, I'm not at all sure that Mrs. Evringham would permit me to smoke in the drawing-room."

"But wouldn't it be nice to go in there just a few minutes before you go to your study? I love to hear cousin Eloise play, but I like to be with you, grandpa."

Mr. Evringham was in a yielding state of mind. He allowed the pressure of the child's hand on his to lead him to the drawing-room, where his entrance made a little stir.

Dr. Ballard was sitting near the piano, listening to the music. Everybody rose as the newcomers entered.

"How are you, Ballard? Jewel wished to hear her cousin's music, and so behold us. If we bring a reminder of the stable, blame her."

"Oh father, that dear horse is all right, I'm sure," gushed Mrs. Evringham, "or else you wouldn't be here!"

"What? Something the matter with Essex Maid?" asked Dr. Ballard with concern.

"Yes." Mr. Evringham seated himself. "A sharp attack, but short. She was relieved before we could get Busby here." The speaker contracted his eyebrows and looked at the child, who was still beside him. "The mare had received mental treatments meanwhile," he added gravely.

Dr. Ballard smiled, and drawing Jewel to him, lifted her upon his knee. "Look here," he said, "can't you let anything around here be sick in peace? We doctors shall have to form a union and manage to get you boycotted."

The child smiled back at him, her head a little on one side, as her manner was when she was in doubt how to respond.

"What a blessing!" exclaimed Mrs. Evringham vivaciously. "Here, father, is the best cup of coffee you ever drank, if I did make it myself."

Many weeks had elapsed since the broker had accepted a cup of coffee from that fair hand, but he rose now to take it with good grace.

"Is there going to be some cambric tea for this baby?" inquired Dr. Ballard.

"You must be hungry, Jewel; you hadn't finished your dinner," said her grandfather, but she protested that she was not.

"How is Anna Belle?" asked Dr. Ballard. "It's a long time since I saw her."

"Would you like to?" asked Jewel doubtfully.

"Why—of—course!—if she's still up. Don't have her dress on my account."

"She doesn't go to bed till I do," responded the child. "I know she'd love to come down!" In a flash she had bounded to the door and disappeared.

Eloise was still sitting on the piano stool, facing the room. "Grandfather," she said, leaning slightly forward in her earnestness, "did Jewel really treat Essex Maid?"

The broker shrugged his shoulders and smiled as he stirred his coffee.

"I believe she did."

"And do you think it did the horse any good?"

"Don't be absurd!" cried her mother laughingly, on nettles lest the girl displease the young doctor.

"Don't crowd me, Eloise, don't crowd me," responded Mr. Evringham. "I'd rather have something a little more substantial doing for a sick horse than the prayers of an infant; eh, Ballard?"

"I've been reading Jewel's Christian Science book a great deal the last few days," said Eloise. "If it's the truth, then she helped Essex Maid."

Mrs. Evringham was dismayed. "What a very large *if*, my dear," she returned lightly.

"She's a bright little girl," said Dr. Ballard, and as he spoke Jewel came back.

She brought her doll straight to him, and he took both child and doll on his lap.

"Dear fellow," thought Mrs. Evringham, "how fond he is of children! I'd like to put Eloise in a strait-jacket. Do play some more, dear, won't you?" she said aloud, eager to return to safe ground.

"Oh yes, cousin Eloise," added Jewel ardently.

"If you will sing afterward. Will you?" asked the girl.

"Can you sing, Jewel?" asked Mr. Evringham.

"No, grandpa, nothing but the tunes in church."

"Well," he responded, half smiling again, "I don't know that a hymn would be so out of place to-night."

"Do play the lovely running thing about spring, cousin Eloise," begged the child.

The girl turned back to the piano. "Jewel is so modern that she doesn't know the Mendelssohn 'Spring Song,'" she said, and forthwith she began it.

Jewel's head lay back against Dr. Ballard's shoulder, and her eyes never swerved from the white-robed musician.

When the player had finished and been thanked, the child and the doctor exchanged a look of appreciation. "That sounds the way it does in the Ravine of Happiness," said Jewel.

"Where is that?"

"Where the brook is."

"Oh!" Dr. Ballard had unpleasant associations with the brook. "I understand you are fond of horses," he added irrelevantly.

"Oh yes."

"Do you want to go driving with me to-morrow morning?"

Jewel's face grew radiant.

"Oh yes!" She looked across at her grandfather.

"I promised to take you driving, didn't I, Jewel? Well, the pleasant weather has come. I guess she'll go with me to-morrow, Ballard."

"Guess again, Mr. Evringham," retorted the doctor gayly. "She has accepted my invitation."

Mrs. Evringham looked on and wondered. "What is it about that child that takes them all?" she soliloquized. "She reminds me of that dreadfully plain Madam what's-her-name, who was so fascinating to everybody at the French court."

Eloise was smiling. "Now it's your turn, Jewel," she said.

The child looked from one to another. "I never sang for anybody," she returned doubtfully.

"Yes indeed, for Anna Belle. I've heard you," said Eloise.

"Oh, she was singing with me."

"Very well. Let her sing with you now."

"What one?"

"The one I heard, — 'Father, where Thine own children are I love to be.'"

"Oh, you mean. 'O'er waiting harpstrings.' All right," and the child, sitting where she was, sang the well-loved hymn to a touched audience.

"Upon my word, Jewel," said her grandfather when she had finished. "Your music isn't all in your soul." His eyes were glistening.

"Those are beautiful words," said Dr. Ballard. "I don't remember any such hymn."

"Mrs. Eddy wrote it," returned the child.

"It wasn't Castle Discord to-night," she said later to Anna Belle, while they were going to bed. "Didn't you notice how much differently people loved one another?"

CHAPTER XIX
A MORNING DRIVE

"I declare, Eloise," said Mrs. Evringham the next morning, "it is almost worth three whole days of storm to have a spell of such heavenly weather to follow. We're sure of several days like this now," She was standing at the open window, having shown a surprising energy in rising soon after breakfast.

She glanced over her shoulder at her daughter, who was picking up the garments strewn about the room. "Now you can live out of doors, I hope, and get yourself toned up again. Really, last evening things were very comfortable, weren't they?"

"Yes. I thought the lump had begun to be leavened," returned the girl.

"Talk English, please," said her mother vivaciously. "Father seemed quite human, and that is all we have ever needed to make things tolerable here. I suppose we reaped the benefit of his relief about the horse."

"It's all Jewel," said Eloise, smiling. "That's English, isn't it?"

"Jewel!" Mrs. Evringham exclaimed. "Why, you're all daffy about that child. What *is* the attraction?"

"That's what I'm trying to find out. It's time for me to go up now and braid her hair and read the lesson."

Mrs. Evringham regarded her daughter. "Young people are eager for novelty, I know," she said, "and it would seem as if an interest in a child was an innocent diversion for you at a time when you were growing morbid, but I do think I'm the most unlucky woman in the world! To think that the child should have to be a Christian Scientist, and that you should take this perverse interest in her ideas just now. I haven't spoken of your remarks about the horse last night, but it was in poor taste, to say the least, to mention such nonsense before Dr. Ballard, and apparently do it so seriously. I knew you had been helping Jewel with lessons, but until last evening I didn't suspect that it might all be on that odious subject. Is it, Eloise?"

"Yes, but it isn't odious. I like the fruit of it in her."

"You've never shown Dr. Ballard your most agreeable side, and now if you're going to parade before him, an Episcopalian and a physician, an interest in this—anarchism, I shan't blame him in the smallest degree if he gives up all thought of you."

Eloise, the undemonstrative, put an arm around her mother. "Shan't you, really?" she replied wistfully. "If I could only hope that."

"Do you want to give me nervous prostration?" rejoined Mrs. Evringham sharply. "Eloise," her voice suddenly breaking, "do you love to torment me?"

"Indeed I don't, poor mother, but I've been so tormented myself, and so desirous not to—oh, not to do anything ignoble! I can't tell you all I've endured since—" She paused, her lips unsteady.

"Since we lost your father," dismally. "Yes, I know it. I'm the most unlucky woman in the world!"

Eloise's arm tightened about her mother as she went on, "Since I was enchanted and thrown into Castle Discord." She looked off at the mental picture of her cousin. "Mother," she turned back suddenly, "what a wonderful thing it is if there really is a God."

"Why, Eloise Evringham, have you ever doubted it! That's positively ill-bred!"

"But One that would be any good to us! Jewel's mother thinks she knows such a One, and so does the child. I wish you'd look into this Christian Science with me. You might find it better than getting grandfather to pay our bills, better than marrying me to Dr. Ballard."

Mrs. Evringham raised her eyes to her deity. "What have I ever done," she ejaculated, "that I should have a queer child! Well, I will not look into it," she returned decidedly; "and if Dr. Ballard were not the broad, noble type of man that he is, he wouldn't take the trouble to notice and entertain a child who has treated him as she has. It might touch even you to see the lengths to which he goes to please you. I hope you will at least have the grace to go down with Jewel to the buggy and see them off."

"I couldn't in this wrapper," replied Eloise, releasing the speaker.

"Of course not, so put on a dress before you go up to Jewel."

"It's too late, dear. He'll be here by half-past ten. I must have her ready."

Mrs. Evringham looked after her daughter's retreating figure, and then her lips came together firmly. She untied the ribbons of the loose gown of lace and silk, in which she had keyed herself up by degrees to face the requirements of luncheon and the afternoon's diversions, and donned a conventional dress, in which she composed herself by the window to watch for the doctor's buggy. There was a vista in the park avenue which afforded a fair look at equipages three minutes before they could reach Mr. Evringham's gateway.

From the moment the doctor's office hour was over this stanch supporter set herself to watch that gap. As soon as she saw Hector's dappled coat and easy stride she sprang up and went downstairs, and when the shining buggy paused at the steps and Dr. Ballard jumped out, she appeared on the piazza to greet him.

"What an inspiring morning!" she said, as he removed his hat. "That insane girl!" she thought. "If he had chanced to be awkward and plain, he would have been just as important to us. His good looks are thrown in, and yet she won't behave herself."

"Glorious indeed!" he replied heartily. "Where's my young lady?"

Mrs. Evringham had plenty of worldly experience, and not even her enemies called her stupid, but at this moment there was but one young lady in the world to her, as she believed there was to him.

"She is upstairs braiding Jewel's hair," she replied before she realized her own insanity. Then she hastened on, coloring under the odd look in his eyes, "But you mean Jewel, of course. She will be down at once, I'm sure. It's so kind of you to take her."

"Not at all. She's an original worth cultivating."

Mrs. Evringham shrugged her shoulders. "I suppose she must be, since you all say so. Eloise gives up a surprising amount of time to her, but I can't judge much from that, because Eloise is so unselfish. For my part, the child's ideas are so strange, and my little girl is still so young and impressionable, I object to having them much together. It may seem very absurd, when Jewel is so young."

"No; I saw last evening how interested Miss Eloise already is."

"Oh," hastily, "she pretends to be, and I assure you I object. Eloise has a good mind, and I hope you will offer a little antidote now and then to the stuff she has begun to read. A word to the wise, Dr. Ballard. I need say no more."

It was true. Mrs. Evringham had no need to say more. Her ideas, and especially those which related to himself, had always been inscribed in large characters and words of one syllable for her present companion, who was a young man of considerable perception and discrimination.

He had not time to reply before Jewel, radiant of face, appeared in the doorway, where she hesitated, her doll in her arms.

"I brought Anna Belle," she said doubtfully, "but I can leave her under the stairs if there isn't room."

"Anna Belle under the stairs on a morning like this! And in such a toilet? Talk about error!" The doctor's tone was tragic as he lifted the happy child into the buggy.

Mrs. Evringham nodded a reply to their smiling farewells as Hector sprang forward, and she looked after them in some perplexity.

"Why should he take the trouble?" she reflected. "It would have been such a splendid morning for them to have gone riding if he had this leisure. Of course it must have been just one of his indirect and lovely ways of trying to please Eloise."

Just as she was solacing herself with the latter reflection, her daughter stepped out on the piazza, a little black book in her hand.

"Warm enough to sit out, isn't it?" she remarked.

Her mother looked at her critically. She had not seen this care-free look on her child's face since Lawrence died. "Why didn't you come out a little sooner?"

"I wasn't presentable. How delicious the air is!"

"Yes. Let us sit here and finish that novel."

"All right."

"What have you there?"

"Mrs. Eddy's book,—'Science and Health.'"

Mrs. Evringham made a grimace. "I read part of it once. That was enough for me. Think of the price they charge for it, too. Think of pretending it is such a good thing for everybody to have, and then putting a price on it that prohibits the average pocketbook." Eloise's smile annoyed her mother. "Weren't you with me the day Nat Bonnell's mother said so much about it?"

"How foolish she was not to try it," said Eloise. "Such a hopeless, monotonous invalid."

"Well, some of her friends worked hard enough to induce her to, but when she found out the mercenary side of it, she saw at once that it couldn't be trustworthy."

"I suppose even Christian Scientists must have a roof and food and clothes," returned Eloise coolly; "but I've thought a good deal the last few days about the criticisms I've heard on the price of the book. The fuss over that three dollars is certainly very funny, when the average pocketbook goes to the theatre sometimes, has flowers for its entertainments, and rejoices to find lace reduced from a dollar and a quarter to ninety-five cents a yard for its gowns. It eagerly hoards and spends three dollars for some passing pleasure or effect, but winces and ponders over paying the same sum for a book that will last a lifetime, and which, if it is worth anything, furnishes the key to every problem in life."

"But why isn't it as cheap as the Bible if it is so beneficial?"

"It will be, probably, when it is generally respected. For the present it wouldn't be wise to cast it about like pearls before swine." Eloise smiled at herself. "You see I'm talking as if I knew it all. My wisdom comes partially from what I have extracted from Jewel, and partly from what is obvious. I haven't reached the place yet where I am convinced, but this book is wonderfully interesting. It came to me in the darkest hour I have ever known, and it has—it has seemed to feed me when I was starving. I don't know how else to put it. I can't think of anything else. Mother, why haven't we a Bible? I was ashamed when Jewel asked me."

Mrs. Evringham, astonished and dismayed by her daughter's earnestness, drew herself up. "We have a Bible, certainly. What an idea!"

"Where is it?" eagerly.

"In the storage warehouse with the other books."

Eloise's laugh nettled her mother.

"The prayer books are upstairs on my table. What more do you want if you are going to take an interest in such things? I wish you would, dear, and embroider an altar cloth while you are here. I'm sure father would gladly contribute the materials and feel a pride in it."

"Oh mother," Eloise still smiled, "you know he never goes to church."

"But he contributes largely."

"Well, I haven't time to embroider altar cloths. Shall I get the story?"

"Yes, do. We'll go around the corner, out of the wind."

Meanwhile Dr. Ballard's buggy was covering the ground rapidly. Through the avenues of the park sped Hector, and joy! Dr. Ballard allowed Jewel to drive as long as they remained within its precincts. Slipping his hand through the reins above where she grasped them, he held Anna Belle on his knee. Jewel had not suspected the size of the park. One could almost see the watered leaves increase in the sunshine, and the birds were swelling their little throats to the utmost. The roses in her cheeks deepened in her happy excitement. She allowed the doctor to do most of the talking, while she kept her eyes on the horse's ears. Just once she ventured to turn enough to glance at him.

"I've had dreams of driving horses," she said.

"Is this the first time you've done it waking?"

"No, the second. Father took me once in Washington Park just before he came away, but the horse didn't pull like this." She smiled seraphically.

"So, boy, steady," said the doctor soothingly, and Hector obeyed the voice.

"Did you play in the Ravine of Happiness when you were a little boy?"

"Where's that?"

"Where the brook is."

"Oh yes. Are you planning to take me to that brook and wet my feet, Jewel?"

"We've gone long past it. Don't you know?"

"I think my education has been neglected. I don't remember it."

"We can go," returned Jewel suggestively.

"Very well, we will; but first I have a couple of visits I must make."

The horse was now trotting toward the park gate. As they reached it Dr. Ballard returned Anna Belle and took the lines.

Jewel gave an unconscious sigh of rapture. "Trolleys and so on, you know," explained Dr. Ballard. "When you come back ten years from now you shall drive outside too. How was Essex Maid this morning?"

"She was all right, but grandpa took only a short ride. I guess he was a little—bit—afraid."

"She's the apple of his eye, or he wouldn't have been so nervous over a trifle last evening," remarked the doctor.

"Well, she made a great fuss," replied Jewel. "She fell down in her stall, and everything like that."

"Did she really?"

"Yes. Zeke said his knees were shaking."

"But she was all right by the time Dr. Busby arrived?"

"Yes."

Dr. Ballard looked at his small companion, a quizzical smile curving his mustache.

"I've never thought of taking a partner, Jewel, but I might consider a mascot. What do you say to sharing my office and being my mascot? Special high chair for Anna Belle, be it well understood."

The little girl eyed him, her head on one side. It was her experience that all men were jokers. "I don't know what a mascot is," she replied.

"It's something or somebody that brings one good luck."

"Do you think I could bring you good luck?"

"It looks that way. Of course there are certain rules you would have to observe. It wouldn't do for you to talk against materia medica to the patients in the anteroom."

"What is an anteroom?"

"The place where my patients wait until I can see them in my office."

Jewel lifted her shoulders and smiled. "I might read them 'Science and Health' while they waited, and then they wouldn't have to go in."

Dr. Ballard's laugh rang heartily along the leafy street. "Is that your idea of mascoting a poor young physician?" he inquired.

Jewel laughed in sympathy. She didn't quite understand him, but she knew that they were having a very good time.

Pretty soon her companion drove in at the gate of an imposing old residence, set back from the street where the trolley ran with an air of withdrawing from the intrusion of these modern tracks.

"I thought it wouldn't injure your conscience to wait for me while I made a couple of professional visits, Jewel, eh?" he asked, as he jumped out and fastened Hector to the ring in the hand of a bronze boy. "I won't be any longer than I can help, and don't you go to hoodooing me, now, while I'm upstairs." The doctor returned to the buggy and took the black case, frowning warningly at the child. "I have troubles enough here without that. This old lady used to trot me on her knee, and she wants to spend half an hour every morning proving that doctors don't know anything before she'll let me get to business."

"It must be hard for doctors," returned Jewel, "going to sorry people all the time, and nothing to give them except something on their tongues."

Dr. Ballard gave his small companion a quick glance. If he secretly considered her beliefs as too richly absurd to excite aught but amusement, she evidently as honestly compassionated the poverty of ideas in his learned profession.

"Well, I'll hurry," he said, and vanished within the house. Time would not have dragged for Jewel had he stayed all the morning. To sit in the shining buggy in close proximity to the dappled gray Hector, and with Anna Belle for a sympathizer, caused the minutes to be winged.

When the doctor returned, a radiant face welcomed him.

"I thought I should never get away," he sighed, "but you don't look bored."

He untied the horse, jumped into the buggy, and they were off again, Hector striding along as if to make up for lost time. "Now only one more call, Jewel, and then we'll get back out of the dust again," said the doctor cheerily.

"I haven't noticed any dust, Dr. Ballard. I'm having the most *fun!*"

"Well now, I'm glad of that. It's a great thing to be eight years old, Jewel."

"That's what cousin Eloise says. She says she'd like to be."

"Indeed? How is the enchanting—excuse me—I mean the enchanted maiden this morning?"

"She's well. She ties my bows now, so grandpa doesn't have to."

"Ties your—" The doctor looked at the speaker, mystified.

Jewel put her hand up to the small billows of silk behind her ear. "My hair bows. They were real hard for grandpa to do."

Dr. Ballard repressed a guffaw, and then turned solemn. "Do you mean to say that Mr. Evringham tied your hair ribbons?"

"Why yes."

"That settles it, Jewel. You must go into partnership with me and wave wands and things. Setting Essex Maid on her legs wasn't a patch on that."

Jewel regarded him questioningly a moment and then repeated, "But it was real hard for grandpa."

"I can believe it!"

"And cousin Eloise is the kindest girl. She's like grandpa about that. Her kindness is inside, too."

"Is it indeed? You don't know how much I thank you for telling me where to look for it."

"Oh, she must be kind to *you*, Dr. Ballard!"

"Once in a while, once in a while," he replied cautiously, but Jewel couldn't get a look into his eyes, though she tried, he was so busily engaged poking an invisible fly from Hector's side with the point of the whip. "If you'll find a way to make her kind to me all the time, Jewel, then you will be my mascot indeed."

"All you have to do is to know she is," replied the child earnestly. "I felt the way you do, at first, but now I've found out just because I stopped being afraid."

"Ah, that's the recipe, eh? All I've to do is to stop being afraid."

"That's all!" cried Jewel, beaming at his ready comprehension. "You'll find out there isn't a thing to be afraid of with Cousin Eloise, and oh, Dr. Ballard," the child smiled at him wistfully, "she's getting so—so—unenchanted."

"You just waved your wand, I suppose, and said 'Presto change,'" returned the young man.

He turned Hector down a side street and drew rein under a large elm. "Here's my rheumatic gentleman," he added, as he jumped from the buggy and fastened the horse. "He won't keep me waiting while he abuses doctors, so I shan't be quite so long this time." The speaker seized his case and went up a garden path to the house, and Jewel, with a luxurious sigh, set Anna Belle in the place he had vacated.

CHAPTER XX
BY THE BROOKSIDE

Scarcely had she seen the doctor admitted and the house door closed when an approaching pedestrian caught her eye. She recognized him at once, and a little more color stole into her round cheeks, while an unconscious smile touched her lips.

The gentleman had observed the doctor enter the house, and glanced idly as he passed, to see what child was waiting in the buggy. The half shy look of recognition which he met surprised him. Somewhere he had seen that rosy face. Going on his way and searching his memory he had left the buggy behind, when in a flash it came to him how, one day, that same shy, pleased smile had beamed wistfully upon him in a trolley car.

Instantly he turned back, and in a minute Jewel saw him standing beside her. He lifted his hat and replaced it as he held out his hand.

"We've met before, haven't we?" he asked kindly.

Jewel shook hands with him, much pleased. "My mother and father have gone to Europe," she said "and it seemed as if there wasn't a Scientist in the whole world until I saw you."

"Another proof of what I always say—that we should all wear the pin. I didn't know that Dr. Ballard had any Science relations."

"Oh, Dr. Ballard and I are not relations," explained Jewel seriously. "I think he wants to marry my cousin Eloise; but he hasn't ever said so, and I don't like to ask him. He's the kindest man. I just love him, and he's letting me ride around with him while he makes calls."

"Why, that's very nice, I'm sure," returned Mr. Reeves, smiling broadly. "Does he know that you're a Christian Scientist?"

"Oh, yes, indeed. I had a claim, and my grandpa called him to help me, so then I told him, but he kept on reflecting love just the same."

Mr. Reeves scented an interesting experience, but he would not question the child. "Nice fellow, Guy Ballard. He deserves a better fate than to bow down to false gods all his days."

"Yes, indeed," returned Jewel heartily.

"But, as you say," continued Mr. Reeves, "he reflects love, and so we shall hear of his being a successful physician."

"Yes, I want him to be always happy," said the child.

"Who is your grandfather, my dear?"

"Mr. Evringham."

"Is it possible? Then you are—whose child?"

"My father's name is Harry."

"Of course, of course." Mr. Reeves nodded, trying to conceal his surprise. "And is he a Scientist now?"

"Yes, my mother is teaching him to be."

"Well, I'm sure I'm very glad to hear this. Your grandfather is not unkindly disposed toward Science?"

"My grandfather couldn't be unkind to anything! I thought you knew him."

Mr. Reeves smoothed his mustache vigorously. "I thought I did," he returned. "You spoke of your cousin. I knew your aunt and cousin were with Mr. Evringham now. Well, I'm glad, I'm sure, that you are so pleasantly situated. You must come to our little hall some Sunday where we have service, you know. It will be rather different from your beautiful churches in Chicago."

"But I'd love to come," replied the child eagerly. "I didn't know there was one here. I'll get grandpa to bring me."

"Mr. Evringham!" The speaker could feel the tendency of his jaw to drop.

"Yes, or else cousin Eloise. She helps me get the lesson every day, and then she takes my book and reads and reads. She told me this morning she read almost all last night."

Mr. Reeves nodded slowly once or twice. "Still they come," he murmured meditatively.

"Would you—would you mind writing down where that hall is?" asked the child.

"Certainly I will." Mr. Reeves suited the action to the word, taking an envelope from his pocket for the purpose. "And if I ever see Mr. Evringham there"—he said slowly, "by the way, please tell your grandfather that we met and had this chat."

"I don't know your name," returned the child.

"Why, of course. Pardon me. Reeves. Mr. Reeves. Can you remember that?"

The little girl flashed a bright look at him. "We can't forget," she reminded him.

"Of course," he nodded. "Exactly. I'm very likely younger in Science than you are, little one. How long have you known about it?"

Jewel thought. "Seven years," she replied.

Her companion gave a laughing exclamation. "There, you see. I've known for only one year. What is your name?"

"Jewel Evringham."

"Good-bye, Jewel, till we meet again, some Sunday soon, I hope."

They shook hands, and Mr. Reeves went smiling on his way.

"Seven years," he reflected. "There's the simon pure article. She can't be over nine. I'll wager Bel-Air Park has had its sensations of late. Evringham! The high ball, the billiard ball, and the race track, and now the reputation of being a difficult old martinet. Never unkind to anything! Why, she's a little feminine Siegfried, that precious Jewel. Ballard and the cousin, eh? I've heard that rumor."

When Dr. Ballard returned to the buggy, Jewel began loquaciously telling him of her pleasant experience.

"And he knows you, Mr. Reeves does, and he said you were a nice fellow," she finished, beaming.

"Very civil of him, I'm sure," returned the doctor as the horse started. "I distinctly remember his having a different opinion one night when he caught me in his favorite cherry tree; but I don't yet understand the levity of his behavior in scraping acquaintance with the young lady I left unprotected in my buggy."

"Oh, we'd met before in a trolley car," explained Jewel. "I wanted to run right to him when I first saw that he was a Scientist."

"A what? Mr. Reeves? Oh, go 'way, my little mascot. Go 'way!"

"Yes, he had on the pin—this one, you know." Jewel touched the small gold symbol, and Dr. Ballard examined it curiously. "So we smiled at each other, and to-day he's told me where I can come to church, and I'm nearly sure cousin Eloise will go with me."

Dr. Ballard's eyes grew serious as he turned Hector's head toward the park. "I can scarcely believe it of Mr. Reeves," he said.

"He says you are too nice to bow down to false gods," added Jewel shyly.

"If mine are false to you, yours are false to me," said the young man kindly. "You can understand that, can't you, Jewel?"

"Yes, I can."

"And we should never quarrel over it, should we?" he went on.

"No—o!" returned Jewel scornfully. "We'd get a pain."

"But you can see," went on the young doctor seriously, "that the more we cared for one another the more we should regret such a wide difference of opinion."

"I suppose so," agreed the child, "and so we'd—"

"You are going back to Chicago after a while, and so you understand that I can better afford to agree to differ with you than I could with some one who was going to stay here—your cousin Eloise, for instance."

The child looked at him in silence. She had never seen Dr. Ballard wear this expression.

"For this reason, Jewel, I want to ask you if you won't do me the favor not to talk to your cousin about Christian Science, nor ask her to read your books, nor to go to church with you."

The child's countenance reflected his seriousness.

"You can see, can't you, that if Miss Eloise should become much interested in that fad it would spoil our pleasure in being together, while it lasted?"

The word fad was not in Jewel's vocabulary, but she grasped the doctor's meaning, and understood that he was much in earnest. She felt very responsible for the moment, and in doubt how to express herself.

"I feel sort of mixed up, Dr. Ballard," she returned after a minute's silent perplexity. "You don't mind cousin Eloise reading the Bible, do you?"

"No."

"You're glad if she can be happy instead of sorry, aren't you?"

"Yes."

Jewel looked at him hopefully. "There won't be anything worse than that," she said.

"Yes, many things worse," he responded quickly. "You might do me that little favor, Jewel. I understand you go to her with your lessons, as you call it, and your questions."

"Yes, she helps me; but she takes my books to her room. I don't see how I can help it, Dr. Ballard."

"Well," he heaved a quiet sigh, "perhaps the attack will be shorter if it is sharp. We'll hope so."

"I wouldn't do any harm to you for anything," said the child earnestly, "but you wait a little while. When people come into Christian Science it makes them twice as nice. If you see cousin Eloise get twice as nice you'll be glad, won't you?"

The young man gave an impatient half laugh.

"I'm not grasping," he returned. "She does very well for me as she is. Now," he turned again to the child, who rejoiced in the recovered twinkle in his eyes, "you have my full permission to convert the error fairy."

"Hush, hush!" ejaculated Jewel, alarmed. "We mustn't hold that law over her."

Dr. Ballard laughed.

"Convert her, I say. Let us see what she would be like if she were twice as nice. She's a very charming woman now, your aunt Madge. If she were twice as nice—who knows? The fairy might spread wings and float away!"

They had entered the park and Jewel suddenly noted their surroundings. "We're coming to the Ravine of Happiness," she said.

"That's the way it's been looking to me ever since last evening," responded her companion meditatively.

The child paid no attention to his words. She was watching eagerly for the bend in the road beside which the gorge lay steepest.

"There!" she said at last, resting her hand on that of her companion. Obediently the doctor stopped his horse. The park was still but for the bird notes, the laughter and babble of the brook far below, and the rustle of the fresh leaves, each one a transparency for a sunbeam.

The two were silent for a minute, Jewel's radiant eyes seeking the pensive ones of her companion.

"Do you hear?" she asked softly at last.

"What?" he returned.

"It is cousin Eloise's Spring Song."

The doctor's words and looks remained in Jewel's mind after she reached home that day. She mused concerning him while she was taking off Anna Belle's hat and jacket up in her own room.

"I don't suppose you could understand much what he meant, dearie," she said, her face very sober from stress of thought, "but I did. If I'd been as big as mother I could have helped him; but I knew I was too little, and when people don't understand, mother says it is so easy to make mistakes in what you say to them."

Anna Belle's silence gave assent, and her sweet expression was always a solace to Jewel, who kissed the hard roses in her cheeks repeatedly before she sat her in the big chair by the window and went down to lunch. Anna Belle's forced abstemiousness had ceased to afflict her. At the lunch table she gave a vivacious account of the morning's diversions, and for once Mrs. Evringham listened to what she said, a curious expression on her face. This lady had expected to endure annoyance with this child on her grandfather's account; but for unkind fate to cause Jewel to be a hindrance and a marplot in the case of Dr. Ballard was adding insult to injury.

The child, suddenly catching the expression of Mrs. Evringham's eyes as they rested upon her, was startled, and ceased talking.

"Aunt Madge does love me," she declared mentally. "God's children love one another every minute, every minute."

"So Mr. Reeves told you where you can go to church," said Eloise, replying to Jewel's last bit of information.

"Yes, and"—the little girl was going on eagerly to suggest that her cousin accompany her, when suddenly Dr. Ballard's eyes seemed looking at her and repeating their protest.

She stopped, and ate for a time in silence. Mrs. Forbes paid little attention to what was being said. She moved about perfunctorily, with an air of preoccupation. She had a more serious trouble now than the care and intrusion of the belongings of Lawrence and Harry Evringham, a worry that for days and nights had not ceased to gnaw at her heart, first as a suspicion and afterward as a certainty.

When luncheon was over, Eloise in leaving the dining-room, put her arm around Jewel's shoulders, and together they strolled through the hall and out upon the piazza.

Mrs. Evringham looked after them. "If only that child weren't a little fanatic and Eloise in such an erratic, wayward state, ready to seize upon anything novel, it would be all very well," she mused, "for Dr. Ballard seems to find Jewel amusing, and it might be a point of common interest. As it is, if ever I wished any one in Jericho, it's that child."

Jewel, happy in the proximity of her lovely cousin, satisfied herself by a glance that aunt Madge was not following.

Eloise looked about over the sunny, verdant landscape. "What a deceitful world," she said. "It looks so serene and easy to live in. So it was very lovely over at your ravine this morning?"

"Oh!" Jewel looked up at her with eager eyes. "Let's go. You haven't been there. It's only a little way. You don't need your hat, cousin Eloise."

Summer was in the air. The girl was amused at the child's enthusiastic tone. "Very well," she answered.

Jewel drew her on with an embracing arm, and they descended the steps and walked down the path.

Suddenly the child stopped. "Doesn't it seem unkind to go without Anna Belle!" she exclaimed.

"Oh, nonsense," returned Eloise, smiling. "You're not going way upstairs to get her. We needn't tell her we went. She's been out driving all the morning. I think it's my turn."

The child looked happily up into her cousin's face. "I love to see you laugh, cousin Eloise," she returned, and they strolled on.

The park drives were deserted. The cousins reached the gorge without meeting any one. Leaning upon the slender fence, they gazed down into the green depths, and for a minute listened to the woodland melody.

"Isn't it just like your Spring Song?" asked the child at last.

"It is sweet and comforting and good," replied the girl slowly, a far-off look in her eyes.

Jewel lifted her shoulders. "Don't you want to get down there, cousin Eloise?" she asked, her eyes sparkling.

"Yes," replied the girl promptly.

"Will it hurt your dress?" added Jewel, with a sudden memory of Mrs. Forbes, as she looked over her cousin's immaculate black and white costume.

"I guess not," laughed the girl. "Are you afraid Mrs. Forbes will put me to bed?"

She bent her lithe figure and was under the wire in a twinkling. Jewel crept gleefully after her, but was careful to hold her little skirts out of harm's way as they climbed down the steep bank and at last rested among the ferns by the brook. Its louder babble seemed to welcome them. Nature had been busy at her miracle working since the child's last visit. Without moving she could have gathered a handful of little blossoms. Instead, she rolled over and kissed a near clump of violets. "You darling, darling things!" she said.

Eloise looked up through far boughs to the fleece-flecked sky. "Everything worth living for is right here, Jewel," she said. "Let's have a tent and not give any one our address."

"I think we ought to let Dr. Ballard come, don't you?"

"Now why did you pick him out?" returned Eloise plaintively. She was resting her head against her clasped hands as she stretched herself against the incline of her verdant couch. Her companion did not reply at once, and Eloise lazily turned her head to where she could view the eyes fixed upon her.

"What are you thinking of, Jewel?"

"I was just thinking that if my mother made you a thin green dress that swept around you all long and narrow, you'd look like a flower, too."

The girl smiled back at the sky. "That's very nice. You can think those thoughts all you please."

"That wasn't all, though, because I was thinking about Dr. Ballard. He feels sorry. I couldn't tell you about it at lunch, because aunt Madge—well, because—"

"Yes," returned Eloise quietly. "It is better for us to be alone."

Jewel's brow relaxed. "Yes," she said contentedly, "in the Ravine of Happiness."

"Look out, though," continued the girl in the same quiet tone and looking back at the sky. "Look out what you say here. It is easy now to feel that all is harmonious, and that discords do not exist. I think even if grandfather appeared I could talk with him peacefully."

"I have thought about it," returned the child, "and it seems hard to know what to say; but I love you and Dr. Ballard both, so it will be sure to come out right. He feels sorry if you are beginning to like to study Christian Science."

"Really, did he speak of that to you? I think he might have chosen a man of his size."

"Of course he spoke of it when he found out I wanted to ask you to take me to our church."

"Where is the church here?" Eloise abandoned her lazy tone.

"They have a hall. Mr. Reeves wrote it down for me. Do you really care, cousin Eloise? You've been so kind and helped me, but do you really begin to care?"

"Care? Who could help caring, if it is true? I've been reading some of the tales of cures in your magazine. If those people tell the truth" —

"Why, cousin Eloise!" The child's shocked eyes recalled the girl's self-centred thoughts.

"I beg your pardon, dear. It was rude to say that. I'm not ill, Jewel. I'm so well and strong that—I've sometimes wished I wasn't, but life turned petty and disgusting to me. I resented everything. It is just as wonderful and radiant a star of hope to read that there is a sure way out of my tangle as if I had consumption and was promised a cure of that. I don't yet exactly believe it, but I don't disbelieve it. All I know is I want to read, read, read all the time. I was just thinking a minute ago that if we had the books here it would be perfect. This is the sort of place where it would be easiest to see that only the good is the real, and that the unsubstantiality of everything evil can be proved."

Jewel gave her head a little shake. "Just think of poor Dr. Ballard being afraid to have you believe that."

"But who wouldn't be afraid to believe it, who wouldn't!" exclaimed the girl vehemently.

"Why, I've always known it, cousin Eloise," returned the child simply.

"You dear baby. You haven't lived long. I don't want to climb into a fool's paradise only to fall out with a dull thud."

Jewel looked at her, grasping as well as she could her meaning. "I know I'm only a little girl; but if you should go to church with me," she said, "you'd see a lot of grown-up people who know it's true. Then we could go on Wednesday evenings and hear them tell what Christian Science has done for them."

"Oh, I'm sure I shouldn't like that," responded Eloise quickly. "How can they bear to tell!"

"They don't think it's right not to. There are lots of other people besides you that are sorry and need to learn the truth."

The rebuke was so innocent and, withal, so direct, that honest Eloise turned toward Jewel and made an impulsive grasp toward her, capturing nothing but the edge of the child's dress, which she held firmly.

"You're right, Jewel. I'm a selfish, thin-skinned creature," she declared.

The little girl shook her head. "You've got to stop thinking you are, you know," she answered. "You have to know that the error Eloise isn't you."

"That's mortal mind, I suppose," returned Eloise, smiling at the sound of the phrase.

"I should think it was! Old thing! Always trying to cheat us!" said Jewel. "All that you have to do is to remember every minute that God's child must be manifested. He inherits every good and perfect thing, and has dominion over every belief of everything else."

Eloise stared at her in wonder. "Do you know what you've talking about, you little thing, when you use all those long words?"

"Yes. Don't you?" asked the child. "Oh, listen!" for a bird suddenly poured a wild strain of melody from the treetop.

"And just think," said Jewel presently, in a soft, awestruck tone, "that some people wear birds sewed on their hats, just as if they were glad something was dead!"

"It *is* weird," agreed Eloise. "I never liked it. Jewel, did Dr. Ballard blame you because I am interested in Christian Science?"

"He said he wished I wouldn't talk to you and go to church and everything."

The girl bit a blade of grass and eyed the child's serious face.

"Well, what are you going to do about it?"

"I asked God to show me. I wish Dr. Ballard would study with you."

"That is impossible. He has spent years learning his science, and he loves it and is proud of it; so what next?"

"Very queer things happen sometimes," rejoined Jewel doubtfully.

"But not so queer as that would be," returned Eloise.

Jewel was pondering. This was very delicate ground, and she still felt some awe of her cousin; however, there was only one thing to consider.

"Do you love him better than anybody, cousin Eloise?" she asked.

A flood of color warmed the girl's face, but she had to smile.

"Would that make the difference?" she asked. "Mustn't we want the truth anyway?"

Jewel heaved a mighty sigh. She was thinking of Dr. Ballard's pensive eyes. "I should *think* so," she answered frankly; "because if you just study the truth, and hold on tight, how can things be anything but happy at last? I wish I was more grown up, cousin Eloise," she added apologetically.

"Oh no, no," answered the girl, with a little catch in her throat. "I've had so much of grown-up people, Jewel! I'm so grown up myself! Just a little while ago I was a schoolgirl, busy and happy all the time. I never even went out anywhere except with father, and with Nat when he was at home from college. You don't know Nat, but you'd like him."

"Why! Is he a Christian Scientist?"

For answer Eloise laughed low but heartily. "Nat a Christian Scientist!" she mused aloud. "Not exactly, my little cousin!"

"Then should I like him as well as Dr. Ballard?" asked Jewel incredulously.

"I don't know. Tastes differ."

"Does he like horses?" asked the child.

"He knows everything about a horse and a yacht except how to pay for them, poor boy," returned Eloise.

"Is he poor?"

"Yes, he is poor and expensive. It is a bad combination; it is almost as bad as being poor and extravagant. His mother is a widow, and they haven't much, but what there was she has insisted on spending on him—that is, all she could spare from the doctor's bills."

"She needs Science then, doesn't she?"

"Jewel, that would be one thing that would keep me from wanting to be a Scientist. What's the fun of being one unless everybody else is? My mother, for instance."

"Yes; but then you'd find out how to help her."

Eloise glanced at the child curiously. She thought it would be interesting to peep into Jewel's mind and see her estimate of Aunt Madge.

"My mother has a great deal to trouble her," she said loyally.

"Yes, I know she thinks she has," returned the child.

Again her response surprised her companion.

"I'll take you as you are, Jewel," she said. "I'm glad you're not grown up. You're fresher from the workshop."

CHAPTER XXI
AN EFFORT FOR TRUTH

When Eloise spoke in the ravine of talking with her grandfather, it was because for a few days she had been trying to make up her mind to an interview with him. A fortnight ago she would have felt this to be impossible; but subtle changes had been going on in herself, and, she thought, in him. If her mother would undertake the interview now and take that stand with Mr. Evringham which Eloise felt that self-respect demanded, the girl would gladly escape it; but there was no prospect of such a thing. Mrs. Evringham was only too glad to benefit by her father-in-law's modified mood, to glide along the surface of things and wait—Eloise knew it, knew it every day, in moments when her cheeks flushed hot—for Dr. Ballard to throw the handkerchief.

The girl wished to talk with Mr. Evringham without her mother's knowledge, and the prospect was a dreaded ordeal. She felt that they had won his contempt, and she feared the loss of her own self-control when she should come to touch upon the sore spots.

"What would you do, Jewel," she asked the next morning, after they had read the lesson; "what would you do if you were afraid of somebody?"

"I wouldn't be," returned the child quickly.

"Well, I am. Now what am I going to do about it?"

Anna Belle, who always gave unwinking attention to the lesson, was in Jewel's lap, and the child twisted out the in-turning morocco foot as she spoke.

"Why, I'd know that one thought of God couldn't be afraid of another," she replied in the conclusive tone to which Eloise could never grow accustomed.

"Oh, Jewel, child," the girl said impatiently, "we'd be sorry to think most of the people we know are thoughts of God."

"That's because you get the error man mixed up with the real one. Mother explains that to me when we ride in cable cars and places where we see error people with sorry faces. There's a real man, a real thought of God, behind every one of them; and when you remember to think right about people every minute, you are doing them good. Did you say you're afraid of somebody?"

"Yes, and that somebody is a man whom I must talk to."

"Then begin right away to know every minute that the real man isn't anybody to be afraid of, for God made him, and God has only loving thoughts; and of course you must be loving all the time. It'll be just as *easy* by the time you come to it, cousin Eloise!"

The girl often asked herself in these days why she should begin to feel unreasonably hopeful and lighter hearted. Her mother no longer complained of her moods. Mrs. Evringham laid the becoming change in her daughter's expression to the girl's happiness in discovering that she did reciprocate Dr. Ballard's evident sentiments.

"Eloise is so high minded," thought the mother complacently. "She would never be satisfied to marry for convenience, like so many;" and considering herself passingly astute, she let well enough alone, ceased to bring the physician's name into every conversation, and bided her time.

One morning Mr. Evringham, coming out of the house to go to town, met Eloise on the piazza.

"You are down early," he said as he greeted her, and was passing on to the carriage.

"Just one minute, grandfather!" she exclaimed, and how her heart beat. He turned his erect form in some surprise, and his cold eyes met the girlish ones.

"She's a stunning creature," he thought, as the sunlight bathed her young beauty; but his face was impenetrable, and Eloise nerved herself.

"Were you thinking of going golfing this afternoon?" she asked.

"Yes."

"I thought you said something about it at dinner last evening. Would you let me go with you?"

Mr. Evringham, much astonished, raised his eyebrows and took off the hat which he had replaced.

"Such a request from youth and beauty is a command," he returned with a slight bow.

Tears sprang to the girl's eyes. "Don't make fun of me, grandfather!" she exclaimed impulsively.

"Not for worlds," he returned. "You will do the laughing when you see me drive. My hand seems to have lost its cunning this spring. Shall we say four-thirty? Very well. Good-morning."

"Now what's all this?" mused Mr. Evringham as he drove to the station. "Has another granddaughter fallen in love with me? Methinks not. What is she after? Does she want to get away from Ballard? Methinks not, again. She's going to ask me for something probably. Egad, if she does, I think I'll turn her over to Jewel."

Eloise's eyes were bright during the lesson that morning.

"It's to-day, Jewel," she said, "that I'm going to talk with that man I'm afraid of."

"Never say that again," returned the child vehemently. "You are not afraid. There's no one to be afraid of. Do you want me to handle it for you?"

"What do you mean, Jewel?"

"To declare the truth for you."

"Do you mean give me a treatment for it?"

"Yes."

"Oh. Do you know that seems very funny to me, Jewel?"

"It seems funny to me that you are afraid, when God made you, and the man, and all of us, and there's nothing but goodness and love in the universe. Fear is the belief of evil. Do you want to believe evil?"

"No, I hate to," returned Eloise promptly.

"Then you go away, cousin Eloise, and I will handle the case for you."

"Oh, are you going golfing?" said Mrs. Evringham that afternoon to her daughter. "Do put on your white duck, dear."

"Yes, I intend to. I'm going with grandfather."

"You are?" in extremest surprise. "Oh, wear your dark skirt, dear; it's plenty good enough. Do you mean to say he asked you, Eloise?"

"No, I asked him."

Mrs. Evringham stood in silent amaze, her brain working alertly. She even watched her daughter don the immaculate white golf suit, and made no further protest.

What was in the girl's mind? When finally from her window she saw the two enter the brougham, Mr. Evringham carrying his granddaughter's clubs, she smiled a knowing smile and nodded her head.

"I do believe I've wronged Eloise," she thought. "How foolish it was to worry. I've been wondering how in the world I was going to get father to give her a wedding, and how I was going to get her to accept it, and now look! That child has thought of the same thing, and will manage it a hundred times better than I could."

Jewel stood on the steps and waved her hand as the brougham rolled away. Eloise had seized and squeezed her surreptitiously in the hall before they came out.

"I do feel braced up, Jewel. Thank you," she whispered hurriedly.

"Is the man over at the golf links?" asked the child, surprised to see that Eloise and her grandfather were going out together.

"He will be by the time I get there," returned the girl.

As soon as the carriage door had closed and they had started, Eloise spoke. "You must think it very strange that I asked this of you, grandfather."

There was a hint of violets clinging to the fresh white garments that brushed Mr. Evringham's knee.

"I would not question the gifts the gods provide;" he returned.

She seemed able to rise above the fear of his sarcasms. "Not that you would be surprised at anything mother or I might ask of you," she continued bravely, "but I have suffered, I'm sure, as much as you have during the last two months."

"Indeed? I regret to hear that."

If there was a sting in this reply, Eloise refused to recognize it.

"In fact I have felt so much that it has made it impossible hitherto to say anything, but Jewel has given me courage."

Mr. Evringham smoothed his mustache. "She has plenty to spare," he returned.

"She says," went on Eloise, "that everything that isn't love is hate; and hate, of course, in her category is unreal. It is because I want the real things, because I long for real things, for truth, that I asked to have this talk, grandfather, and I wanted to be quite alone with you, so I thought of this way."

"It's the mater she's running away from, then," reflected her companion. He nodded courteously. "I am at your disposal," he returned.

Subtly the broker's feeling toward Eloise had been changing since the evening in which Jewel wrote to her parents. His hard and fast opinion of her had been slightly shaken. The frankness of her remarks on Christian Science in the presence of Dr. Ballard the other evening had been a surprise to him. The cold, proud, noncommittal, ease-loving girl who in his opinion had decided to marry the young doctor was either less designing than he had believed, or else wonderfully certain of her own power to hold him. He found himself regarding her with new interest.

"I've been waiting for mother to talk with you," she went on, "and clear up our position; but she does not, and so I must." The speaker's hands were tightly clasped in her lap. "I wish I had Jewel's unconsciousness, her certainty that all is Good, for I feel—I feel shame before you, grandfather."

It seemed to Mr. Evringham that Jewel's eyes were appealing to him.

"She says," he returned with a rather grim smile, "Jewel avers that I am kindness itself inside. Let us admit it for convenience now, and see if you can't speak freely."

"Thank you. You know what I am ashamed of: staying here so long; imposing upon you; taking everything for granted when we have no right. I want to understand our affairs; to know if we have anything, and what it is; to have you help me, *you*; to have you tell me how we can live independently, and help me to make mother agree to it. Oh, if you would—if you *could* be my friend, grandfather. I need you so!"

Mr. Evringham received this impetuous outburst without change of countenance. "How about Ballard?" he said. "I thought he was going to settle all this."

There was silence in the brougham. The flash of hurt in the girl's eyes was quenched by quick tears. Her companion reddened under the look of surprise she bent upon him, her lovely lips unsteady.

"No offense," he added hastily. "Ballard's sentiments are evident enough, and he is a fine fellow."

Eloise controlled herself. "Will you take the trouble to explain our affairs to me?" she asked.

"Certainly," responded Mr. Evringham quickly. "I wish for your sake there was more to explain, more possibilities in the case."

"We have nothing?" exclaimed the girl acutely.

"Your father took heavy chances and lost. His affairs are nearly settled, and what there is left is small indeed." The speaker cast a quick glance at the girl beside him. She had caught her lip between her teeth. Jewel's soft voice sounded in his ears. "Cousin Eloise feels sorry because she isn't your real relation." An inkling of what the girl might suffer came to him.

"Your mother and you have a claim upon me," he went on. "I should certainly feel a responsibility of all my son's debts, and the one to his wife and daughter in particular. I will try to make the situation easier for you in some way."

"Manage for us to go away, grandfather. Haven't you a little house somewhere?"

The beseeching in her tone surprised Mr. Evringham still more. What did the girl mean? Didn't she intend to marry Ballard? He had believed her to be planning to preside in the Mountain Avenue mansion.

"Yes, it can be arranged, certainly," he answered vaguely; "but there's no hurry, Eloise," he added, in the kindest tone he had ever used toward her. "Some evening we will go over the affairs, and I will show you where your mother stands financially, and we will try to make some plan that shall be satisfactory."

Eloise gave him a grateful look, as much in response to his manner as to his words. "Thank you. The present condition is certainly—error," she said.

"Well, we'll try to find harmony," replied the other. "Jewel would say it was easy. I should like to have you remain at my house at least as long as she does, Eloise. I should probably have to tie her hair ribbons again if you went."

The two found themselves smiling at each other. The atmosphere was lightened, and the brougham drew up at the clubhouse.

Mr. Evringham handed out the girl, gave Zeke the order to return for them, and they went up the steps.

"I would drive back with him, grandfather, only that mother would wonder, and ask questions," said Eloise. "Don't let me detain you in any way. I'll just sit here on the piazza."

"Not play? Nonsense!" returned Mr. Evringham brusquely.

"Please don't feel obliged"—Eloise began humbly.

"But I can't help being obliged if you'll play with me," interrupted her companion.

Some men observed the confidential attitude of the broker and the beautiful girl. "What's doing over there?" asked one. "Is Evringham beginning to take notice?"

"Why, don't you know?" returned the other. "That's his granddaughter."

"His daughter, do you mean? Didn't know he had one."

"Not a bit of it. She's Lawrence's stepdaughter."

The other shook his head. "That's too involved for me. She's a queen, anyway."

"Going to marry Ballard, they say."

"That so? Then I won't go up and fall on Evringham's neck. My bank book isn't in Ballard's class. She can play, too," as he observed Eloise make a drive while she waited the reappearance of her companion from the clubhouse. "Isn't that a bird!—and say, there's young Lochinvar himself!" for here a light automobile whizzed briskly up to the clubhouse.

Dr. Ballard sprang out, for he had recognized the figure at the first teeing ground.

"You gave me the slip!" he cried as he approached.

"Oh, I just went with a handsomer man," returned Eloise, smiling, as they shook hands.

"I didn't know I could come until the last minute, then I went to the house for you and found I had missed you."

Mr. Evringham and the caddy approached. "I cut you out for once, Ballard," he said. "Well, we're off, Eloise. I saw you drive. I doubt if he catches us."

Jewel's eyes questioned Eloise that evening when she reached home, and she received the smiling, significant nod her cousin gave her with satisfaction.

It was an apparently united family party that gathered about the dinner table. Mr. Evringham and Eloise discussed their game, while Mrs. Evringham fairly rustled with complacence.

As Jewel clung to her grandfather's neck that evening in bidding him good-night, she whispered:—

"How happy we all are!"

"Are we, really? Well now, that's very gratifying, I'm sure. Good-night, Jewel."

CHAPTER XXII
IN THE HARNESS ROOM

"Mother, can I have three dollars?" asked Eloise the next morning.

"Were you thinking of a new riding hat, dear? I do wish you had it to wear this afternoon. Yours is shabby, certainly, but you can't get it for that, child."

"No; I was thinking of a copy of 'Science and Health.' I don't like to take Jewel's any longer, and I'm convinced."

"What of—sin?" asked Mrs. Evringham in dismay.

"No, just the opposite—that there needn't be any. The book teaches the truth. I know it."

"Well, whether it does or doesn't, you haven't any three dollars to spend for a book, Eloise," was the firm reply. "The *idea*, when I can barely rake and scrape enough together to keep us presentable!"

"Where do you get our money?" asked the girl.

"Father gives me a check every fortnight. Of course you know that he has charge of our affairs."

Eloise's serene expression did not change. She looked at the little black book in her hand. "This edition costs five dollars," she said.

"Scandalous!" exclaimed Mrs. Evringham. "I can tell you this is no time for us to be collecting *editions de luxe*. Wait till you're married."

"I'm going to run in town for a while this morning, mother."

"You are? Well don't get belated. You know that you are to ride with Dr. Ballard at half past four. Dear me," her brow drawn, "you ought to have that hat. Now I think that I *could* get on without that jet bolero."

Eloise laughed softly and drew her mother to her. "Have your jet bolero, dear," she answered. "My hat isn't bad."

Eloise went to her room, and closing the door, took from one of her drawers a box. It contained her girlish treasures, the ornaments and jewels her father had given her from time to time. She took out a small diamond ring and pressed it to her lips.

"Dear papa! I love it because you gave it to me, but I can get with it a wonderful thing, a truth which, if we had known it, would have saved you all those torturing hours, would have saved your dear life. I know how gladly you would have me get it now, for you are learning it too; and it will be your gift, dear, *dear* papa, your gift just the same."

Jewel had to study the lesson with only Anna Belle's assistance that morning, but she received the third letter from her mother and father. Their trip was proving a success from the standpoints of both business and pleasure, but their chief longing was to get back to their little girl.

It was very like visiting with them to read it over, and Jewel did so more than once. "I'll show it to cousin Eloise as soon as she comes home," she reflected. Then she dressed Anna Belle to go out.

Running downstairs the child sought and found Mrs. Forbes in the kitchen. The housekeeper no longer questioned her going and coming, although she still considered herself in the light of the child's only disciplinarian, and was vigilant to watch for errors of omission and commission, and quick to correct them.

"Mrs. Forbes, may I have an old kitchen knife?"

"Certainly not. You'll cut yourself."

"I want it to dig up plants."

Mrs. Forbes stared down at her. "Why, you mustn't do any such thing."

"I mean wild flowers for a garden that Anna Belle and I are going to make."

"Oh. I'll see if I can't find you a trowel."

There was one at hand, and as the housekeeper passed it to the child she warned her:—

"Be careful you don't make a mistake, now, and get hold of anybody's plants. What did your cousin Eloise go to New York for?"

"I don't know."

"Well I hope it's for her trousseau."

Jewel smiled. "My mother makes those."

"I don't believe she'll ever make one for you, then," returned Mrs. Forbes, but not ill-naturedly. She laughed, glancing at Sarah, who stood by.

"But I think she will for Anna Belle," returned Jewel brightly, "when she gets older."

The housekeeper and maid both laughed. "Run along," said Mrs. Forbes, "and don't you be late for lunch."

"She's an awful sweet child," said Sarah half reproachfully. "Just the spirit of sunshine."

"Oh well, they'd turn her head here if it wasn't for me," answered the other complacently.

Jewel was not late to lunch, but eating it tete-a-tete with aunt Madge was not to her taste.

Mrs. Evringham utilized the opportunity to admonish her, and Mrs. Forbes for once sympathized with the widow's sentiments.

Aunt Madge took off her eyeglasses in a way she had when she wished to be particularly impressive.

"Jewel," she said, "I don't think any one has told you that it is impolite to Dr. Ballard to say anything about Christian Science in his presence."

"Why is it?" asked the child.

"Because he is a learned physician, and has, of course, a great respect for his profession."

"I have a great respect for him," returned the child, "and he knows I wouldn't hurt his feelings."

"The idea!" exclaimed Mrs. Evringham, looking down from a height upon the flaxen head. "As if a little ignorant girl could hurt the feelings of a man like Dr. Ballard!"

Mrs. Forbes also stared at the child, and she winced.

"I do love them, and they do love me," she thought. "I don't remember ever speaking about it before the doctor unless somebody asked me," she said aloud.

"Your cousin Eloise may ask you," returned Mrs. Evringham. "Nobody else would. She does it in a spirit of mischief, perhaps, but I shall speak to her. She has a passing curiosity about your ideas because it is odd and rather amusing to find a child who has such unnatural and precocious fancies, and she tries to draw you out; but it will not last with her. Neither will it with you, probably. You seem to be a sensible little girl in many ways." Mrs. Evringham made the addition magnanimously. She really was too much at peace with all the world just now to like to be severe.

Outwardly Jewel was silent. Inwardly she was declaring many things which would have surprised her companions.

"Does your cousin Eloise pretend to you that she is becoming seriously interested in your faith?" pursued Mrs. Evringham.

"She will tell you all about it," returned Jewel.

Aunt Madge shrugged her shoulders and laughed a little. Her thoughts reverted to her daughter's trip to the city. She had wondered several times if it had any pleasant connection with her sudden good understanding with Mr. Evringham.

To Jewel's relief her thoughts remained preoccupied during the remainder of the meal; and as soon as the child could leave, she flew to the closet under the stairs, where Anna Belle often went into retreat during the luncheon hour, and from thence back to the garden she was making by the brookside.

When she returned to the house her eyes lighted as she saw two horses before the piazza, and Dr. Ballard standing beside one of them.

"How are you, Jewel?" he asked, as she danced up to him smiling. Stooping, he lifted her into the side saddle, from whence she beamed upon him.

"Oh, what fun you're going to have!" she cried.

"I'd like to be sure of that," he answered, his gloved hand on the pommel.

"What do you mean?" incredulously. "You don't like that automobile better, do you? They're so—so stubby. I must have a horse, a horse!" She smoothed and patted her steed lovingly.

"You ought to have—Jewel of the world," he said kindly. "My bad angel!" he added, looking up quizzically into her eyes, and smiling at the widening wonder that grew in them.

"Your—what?" she asked, and then Eloise came out in her habit.

"I'm going instead of you," cried the child gayly, "to pay you for staying away all day."

"Did you miss me?" asked the girl as she shook hands with her escort.

"I tried not to. Anna Belle and I have something to show you in the ravine." As she spoke, Jewel slid down into the doctor's arms, and stood on the steps watching while he put Eloise up and mounted himself.

The child's eyes dwelt upon the pair admiringly as they waved their hands to her and rode away. Little she knew how their hearts were beating. Mrs. Evringham, watching from an upper window, suspected it. She felt that this afternoon would end all suspense.

The child gave a wistful sigh as the horses disappeared, and jumping off the piazza, she wandered around the house toward the stable. There had been no rules laid down to her since the night of Essex Maid's attack, and Zeke was always a congenial companion.

As she neared the barn a young fellow left it, laughing. She knew who he was,—one of the young men Zeke had known in Boston. He had several times of late come to call on his old chum, for he was out of work.

As he left the barn he saw the child and slouched off to one side, avoiding her; but she scarcely noticed him, congratulating herself that Zeke would be alone and ready, as usual, to crack jokes and stories.

The coachman was not in sight as she entered, but she knew she would find him in the harness room. Its door stood ajar, and as the child approached she heard a strange sound, as of some one weeping suppressedly. Sturdily resisting the sudden fear that swept to her heart, she pushed open the door.

There stood Mrs. Forbes, leaning against a wooden support, her forehead resting against her clasped hands in a hopeless posture, as she sobbed heavily. The air was filled with an odor which had for Jewel sickening associations. The only terror, the only tragedy, of her short life was wrapped about with this pungent smell. She seemed again to hear her mother's sobs, to feel once more that sensation of all things coming to ruin which descended upon her at the unprecedented sight and sound of her strong mother's emotion.

All at once she perceived Zeke sitting on a low chair, his arms hanging across his knees and his head fallen.

The child turned very pale. Her doll slid unnoticed to the floor, as she pressed her little hands to her eyes.

"Father, Mother, God," she murmured in gasps. "Thou art all power. We are thy children. Error has no power over us. Help us to waken from this lie."

Running up to the housekeeper, she clasped her arms about her convulsed form. "Dear Mrs. Forbes," she said, her soft voice trembling at first but growing firm, "I know this claim, but it can be healed. It seems very terrible, but it's nothing. We know it, we must know it."

The woman lifted her head and looked down with swollen eyes upon the child. She saw her go unhesitatingly across to Zeke and kneel beside him.

"Don't be discouraged, Zeke," she said lovingly. "I know how it seems, but my father had it and he was healed. You will be healed."

The coachman lifted his rumpled head and stared at her with bloodshot eyes.

"Great fuss 'bout nothing," he said sullenly. "Mother always fussing."

Something in his look made the child shudder. Resisting the sudden repugnance to one who had always shown her kindness, she impulsively took his big hand in both her little ones. "Zeke, what is error saying to you?" she demanded. "You can't look at me without love. I love you because God does. He is lifting us out of this error belief."

The young fellow returned the clasp of the soft hands and winked his eyes like one who is waking. "Mother makes great fuss," he grumbled. "Scott was here. We had two or three little friendly drinks. Ma had to come in and blubber."

"What friendly drinks? What do you mean?" demanded Jewel, looking all about her. Her eyes fell upon a large black bottle. She dropped the coachman's hand and picked it up. She smelled of it, her eyes dilated, and she began to tremble again; and throwing the whiskey from her, she buried her face for a moment against Zeke's shirt sleeve.

"Is it in a bottle!" she exclaimed at last, in a hushed voice, drawing back and regarding the coachman with such a white and horrified countenance that it frightened the clouds from his brain. "Is that terrible claim in a bottle, and do people drink it out?" she asked slowly, and in an awestruck tone.

"It's no harm," began Zeke.

"No harm when your mother is crying, when your face is full of error, and your eyes were hating? No harm when my mother cried, and all our gladness was gone? Would you go and drink a claim like that out of a bottle—of your own accord?"

Zeke wriggled under the blue eyes and the unnatural rigidity of the child's face.

"No, Jewel, he wouldn't," groaned Mrs. Forbes suddenly. "Zeke's a good boy, but he's inherited that. His father died of it. It's a disease, child. I thought my boy would escape, but he hasn't! It's the end!" cried the wretched woman. "What will Mr. Evringham say! To think how I blamed

Fanshaw! Zeke'll lose his place and go downhill, and I shall die of shame and despair." Her sobs again shook her from head to foot.

Jewel continued to look at Zeke. A new, eager expression stole over her face. "*Is* it the end?" she asked. "Don't you believe in God?"

"I suppose so," answered the coachman sullenly. "I know I'm a man, too. I can control myself."

"No. Nobody can. Even Jesus said, 'Of myself I can do nothing.' Only God can help you. If you can drink that nasty smelling stuff, and get all red and rumply and sorry, then you need God the worst of anybody in Bel-Air. You look better now. It's just like a dream, the way you lifted up your face to me when I came in, and it *was* a dream. I'll help you, Zeke. I'll show you how to find help." The child suddenly leaned toward the young fellow, and then retreated. "I can't stand your breath!" she exclaimed, "and I like to get close to the people I love."

This seemed to touch Zeke. He blushed hotly. "It's a darned shame, kid," he returned sheepishly.

"Mrs. Forbes, come here, please," said Jewel. The housekeeper had ceased crying, and was watching the pair. She saw that her boy's senses were clearer. She approached obediently, and when the child took her hand her own closed tightly upon the little fingers.

"Zeke, you're a big strong man and everybody likes you," said Jewel earnestly. "Isn't it better to stay that way than to drink out of a bottle, no matter *how* much you like it?"

"I don't like it so awfully," returned Zeke protestingly. "I like to be sociable with the boys, that's all."

"What a way to be sociable!" gasped the child. "Well, wouldn't you rather be nice, so people will like to get close to you?"

"Depends on the folks," returned the boy with a touch of his usual manner. "You're all right, little kid." He put out his hand, but quickly withdrew it.

Jewel seized it. "Now give your other one to your mother. There now, we're all together. If your mother thinks you have a disease, Zeke, then she must know you haven't. If you want me to, I'll come out here every day at a quiet time and give you a treatment, and we'll talk all about Christian Science, and we'll know that there's nothing that can make us sick or unhappy—or unkind! Think of your unkindness to your mother—and to me if you go on, for I love you, Zeke. Now *may* I help you?"

The soft frank voice, the earnest little face, moved Zeke to cast a glance at his mother's swollen eyes. They were bent upon Jewel.

"Do you say your father was cured that way, child?" asked Mrs. Forbes.

"Yes. Oh yes! and he's so happy!"

"Zeke, let's all be thankful if there's *anything*," said the woman tremulously, turning to him appealingly.

"I'd just as soon have a visit from you every day, little kid," said the young fellow. "You're a corker."

"But you must want more than me," returned the child. "God and healing and purity and goodness! If you're in earnest, what are you going to do with that?" She touched the black bottle with the toe of her shoe.

Zeke looked at the whiskey, then back into her eyes. They were full of love and faith for him.

He stooped and picked up the bottle, then striding to a window, he flung it out toward the forest trees with all the force of his strong arm.

"Damn the stuff!" he said.

Mrs. Forbes felt herself tremble from head to foot. She bit her lip.

Her son turned back. "Getting near train time," he added, not looking at his companions. "Guess I'll go upstairs."

When he had disappeared his mother stooped slowly and kissed Jewel. "Forgive me," she said tremulously.

"What for?" asked the child.

"Everything."

The housekeeper still stood in the harness room after Jewel had gone away. She bowed her head on her folded hands. "Our Father who art in heaven, forgive me," she prayed. "Forgive me for being a fool. Forgive me for not recognizing Thine angel whom Thou hast sent. Amen."

CHAPTER XXIII
MRS. EVRINGHAM'S CALLER

Mrs. Evringham was busily chewing the cud of sweet fancies only, that afternoon. Following the equestrians in their leafy woodland path, she pictured them as talking of their future, and herself built many castles in the air. "Ah," she thought sentimentally, leaning back in her reclining chair, "how charming is youth—with plenty of money!"

She was roused from these luxurious meditations by the appearance of Sarah, bearing a card on a salver.

"A man!" she exclaimed with annoyance. "I'm not dressed."

Lifting the card, she read it with a start.

"Mr. Nathan Wycliffe Bonnell."

"Tell him I'll be down soon," was all she said; but her thoughts ran swiftly as she hurriedly slipped into her gown. "How in the world comes the boy out here? Just as well that Eloise is away. It would only be painful to her, all the old associations." But old associations cropped up more and more enticingly for Mrs. Evringham as she made her swift toilet, and by the time she reached the drawing-room her eagerness lent her cordiality a very genuine tone.

"Nat, dear boy, how are you?"

The young man who rose eagerly to meet her would have been noticeable in any crowd. She gazed up into his smooth-shaven, frank face, with its alert eyes and strong chin, and felt a yearning affection for all which he represented to her. "What are you doing out here?"

"Visiting you and Eloise," he answered, with the hearty relish which always characterized his manner when circumstances were agreeable. "Where is she?"

"Riding. I don't know when they will come home, either. It's such a charming day, isn't it? So good of you to hunt us up, Nat. We've been out of the world so long. I can't tell you what a rush of memories comes over me at sight of you, you nice, big boy. I do believe you've been growing." She gave a glance of approval at the young man's stalwart proportions.

"Oh, don't humiliate me," he laughed, as she drew him to a divan, where they seated themselves.

"How could you get away at this hour?"

"I'm changing my business, and get a week's vacation thereby. Great luck, isn't it?"

"I hope so. Are you going to do better?"

"Much better. It's only a little matter of time now, Mrs. Evringham—automobiles, steam yachts, and all the rest of it."

"Ah, the optimism of youth!" she sighed, gazing at the dancing lights in his eyes. "It's very beautiful, and usually entirely unfounded. You look so radiant, my dear. Perhaps you have come out here to let us congratulate you. Have you found that desirable girl? I certainly should be the first to be told, for I always talked to you very plainly, didn't I?"

"Indeed you did, Mrs. Evringham. You always kept my ineligibility before me strenuously."

"A certain *sort* of ineligibility, dear boy," returned the lady with a flattering cadence. "Your capital did not happen to consist of money. Tell me all, Nat. Who is she?"

He shook his head. "She's still not impossible, but improbable," he returned.

"Oh, you are too difficult, my dear. Really, I thought at the time our misfortunes fell upon us that it was going to be Miss Caton. She would have been a great assistance to you, Nat. It isn't as if you could even afford to be a bachelor. In these days so much is expected of them. How is your mother?" Mrs. Evringham made the addition in that tone of fixed sympathy which one employs when only a depressing answer can be expected.

"Very well, thank you."

"You mean as well as usual, I suppose."

"No, I mean well. Wonderful, isn't it?"

"Really, Nat?" Mrs. Evringham straightened up in her interest. "Who did it?"

"She was healed by Christian Science."

"You don't mean it!"

"Indeed I do."

Mrs. Evringham thanked her holy stars that Eloise was absent.

"Well! I never for one moment classed your mother as a *malade imaginaire*!" exclaimed the lady.

Her companion raised his eyebrows. "I fancy no one did who knew her."

"You believe it, then?"

"I should be an idiot if I didn't."

"Do you mean to say she is out of her wheeled chair?"

"No chairs for her now. When she wishes to walk she walks."

"Then she always could!" declared Mrs. Evringham.

"I think you know better than that," returned the other calmly.

"How long since?" asked Mrs. Evringham.

"Three months."

Silence.

"Aren't you glad for her?" asked Bonnell with a slight smile of curiosity into the disturbed face. "I ought to have told you at first that osteopathy did it; then after your joy had subsided, break the truth gently."

"Of course I'm glad," returned the other stiffly, "but I'd rather Eloise did not hear of it at once."

"May I know why?"

"Certainly. We have a very dear friend who is a physician. It looks very much as if he might be something nearer than a friend. It is he with whom Eloise is riding this afternoon. It is very distasteful, naturally, to have these alleged cures discussed in our family. We have had some annoyance in that line already. You can understand how doctors must feel."

"Yes, so long as they believe a cure to be only alleged; but where one is convinced that previously hopeless conditions have been healed, and it does happen once in a while, they are glad of it, I'm confident. We haven't a finer, broader minded class of men in our country than our physicians."

"I think so," agreed Mrs. Evringham, drawing herself up with a fleeting vision of the Ballard place on Mountain Avenue.

"But they are not the wealthiest at the start," said Nat. "Is it possible that you are allowing Eloise to ride unchaperoned with a young physician?"

Mrs. Evringham did not remark the threatening curves at the corners of the speaker's lips.

"Oh, this one is different," she returned seriously; "very fine connections, and substantial in *every* way."

Her companion threw back his head and laughed frankly.

"We have to smile at each other once in a while, don't we, Mrs. Evringham?" he said, in the light, caressing manner which had for a few years been one of her chief worries; "but all the same, you're fond of me just as long as I don't forget my place, eh? You're glad to see me?"

"You know I am." Mrs. Evringham pressed her hand against the laces over her heart. "Such a bittersweet feeling comes over me at the very tones of your voice. Oh, the happy past, Nat! Gone forever!" She touched a dainty handkerchief to her eyes. "I suppose your mother is still in her apartment?"

"She has taken a place at View Point for the summer, and has set her heart on a long visit from you."

"How very kind of her," responded Mrs. Evringham with genuine gratitude. "I don't know what father means to do in the hot weather or whether he—or whether I should wish to go with him. Your mother and I always enjoyed each other, when she was sufficiently free from suffering."

"That time is always now," returned Nat, a fullness of gratitude in his voice.

His companion looked at him curiously. "I can't realize it."

"Come and see," was his reply.

"I will, I certainly will. I shall anticipate it with great pleasure."

A very convenient place to prepare a part of Eloise's trousseau, Mrs. Evringham was considering, and the girl safely engaged, Nat's presence would have no terrors. "You think you are really getting into a good business arrangement now?" she asked aloud.

"Very. I wake up in the morning wondering at my own good fortune."

"I am so glad, my dear boy," responded the other sympathetically. "Perhaps, after all, you will be able to wait for a little more chin than Miss Caton has. Of course she's a very *nice* girl and all that."

Bonnell smiled at the carpet.

They talked on for half an hour of mutual friends over cups of tea, and then he rose to go.

"Eloise will be sorry!" said Mrs. Evringham effusively. "It's such a long way out here and so difficult for you to get the time. It isn't as if you could come easily."

"Oh, I have several days here. I'm staying at the Reeves's. Do you know them?"

"No," returned the lady, trying to conceal that this was a blow.

"It is Mr. Reeves with whom I am going into business, and we are doing some preliminary work. I shall see Eloise soon. Remember me to her."

"Yes, certainly," replied Mrs. Evringham. She kept a stiff upper lip until she was alone, and then a troubled line grew in her forehead.

"It will be all right, of course, if things are settled," she thought. "I can scarcely wait for Eloise to come home."

Jewel had come from the barn straight to her room, where she thought upon her problem with the aids she loved.

At last she went downstairs to a side door to watch for Zeke as he drove from the barn on his way to the station to meet Mr. Evringham. As the horse walked out of the barn she emerged and intercepted the coachman.

Mrs. Forbes at a window saw Zeke stop. She wondered what Jewel was saying to him, wondered with a humble gratitude novel to her dominating nature.

"Wait one minute, Zeke," said the child. "I've been wondering whether I ought to say anything to grandpa."

"If you do I'll lose my place," returned the young fellow; "and I've never done wrong by the horses yet."

"I know you haven't. God has taken care of you, hasn't he, Zeke? Do you think it's right for me not to tell grandpa? I've decided that I'll do whatever you say."

It was the wisdom of the serpent and the harmlessness of the dove. Zeke, nervously fingering the whip handle, looked down into the guileless face and mentally vowed never to betray the trust he saw there.

"Then don't tell him, Jewel," he returned rather thickly, for the fullness in his throat. "You come out to the barn the way you said you would, and we'll talk over things. I don't care if the boys do laugh. I've sworn off. I believe you helped Essex Maid the other night. I believe you can help me."

Jewel's eyes were joyful. "If you know you *want* help, Zeke, then you'll get it. Mother says that's the first thing. Mortal mind is so proud."

"Mine ain't strutting much," returned Zeke as he drove on.

Jewel amused herself about the grounds until the phaeton should return with her grandfather.

When she saw it coming she ran down to the gate and hopped and skipped back beside it, Mr. Evringham watching her gyrations unsmilingly.

As he dismounted at the piazza she clung to his hand going up the steps. "Which are you going to do, grandpa, go riding or play golf?"

"Which do you want me to do?" he asked.

"When you ride it's more fun for me," she replied.

He seated himself in one of the chairs and she leaned against its broad arm.

"It's rather more fun for me, too. I'm growing lazy. I think I'll ride."

"Good!"

"What have you been doing to-day, Jewel?"

"Well," —meditatively,— "cousin Eloise went to New York, so I had to get my lesson alone. And I didn't braid my hair over."

Mr. Evringham looked startled. "She'll do it, I dare say, before dinner," he replied.

"If she has time. She has gone riding with Dr. Ballard. They just trotted away together. Oh, it was lovely!"

Mr. Evringham, leaning his head back, looked off under his heavy brows as he responded:—

"Across the hills and far away,

Beyond their utmost purple rim,

And deep into the dying day

The happy princess followed him,

"and all that sort of business, I suppose."

"I don't know what you mean," said Jewel doubtfully.

"I should hope not. Well, what else have you done? Been treating any rheumatism? I haven't had it since the sun shone."

"You never asked me to," returned the child.

Mr. Evringham smiled. "The sunshine is a pretty good treatment," he observed.

"Sometimes your belief comes into my thought," said Jewel, "and of course I always turn on it and think the truth."

"Much obliged, I'm sure. I'd like to turn on it myself at times."

"You can study with cousin Eloise and me, if you'd like to," said Jewel eagerly.

"Oh, thank you, thank you," rejoined the broker hastily. "Don't disturb yourself. There must be some sinners, you know, or the saints would have to go out of business—nobody to practice on. Well, have you been to the ravine?"

"Oh yes! Anna Belle and I, and we had more *fun*! We made a garden."

"Morning or afternoon?"

"Morning."

"Well I wish to know," said Mr. Evringham in a suddenly serious and impressive tone, "I wish to know if you reached home in time for lunch."

Jewel felt somewhat startled under the daze of his piercing eyes, but her conscience was clear. "Yes, I was here in plenty of time. I wanted to surely not be late, so I was here too soon."

"That's what I was afraid of," returned Mr. Evringham gravely. "I don't wish you to be unpunctual, but I object equally to your returning unnecessarily early when you wish to stay."

"But I couldn't help it, grandpa," Jewel began earnestly, when he interrupted her.

"So I've brought you this," he added, and took from his pocket an oblong package, sealed at each end.

The child laid her doll in the broker's lap,—he had become hardened to this indignity,—and her fingers broke the seals and slipped the paper from a morocco case.

"Push the spring in the end," said Mr. Evringham.

She obeyed. The lid flew up and disclosed a small silver chatelaine watch. The pin was a cherub's head, its wings enameled in white, as were the back and edges of the little timepiece whose hands were busily pointing to blue figures.

Jewel gasped. "For me?"

Her grandfather smoothed his mustache. He had presented gifts to ladies before, but never with such effect.

"Grandpa, grandpa!" she exclaimed, touching the little watch in wondering delight. "See what Divine Love has sent me!"

Mr. Evringham raised his eyebrows and smiled, but he was soon assured that Love's messenger was not forgotten. He was instantly enveloped in a rapturous hug, and heroically endured the bitter of the watchcase pressing into his jugular for the sweet of the rose-leaf kisses that were assaulting his cheek like the quick reports of a tiny Gatling gun.

"See if you can wind it," he said at last.

Jewel lifted her treasure tenderly from its velvet bed, and he showed her how to twist its stem, and then pinned it securely on the breast of her light sailor suit, where she looked down upon it in rapt admiration.

"Now then, Jewel, you have no excuse!" he said severely.

She raised her happy eyes, while her hand pressed the satin surface of her watch. "Grandpa, grandpa!" she said, sighing ecstatically, "you're such a joker!"

CHAPTER XXIV
THE RAVINE GARDEN

Mrs. Evringham tried heroically to look impassive when her daughter returned from the ride. There was barely time then to dress for dinner, and no opportunity for confidences before the meal, nor afterward until bedtime; but the look of peace and sweetness in Eloise's face could have but one significance to the mother, who believed that peace lay only in the direction upon which she had set her heart.

Mr. Evringham took coffee with them after dinner in the drawing-room, while Jewel caressed her watch, never tiring of looking at its clear face and the little second hand which traveled so steadily its tiny circuit.

Mrs. Evringham looked often toward the door, expectant of the doctor's entrance. The evening wore on and he did not come. Still Eloise's face wore the placid, restful expression. A gentle ease with her grandfather replaced her old manner.

Her mother determined to try an experiment.

"You could never guess who called to-day, Eloise," she said suddenly.

Her daughter looked up from her coffee. "No. Who was it?"

"Nat Bonnell."

"Really!" The girl's tone indicated great surprise, and that only. "I wish I might have seen him."

The addition was made so calmly, almost perfunctorily, that Mrs. Evringham smiled with exultation.

She turned to her father-in-law. "Who would believe that Mr. Bonnell was Eloise's brightest flame a year ago? 'How soon are we forgot!'" she said lightly.

When Jewel had kissed them all good-night and gone upstairs, and Mr. Evringham had withdrawn to his library, Mrs. Evringham took her child's hand and looked fondly into her eyes.

"Well?" she asked.

"Well," returned Eloise, "do tell me everything Nat said."

"After you've told me everything Dr. Ballard said. I supposed you'd fly to tell me, dear."

The girl looked tenderly back into the eyes that were sharp with inquiry. "Dear little mother," she returned, "it can't be."

"What can't be?"

"What you wish. Dr. Ballard."

"Have you—refused him—!" Mrs. Evringham's face whitened, and unconsciously she stepped back.

"It didn't have to come to that. Dr. Ballard is so fine—such a wise man in so many ways. I do admire him so much."

"What did you say to him? I will know!" exclaimed Mrs. Evringham passionately.

Eloise was mute, and her eyes besought her mother.

"Speak, I say! Was it Christian Science? Did you dare, Eloise Evringham, did you *dare* spoil your life—my life—our future, by scaring Dr. Ballard with that bugbear?" The angry woman was breathing fast.

"Mother dear, don't give us something so painful to remember. Don't, I beg of you. Dr. Ballard does not reproach me. He thinks I shall change, and he wishes to give me time to see if I do. Think of him, if you will not think of me. He would be so shocked to have you take it this way. If you could have seen how kind he was, how patient. Dear mother, don't cry. It isn't anything I can help, unless I should deliberately turn dishonest."

But Mrs. Evringham did cry, and heartily. She hurried away to her own room as quickly as possible, and locked the door against Eloise, who lay awake for hours with a strange mingling of regret and joy at her heart, and a constant declaring of the truth.

At midnight the girl heard the door unlock and saw her mother emerge.

"Darling mamma!" she exclaimed, springing out of bed.

"Oh, Eloise," moaned the poor woman, dissolving again upon her child's shoulder. "I never went to bed without your kiss, and I can't bear it. How can you be so cru—cru—cruel!"

"Darling, everything is going to come right," returned Eloise, holding her close. "Nothing good would come of doing wrong. I never loved you so much as now. I never saw duty so plainly. Dearest, in one way I suffer for you, but still I was never so happy. I have grasped the end of the clue that will surely lead us safely through the labyrinth, no matter what life brings. You will see, mamma dear, after a while you will see. Don't go back. Come into my bed."

Disconsolately Mrs. Evringham obeyed, and in a few minutes, worn out with emotion, she had sobbed herself to sleep in her child's arms; and although for many days afterward she wore a languid air, and declared that there was nothing to live for, she yielded herself to Eloise's courageous and quietly joyful atmosphere, with silent wonder at her child's altered outlook.

On the morning following the painful interview with her mother, Eloise presented herself in Jewel's room at the usual hour.

Smiling, she approached the child and exhibited three fresh new books. India paper editions of the Bible and "Science and Health," and the little brown pamphlet were in her hands.

"Yours?" exclaimed the child.

Eloise nodded.

"Good, good!" Jewel hopped up and down, and forthwith brought Anna Belle to have her share in the rejoicing.

"You were afraid you couldn't get them. Now see!" cried the child triumphantly. "As if Divine Love couldn't send you those books!"

"He showed me a way," returned the girl. "See where I've written my name. I want you to put 'Jewel' right under it in each one."

"Oh, in those lovely books?" said the child doubtfully. "I don't write very well."

"Yes, I want it, dear, when we go downstairs and can get some ink. Did anybody fix your hair yesterday?"

"I just brushed it down real smooth on the outside," returned the child.

"It looks so," said Eloise, laughing. "Let's fix it before we have the lesson. By the way, what time is it, Jewel?"

The little girl smiled back at her cousin's reflection in the glass, and took the open morocco case from the bureau. "Anna Belle and I put him to bed last night," she said, looking fondly at the silver cherub on its velvet couch. "We've named him Little Faithful. He'll come to the lesson, too. I know he's going to be a lovely Scientist."

"I'm sure I hope he will, and neither be fast nor lazy," returned Eloise, as she unbraided the short pigtails.

"I tell you it wasn't so nice getting the lesson alone yesterday," said Jewel. "You were away all day! Did you have a nice ride?"

"Yes," Eloise responded slowly. "The day was very nice—and so is Dr. Ballard."

"Did he enjoy it?" asked the child hopefully. The doctor had been a good deal on her mind.

"Some of the time," responded Eloise soberly.

"Why not all the time? Did error creep in?"

The older girl brushed away in silence for a minute.

"I didn't mean to talk about grown-up things," said the child, somewhat abashed. "Mother says I must be careful not to."

"It is all right, Jewel. The new ideas I have been learning have made me see some things so clearly. One is to perceive what it is that really draws people together in a bond that cannot be broken. There is only one thing that can do it and will do it, and that is loving the same truth. Two people can have a very good time together for a while, and like each other very much, but the time comes when their thoughts fly apart unless that one bond of union is there—unless they love the same spiritual truth."

The speaker caught, in the glass, the child's eyes fixed attentively upon her.

"Wouldn't Dr. Ballard look at our book?" asked Jewel softly.

"No, dear."

The child reflected a minute, and her eyes filled. "I just love him," she said.

Her cousin stooped and kissed her cheek. "You well may," she returned quietly. "He deserves it."

They studied the lesson and then went downstairs, where Jewel in her very best hand slowly transcribed her name in the new books; then she told Eloise that she was going out to the barn.

"I'm going to visit with Zeke," she said. "He has a claim of error, and he is willing Science should help him."

"Is he ill?"

Jewel looked off. "It isn't that kind of error."

"There are plenty worse," rejoined Eloise. She looked doubtfully at the little girl. "Wouldn't you better tell me, dear? Is it right for you to go?"

"Yes, it's right. His mother knows it, and she's so kind to me. What do you think! At breakfast she asked me if I wouldn't like to bring Anna Belle down. She says I can bring her to the table whenever I want to. Isn't it nice? The dear little creature has been so patient, never having a thing to eat!"

Eloise could not help laughing, the manner in which Jewel finished was so suddenly quaint; but she shook her head in silent wonder as she watched the short skirted figure setting forth for the barn.

"Oh cousin Eloise." Jewel turned around. "Will you come to the ravine after lunch, and see what Anna Belle and I have done?"

"Yes."

Jewel walked on a little further and turned again. "You won't wear your watch, will you?" she called.

"No, I'll surely forget it," returned the girl, smiling.

The small figure went on, well content.

"Oh, if I could only be invisible in that barn!" soliloquized Eloise. "How I would like to hear what she will say. How wonderful it is that that little child has more chance of success, whatever trouble Zeke has been getting into, than any full-grown, experienced sage, philosopher, or reformer, who is a worker in mortal mind."

Anna Belle came to luncheon that day. Mrs. Forbes actually put a cushion in one of the chairs to lift the honored guest to such a height that her rosy smile was visible above the tablecloth. Not content with this hospitality, the housekeeper brought a bread-and-butter plate, upon which she placed such small proportions of food as might be calculated to tempt a dainty appetite. Jewel felt almost embarrassed by the eminence to which her child was suddenly raised.

"Oh, thank you, Mrs. Forbes," she said; "you needn't take so much trouble. Anna Belle's just used to having a part of mine."

But nothing now was too good for Anna Belle. "She shall have a cup-custard to-morrow," returned the housekeeper.

Mrs. Evringham looked on with lack-lustre eyes. As well make much of Anna Belle as any other idol. Everything was stuffed with sawdust!

How the sunbeams glanced in the woods that day as Jewel, one hand clasping her doll and the other in Eloise's, skipped along the road to the ravine!

When they had stooped under the wire and gone down the bank, how the brook sang, and how the violets bloomed in Jewel's garden!

"It's very pretty," said Eloise, regarding the paths and flower beds which Jewel exhibited with pride. "It's very pretty, but it lacks one thing."

"What?" asked the child eagerly.

"A pond."

"But it is by the side of a rushing river," returned Jewel.

"Yes, but all the more easy to have a pond."

"How?"

"We'll set a shallow pan, and sink it in the ground, and plant ferns about it to hang over. Anna Belle can have some little china dolls to go in wading in it."

"Oh yes, yes!" cried Jewel delighted. "Hear that, dearie? Hear what Love is planning for you?"

Anna Belle's nose was buried in the grass and her hat was awry. If she had a fault, it was a tendency to being overdressed. At present her plumed hat and large fluffy boa gave her an aspect unsympathetic with the surroundings. Jewel pulled her upright and placed her on the mossy divan.

"If I'd only brought the trowel I could get the hole ready," Jewel was saying, when a whistle, soft and clear as a flute, sounded above the brook's gurgle.

She lifted a finger in caution. "Oh," she whispered, looking up into her cousin's face, "the loveliest bird! Hush."

Clear, sweet, flexible, somewhere among those high branches sounded again the same elaborate phrase.

Jewel was surprised to see her cousin's pleased, listening expression alter to eager wonder, then the girl flushed rosy red and started up. "Siegfried!" she murmured.

Again came the bird motif sifting down through the rustling leaves.

"Nat!" called Eloise gladly.

"Any nymphs down there?" questioned a man's voice.

"Oh yes!"

"May Pan come down?"

"Yes indeed."

Jewel, watching and wondering, saw a young man in light clothes swing himself down from tree to tree, and at last saw both his hands close on both her cousin's.

The two talked and laughed in unison for a minute, then Eloise freed herself and turned to the serious-faced child. "You remember my speaking of Nat the other day?" she asked. "This is he. Mr. Bonnell, this is my cousin Jewel Evringham. She is landscape gardening just now, and may not feel like giving you her hand."

"I can wash it," said Jewel, dipping the earthy member in the brook, wiping it on the grass, and placing it in the large one that was offered her.

"How did you ever find us? I thought you'd gone back to New York. I had no idea of seeing you," said Eloise in a breath.

"Didn't your mother tell you? I have a week off."

The girl's bright face sobered. "Poor mother! She had a—a shock after you were here yesterday. I suppose it put everything out of her head. Was it she who sent you to find us?"

"No; a massive lady met me at the door and informed me that your mother wished to be excused from every one to-day, but that you had fallen down a crack in the earth which could be reached up this road." The speaker looked about. "As there doesn't seem any place to stand here, hadn't we better sit down before we fall in the brook? I might rescue you, but the current is swift."

Eloise at once sank upon the green incline, and he followed her example. Jewel watched him with consideration, and he became aware of her gaze.

"What are you making, little girl?" he asked, with his sunshiny smile.

"A garden; and I could dig the pond if I had brought the trowel."

"Perhaps my knife will do." He took it out and opened the largest blade. "What do you think of that?"

"Do you suppose I should break it?" asked the child doubtfully.

"You're welcome to try," he replied.

She leaned forward and accepted it from his outstretched hand.

CHAPTER XXV
MUTUAL SURPRISES

"I thought I knew Bel-Air Park," said Bonnell looking about him. "I never suspected this."

"Jewel is the Columbus of this spot. She has named it the Ravine of Happiness."

Nat looked at his speaker. "That's rather ambiguous. Does she mean where happiness is buried or where it is found?"

Eloise smiled. "Jewel never buries any happiness. Well, how is everybody, Nat? Your mother, first of all."

"Didn't Mrs. Evringham tell you?"

The girl's face clouded with apprehension at his surprised tone. "No. You will think it very strange, but poor mamma was under such excitement, you must pardon her. Everything went out of her head. Don't tell me that dear Mrs. Bonnell"—she lowered her voice—"that you have lost her!"

He shook his head. "No, I've gained her. She's well."

"Well!" repeated the girl amazed. "Why, what do you mean? How glorious! How long since?"

"About three months."

"I am so glad! Tell me more good news. Tell me about your own frivoling, and then I shall hear about the other people."

The young man shook his head. "I observed Lent this year scrupulously, and I haven't changed my tactics since Easter. I've been keeping my nose to the grindstone. Began to see things a little differently, Eloise. I decided it was mother's innings—decided to drop the butterfly and do the bee act."

"Is it possible!" The girl laughed. "Will wonders never cease! What was the matter? Did the heiresses cut you?"

"I cut the whole thing, and I have my reward. I suppose your mother didn't tell you that, either. I'm going into business with Mr. Reeves. Do you know him? Jewel does." He smiled toward the child, who lifted an interested face.

"Yes, I do," she said. "You remember about him, cousin Eloise."

"Certainly." The girl looked at her friend questioningly.

"I'm spending this week at his house."

"And you know about Jewel? He has told you?"

"Certainly. The one person of his acquaintance who hasn't to unlearn anything."

"You mean he talked to you of Christian Science?"

Bonnell's hands were clasping his knees. His hat lay on the bank beside him and the thick hair tossed away from his brow. He nodded slowly, wondering at the sudden attentive interest of her look.

"Yes," he replied. "We talked on the tabooed subject."

"Tabooed with whom? You?" she asked disappointedly.

"No, with you I understand."

Color flew into Eloise's face. "Who told you that? Mother of course."

Bonnell nodded, giving a fleeting glance toward the child, who was again busy at her excavation.

"Are congratulations in order, Eloise?" he asked quietly.

"Yes, congratulations." Her eyes grew full of light. "For I have come to see the truth. That child has shown me."

The young man's lips remained apart for a second in his surprise at this declaration, after Mrs. Evringham's detailed representations.

"Then I may tell you how my mother was healed," he said at last.

"Oh, was it really so?"

"Yes."

"And you, Nat?" Unconsciously Eloise leaned her whole body toward him, supporting her hand on the ground. "You know about it yourself? You understand?"

"Yes."

"And you believe in it?"

"With all my heart."

Her face shone. "Oh, Jewel, do you hear? Mr. Bonnell is a Scientist." The girl's breathing was hastened. Her eyes were like stars.

The child sank back from her work and regarded the visitor, smiling. She was glad, but she was not astonished. In her world a great many young men had found the key to life, but to Eloise it was something wonderful. She looked at her old friend as if she had never seen him before. She reviewed all she knew of his gay life with its background of suffering.

"Do you study the lessons?" she asked incredulously. "*You?*"

"Every day. I am surprised beyond measure to find you interested, for your mother told me—And the doctor—?"

"Is a very fine man," returned Eloise gravely, as he paused.

Bonnell's mental questions were answered by her manner. He put his hand in the pocket of his sack coat and drew out a small, thin, black book.

Eloise took it. "'Unity of Good,'" she read on its cover. "I haven't seen this one," she said eagerly.

"You will," he replied.

She looked up. "Do you know, I thought just now you were going to take out your pipe?" she said naively. "That's where you used to keep it."

"My pipe doesn't like me any more," he rejoined quietly.

"Are you happy, Nat?" she asked, scrutinizing his face with childlike, searching eyes.

"I was never a very solemn codger, was I?" he returned.

"But are you happier? Does the world look different? Of course it does, with your mother well."

"Oh yes," he answered in a changed tone, tossing his head back, and making a gesture as of throwing away something. "There was nothing in it before, nothing in it."

"Yes, yes, I know," she returned comprehendingly.

Jewel had watched them, and now, as they paused, her voice broke the silence in which the two friends looked into each other's faces.

"Cousin Eloise is going to church with me on Sunday," she announced.

"Oh, certainly." Bonnell smiled. "Wednesday evening meetings and all now, Eloise. Haven't you attended yet?"

"No, I've only just learned. I've only just seen. I'm only beginning to see, Nat. Your mother was healed. Oh, it is *true*, isn't it! It's so wonderful to find that you, *you*, know more about it than I do, when I supposed you would scorn it. I can't help expecting to wake up."

"That is just what you will do," returned Bonnell. "You will waken—to a thousand things. So your mother objects."

"Poor little mother," returned Eloise, looking down with sudden sadness.

"My mother wants you and yours to make us a long visit at View Point this summer."

The girl's lovely eyes raised hopefully. "The best thing that could happen," she exclaimed.

"I think so," responded her companion.

When Mr. Evringham returned from golf that afternoon, only his daughter-in-law was in sight. She inclined her head toward him with the air of a Lady Macbeth.

"Have you seen anything of the girls?" she asked as he approached her.

"Nothing. Where are they?"

She slowly shrugged her shoulders. "I'm the last one to ask. They wouldn't think of telling me," she returned.

"What's up now?" thought Mr. Evringham. "You don't look well, Madge," he said aloud.

Once she would have welcomed the evidence of solicitude. Now nothing mattered.

"I don't feel well," she replied, "and I can't even call the physician I prefer."

Mr. Evringham stared down at her for a silent minute, and light broke upon him.

"Is it all off with Ballard?" he asked bluntly.

"Yes; and that's what you have done, father, by allowing that child Jewel to come here."

Mr. Evringham bit his lip. This amused him.

"Eloise has mounted the new hobby, and is riding for dear life away from common sense, away from everything that promised such happiness."

"Do you mean Christian Science?"

"Of course I do."

"It's a strange thing, Madge. Do you know, it captures people with good heads." Mr. Evringham seated himself near his daughter's chair. "I came out on the train with my friend Reeves. He was talking about young

Bonnell, of whom you spoke last night. Said his mother was cured when the doctors couldn't do anything. You know her, eh?"

"As well as if she were my own flesh and blood."

"Is it a fact, what they say?"

"She was considered incurable. I know nothing about the rest of it. Nat was telling me yesterday. Now he is probably infatuated also, and, sooner or later, Eloise is sure to meet him."

"H'm, h'm. An old flame, you said," remarked Mr. Evringham. "Indeed! In—deed! I trust for your sake, Madge, that his is not objectionable to you."

"He is," snapped Mrs. Evringham. "A poor fellow, with his way to make in the world. He's been out of college a couple of years and hasn't done anything worth speaking of yet."

"Reeves is going to take him into the business," returned Mr. Evringham. "I don't know why or wherefore, but the mere fact is decidedly promising."

"Oh, who can tell if that will last!" returned the other with scornful pessimism. "Nat has let too many cotillions to do anything else well. I can only pray that he will get away without seeing Eloise. Mrs. Bonnell has invited us to make her a visit this summer. I certainly shall not go one step!"

A sudden sound of laughter was heard on the quiet air. Mrs. Evringham leaned forward. "There are the children now," she said, as figures turned in at the gateway; "and who is that? It is" —with desperation,—"he's here! Nat Bonnell is with them!"

She sat upright with disapproval, clasping the arm of her chair, while her father-in-law looked curiously at the approaching group. His gaze fixed on the young man with the well-set head who, swinging his hat in his hand, was talking fast to Eloise of something that amused them both. Jewel apparently interrupted him and he stooped with a quick motion, and in a second she was sitting on his shoulder, shrieking in gleeful surprise.

Thus they approached the piazza and came close before noting that it was occupied.

"Grandpa, see me!" cried Jewel delightedly.

Bonnell met the unsmiling gaze of his host as Mr. Evringham rose, and then caught sight of Mrs. Evringham stonily gazing from her chair.

"Ah, how do you do?" he called laughingly.

"Jove, he is a good looking chap!" thought the host, and Bonnell set Jewel down at his feet with such velocity that Anna Belle was cast heavily to earth.

"A thousand pardons!" exclaimed Nat, catching up the doll by the skirt and restoring her.

Jewel gave him a bright look. "*She* knows there is no sensation in matter," she said scornfully.

Poor Anna Belle! The topography of the ravine was full of hazards for her, and her seasons there were always so adventurous and full of sudden and unlooked-for bumps that her philosophy was well tested, and she might reasonably have complained of this gratuitous blow; but she smiled on, as Jewel hugged her. Her mental poise was marvelous, whatever might be said of the physical.

Eloise introduced her friend and went to her mother's side, while Bonnell shook hands with Mr. Evringham and exchanged some words concerning Mr. Reeves and business matters.

"Wide awake," was the older man's mental comment. "Doesn't seem at all the sort of person to be fooled about that healing business. Good eye. Good manner. Perhaps this was Ballard's handicap all the time. I guess you're in for it, Madge."

Nat moved to greet Mrs. Evringham, who gave him no welcoming smile. She leaned back listlessly, not caring what effect she produced. He seemed to her a part of the combination entered into by the Fates to thwart and annoy.

Bonnell knew her nearly as well as Eloise did. "I'm sorry you're under the weather," he said sympathetically, when he had discovered that, in his own phrase, there was "nothing doing." "I received a letter from my mother to-day, in which she impressed upon me that she expected you both by the middle of June."

"My plans have changed since yesterday, Nat," returned Mrs. Evringham dismally. "Yes. We shall not be able to go to your mother's, as I had hoped. Some time during the season I shall try to look in on her of course. You tell her so, Nat, when you write."

"Nonsense, nonsense, Mrs. Evringham. You don't in the least mean it," he returned cheerfully, with the smile and manner which she could not and would not endure.

"I do mean it, Nat. I tell you my plans are changed. Eloise and I may go to Europe."

Naturally she had never thought of Europe until that moment, but that laughing, caressing light in Nat Bonnell's eyes was insufferable.

"Ah, in that case, of course," he returned, "we couldn't say a word," and then he moved to go.

Mr. Evringham urged the visitor to stay to dinner, but he declined and once more shook hands.

"Good-by, Jewel," he said to the child. "Sunday, you know."

"Yes indeed, I know," she returned, an irresistible tendency to hop moving her feet. On nearer acquaintance she had found Mr. Bonnell exhilarating.

"Good-by, Nat," said Eloise.

He looked into the face on which rested a cloud. "I think you might be a degree more attentive," he suggested.

"How?"

"Oh—take me to the gate, for instance."

Eloise smiled and went with him. He turned with a slight bow that included the group, and they strolled down the path.

"It's all up, Madge," remarked Mr. Evringham, half smiling. "No use wriggling, no use staying away from the mother. Might as well yield gracefully. I think Ballard might have been told, that's all."

"There was nothing to tell, father! How can you be so unkind? That's just Nat's manner. He is used to everybody liking him, and always having his own way; but Eloise never—she *never*"—the speaker saw that if she continued, in a moment more she would be weeping, and she certainly was not going to weep in this company. So she contented herself by glaring toward the gate, where could be seen two figures in earnest conversation.

"I had counted so much on Mrs. Bonnell's influence," Eloise was saying. "What does mother mean? She knows my mind is made up as to Christian Science. What is she afraid of?"

Bonnell caught his thumbs in his coat pockets and lifted himself slightly on his toes. "She is afraid of me."

"Of you?" The girl lifted surprised eyes to his and let them fall again, her grave face coloring.

"She has always been more or less afraid of me. I'm ineligible, you know."

"Yes, you are, awfully, Nat," returned Eloise earnestly. "That's what makes you so nice. Didn't we always have a good time together?"

"Yes, on those rare occasions when we had a chance, but Mrs. Evringham always suspected me. She never felt certain that I wasn't waiting for your skirts to be lengthened and your hair to go up in order to steal you."

Eloise tried to look at him, but found it more comfortable to examine the inexpressive gravel path. "But now you have something to think of besides girls," she said gently.

"Yes. Do you know, Eloise, if I had been promised the granting of one wish as I took the cars for Bel-Air, it would have been that I might find you convinced of the truth of Christian Science."

She looked at him now brightly, gladly. "It is such a help to me to know that you are in it," she returned. Their hands simultaneously went forth and clasped. "What shall we do about mother?"

He smiled. "That will all come right," he returned confidently.

"There are classes, Nat," she said. "Have you been through one?"

"Not yet. Perhaps we could enter together."

"Do you think so?" she returned eagerly.

He was looking down at her still—calm, strong.

She started. "I mustn't be late to dinner. Good-by. Sunday, Nat."

"Not to-morrow? I want some golf."

"Yes, go. It's a fine links. I'm sorry, but I'd better not go there for the present. Good-by."

She was gone, so he strolled on and out through the park, and as he went he put two and two together, and suspected the cause of the girl's objection to golf.

CHAPTER XXVI
ON WEDNESDAY EVENING

"This is my silk dress, grandpa," said Jewel, coming out on the piazza Sunday morning.

Mr. Evringham was sitting there reading the paper. He looked up to behold his granddaughter standing expectantly.

She had on the cherished frock. Her plump black legs ended in new shoes, the brim of her large hat was wreathed with daisies, snowy ribbons finished her well-brushed braids, while, happiest touch of all, Little Faithful was ticking away on her breast.

"Well, who is this bonnie lassie?" asked Mr. Evringham, viewing her.

"It's my best one," said Jewel, smilingly, coming close to him.

"I should hope so. If you were anything grander I should have to put on smoked glasses to look at you. Church, eh?" He took the brown pamphlet she carried and examined it.

"Yes. I wish you were coming."

"Oh, I have an important engagement at the golf club this morning."

"Have you? Well, grandpa, I was thinking you can't play golf or ride at night, and wouldn't you take me Wednesday evening?"

"Where to?"

"Church."

"Heavens, child! Wednesday evening prayer meeting?" asked the broker in perturbation.

"No. It's just lovely reading and singing and interesting stories," replied Jewel, endeavoring to paint the picture as attractively as possible.

"H'm. H'm. Do you suppose Mr. Reeves goes?"

"Why, of course," replied the child. "Scientists never stay away."

"Then should I be considered a Scientist if I went? I still have some regard for my reputation."

"A great many visitors go," replied the child earnestly. Then she added, with unmistakably sincere naivete, "I don't mind leaving you in the daytime, because we're used to it; but I was thinking it would make me homesick, grandpa, to go away in the evening and leave you in the library."

Mr. Evringham took her little hand in his. "Have you thought, Jewel," he asked, "how it will be when you leave me altogether?"

"I shall have mother and father then," returned the child.

"Yes; but whom shall I have?"

The question came curtly, and Jewel looked into the deep-set eyes in surprise. "Shall you miss me, grandpa?" she asked wonderingly.

"Whom shall I have, I say?" he repeated.

The child thought a minute. "Just who you had before," she answered, slipping her arm around his neck. "There's Essex Maid, you know."

The broker gave a short laugh. "Yes. It's lucky, isn't it?" he returned, rather bitterly.

"Do you like to have me with you, grandpa?" pursued the child, pleased.

"Yes; confound it, Jewel, yes."

"Then Divine Love will fix it somehow, for I love to be with you, too."

"You do, eh? Then I'll tell you that I received a letter from your father yesterday. It was a very pleasant letter, but it said they felt obliged, if they could, to stay over a little longer—two or three weeks longer."

The child's face grew thoughtful.

"He said they had just received your letter, and were very pleased and thankful to know that you were happy. He said it would be a business advantage to them to stay, but that they could come home at the appointed time if you wished it. I am to cable them to-morrow, if you do." Silence for a minute while Jewel thought. "Do you think you can be happy with me a little longer than you expected?"

"I do want to see mother and father very much," returned the child, "but I'm just as happy as anything," she added heartily, after a pause.

Mr. Evringham had listened with surprising anxiety for the verdict. "Very well, very well," he returned, with extra brusqueness, picking up his newspaper. "I guess there won't be anything to prevent my going to that meeting with you Wednesday evening, Jewel. Just once, you understand, once only."

At this moment the brougham drove around to the steps, and Eloise came out upon the piazza. She was a vision of dainty purity in her white gown, white hat, and gloves.

Mr. Evringham rose, lifted his hat, and going down the steps opened the door of the carriage. "A man need not be ashamed to have these two ladies represent him at church," he said, looking into Eloise's calm eyes.

She smiled back at him. There was no suspicion now of sarcasm or stings. The air she breathed was wholesome and inviting. The lump had been leavened.

Arrived at the hall where the services were held, the girls were ushered into good seats before the room rapidly filled.

They saw Mr. Reeves and his family and Mr. Bonnell come in on the other side, and the latter did not rest until he had found them and sent over a bright, quick nod.

The platform was beautiful by a tall vase of roses at the side of the white reading-desk, and Eloise listened eagerly to the voices of the man and woman who alternately read the morning lesson. The peace, simplicity, and quiet of the service enthralled her. She looked over the crowd of listening, reverent faces with wistful wonder. Nat was among them, *Nat!* Sometimes she glanced across at his attentive face. Nat at church, in the morning; thoroughly interested! She pinched her arm to make quite certain.

Once when they rose to sing, it was the hymn she had heard. The voices swelled: —

> "O'er waiting harpstrings of the mind
> There sweeps a strain,
> Low, sad, and sweet, whose measures bind
> The power of pain."

The girl in the white dress did not sing. She swallowed often. The voice of the child at her side soared easily.

> "And o'er earth's troubled, angry sea,
> I see Christ walk;
> And come to me, and tenderly,
> Divinely, talk."

What a haven of promise and peace seemed this sunny, simple place of purity.

> "From tired joy and grief afar,
> And nearer Thee,
> Father, where Thine own children are
> I love to be."

Jewel, looking up at her companion, was surprised to see her lashes wet and her lower lip caught between her teeth.

"What's the matter, cousin Eloise?" she whispered softly as they sat down.

The girl tried to smile. Words were not at her command. "Gladness," she returned briefly; which reply caused Jewel to meditate for some time.

They had a talk with Nat and were presented to the Reeves family after church, and Eloise felt herself in an atmosphere of love.

Jewel left the group for a private word to Zeke before her cousin should come to enter the brougham. 'Zekiel sat bolt upright in the most approved style, and did not turn his face, even when the child addressed him.

"I've been wondering this morning," she said, "how we can manage for you to come to church, 'Zekiel."

"Oh, I have it six times a week," returned the coachman.

"But it's so lovely just to listen to them read and not have to hunt up the places or anything."

"I'm satisfied with my minister," returned Zeke, almost smiling.

Eloise and Mr. Bonnell came out to the carriage, so there was no further time for talk.

The subject remained in Jewel's mind, however. On Wednesday morning, just before Mr. Evringham went to the station, the child seized him in the hall.

"Grandpa, don't you think it would be nice to go in the trolley car to church to-night?"

"To—where?" asked the broker, frowning.

"This is the night we're going to church, you know."

"The dev—Ah, to be sure. So we are. Well—a—what did you say? Trolley car? Why?"

"Well, we could all go then, you know," returned Jewel. "Cousin Eloise wants to go, but," the child's honesty compelled her, "she wouldn't have to go with us because it is Mr. Bonnell's last night in Bel-Air, and I heard him ask if he might come for her; but I do so want Zeke to go, grandpa!"

"Well, for the love of"—began the broker slowly.

"Yes, Zeke is getting to understand a good deal about Christian Science. He has some claims of error that his mother knows about, and they make her sorry, and I've been helping him and reading to him out of my books, and I do want him to go to the testimonial meeting so much."

The child looked wistfully up into the dark eyes that rested upon her. Mr. Evringham had remarked his housekeeper's change of spirit toward the little girl, had wondered at the increasing and even reckless indulgence of Anna Belle, who from being an exile in the stair closet had now arrived at a degree of consideration and pampering which threatened to turn her head.

"Jewel," he said impressively, "I wish you to understand one thing distinctly. You are not now or at any future time to try to make a Christian Scientist of Essex Maid."

From wondering sobriety Jewel's lips broke into a gleeful smile. "I don't have to," she cried triumphantly. "She is one! Anyway, she has demonstrated everything a horse ought to!"

Mr. Evringham flung his hands over his head despairingly. "Great heavens!" he exclaimed tragically, rushing out to the brougham, Jewel at his heels in peals of laughter.

But they went to church in the trolley car. Eloise reached the same place with Mr. Bonnell, but whether she walked or drove or rode nobody ever knew, and it didn't matter much, for a full moon illuminated the night.

Early in the evening a young man entered the hall quietly and took a back seat. It was Zeke.

Mr. Reeves saw Jewel and her grandfather come in, and softly he smote his knee. "She's done it!" he ejaculated mentally. He noted the broker's haughty carriage, the half challenging glances he threw to right and left as he proceeded up the aisle to the position of Jewel's choice.

Mr. Reeves composed his countenance with some difficulty, and catching the wandering eye, gave his friend a grave bow.

Testimonial meetings differ in point of continued interest. This proved to be a good one. The most interesting narrative of the evening was Nat Bonnell's. His self possession, fine presence, and good voice made more effective the marvelous story of his mother's resurrection to strength. He told it with dignity and directness, and Mr. Evringham was impressed.

"What's my rheumatism to that, eh, Jewel?" he whispered, as Nat sat down.

"Just nothing, grandpa," replied the child.

"You think the Creator'd consider me worth attending to, eh?"

"God doesn't know you have the rheumatism," exclaimed Jewel with soft scorn.

"Doesn't? Well! I've always supposed He thought I needed reminding on account of a number of things, and so touched me up with that. I didn't blame Him much.

"If He knew it, it would be real, and then it couldn't be changed," returned Jewel earnestly in the ear he bent to her.

The broker sat up and looked down on her large hat and short legs. "Whew, but I'm a back number!" he mused.

The next testimonial made Jewel's eyes brighten. It was given by a man who told a story of hopeless intemperance and his family's want. The unaffected humility and gratitude that sounded in his voice as he described the changed conditions which followed his cure caused the roses to deepen in Jewel's cheeks. She wondered where Zeke was sitting.

Altogether she was happy over the meeting, and her grandfather's attitude was as kindly as could have been expected.

Eloise came into her mother's room that night, beaming.

"I wish you had come with us," she said. "It was wonderful."

Mrs. Evringham turned to her with a lofty air. "I have too much loyalty to friendship to be seen in such a place," she returned.

"Nat said he wouldn't ask you to come down to bid him good-by, because he expects to come out to spend Sundays for a while."

Mrs. Evringham looked at her daughter. All the girl's face had lacked of vivacity and happy expression it wore now, making her radiant.

"You could never guess the news I have for you, mother."

Mrs. Evringham's lips tightened. "Eloise, if you will not marry the fine man who had my entire approval, it will be outrageous for you to marry an ineligible, a young fellow whose goods are all in the show window, who has not proved himself in any way. I refuse to hear your news," she returned impetuously.

The girl laughed. "Do you mean Nat, dear?" she asked, her rosy face coming close. "I'm afraid he's going to spoil himself by becoming eligible. He has been telling me a lot about the business to-night."

"Ho! Nat Bonnell could always talk."

Eloise's arms closed around her. "There's only one source of supply, mother. Nat has found Him. I am finding Him. We shall not want. What do you think I have here for you? Grandfather gave it to me." Eloise put into her mother's hands a draft for a thousand dollars.

Mr. Evringham appeared to lose sight of the dagger she had been seeing before her for days. "What is this?" she ejaculated. "A present from father?"

"Not at all. Some unknown man owed it to papa, and his conscience made him pay the debt. It came in grandfather's evening mail, and he has only just opened it."

Mrs. Evringham examined the paper eagerly.

"How wonderful!" she exclaimed.

"How natural," returned Eloise. "That is the wonderful part of it."

CHAPTER XXVII
A REALIZED HOPE

One afternoon Mr. Evringham did not return from the city at the usual time. Jewel, watching for him, was surprised after a while to see him walking up from the gate.

"Why, what's happened?" she asked. "Zeke went for you."

"Yes; but he found he had to leave Dick to be shod."

"Then are you going to saddle Essex Maid yourself? Oh, can I see you do it, grandpa?" She hopped with anticipation.

"I don't know that I'll ride just now. It's an excellent day for walking. It seems rather strange to me, Jewel, that you've never shown me the Ravine of Happiness. You talk a good deal about it."

"Oh, would you like to come?" cried the child, flushing. "Good! I have the pond all fixed in Anna Belle's garden, and the ferns droop over it just like a fairy story."

"Have you put up a sign for the fairies to keep out?"

"No—o," returned Jewel, drawing in her chin and smiling.

"Oh well, you may be sure they're at it, then, every moonlight night. They haven't a particle of respect, you know, for anything. If I were in Anna Belle's place, I should put up a sign, 'Private Grounds.'"

"Oh, she's so unselfish she wouldn't. If they only won't break the flowers she won't care," returned the child, entering into the fancy with zest.

Mr. Evringham took the doll from her arms, and carrying it up the steps deposited it in the piazza chair.

"Isn't she going?" asked Jewel soberly.

"No, not this time. She doesn't care, she's been there so much. Just see how cheerful and comfortable she looks!"

There was, indeed, a smile of almost cloying sweetness on Anna Belle's countenance, and she seemed to be seeing pleasing visions.

"I never saw such a good child!" said Jewel with an admiring sigh; then she put her hand in her grandfather's and they strolled out into the park and up the shady road. Just before reaching the bend around which lay the gorge, Mr. Evringham surprised his companion by breaking in upon her lively chatter with a tune which he whistled loudly.

It was such an unusual ebullition that Jewel looked up at him. "Why, grandpa, I never heard you whistle before," she said.

"You didn't? That's because you never before saw me out on a lark. I tell you, I'm a gay one when I get started," and forthwith there burst again from his lips a gay refrain, that sounded shrilly up the leafy path. They rounded the bend in the road, and the broker looked down into the eyes that were bent upon him in admiration.

"You whistle almost as well as Mr. Bonnell," said the child.

"Give me time and I dare say I shall beat him out," was the swaggering response. "Ah, here's your ravine, is it?"

"Yes, that's" —began Jewel, and went no further.

A couple of rods from where she suddenly came to a standstill was an object which for a moment rooted her to the spot. A small horse, black as jet, with a white star in his forehead and a flowing, wavy mane and tail, stood by the roadside. His coat, gleaming like satin, set off the pure white leather of his trappings. On his back was fastened a side saddle, and he was tethered to the rail of the light fence.

Mr. Evringham appeared not to see him. He was looking down the rocks and grass of the steep incline.

"Is there any sort of a path?" he asked, "or do you descend it as you would a cellar door? I think you might have told me, so I could change these light trousers."

"Grandpa!" exclaimed Jewel in a hushed tone, pointing before her. "See that horse—just like the coal black steed the princess rides in a fairy story."

"Why, that's so. He is a beauty. Where do you suppose the princess is?"

"She's probably gone down the ravine," returned the child, her feet drawn forward as if by a magnet. "Let's not go down yet."

The broker allowed himself to be led close to the pony, who turned his full bright eyes upon the pair curiously.

"Do you think I might touch him, grandpa?" asked the child, still in the hushed voice.

"If he's a fairy horse he might vanish," returned Mr. Evringham. "Let's see how he stands it." So saying he gave the shining flank some sturdy love pats. "Oh, he's all right. He's good substantial flesh and blood."

"But the lady," said Jewel, looking about, the pupils of her eyes dilated with excitement.

"Oh, I don't think a very big lady has been riding in that saddle. You can do as you'd be done by, I fancy."

Upon this Jewel stroked the pony over and over lovingly, and he nosed about her in a friendly way.

"Grandpa, see him, see him! And oh grandpa, see his beautiful star, white as a snowflake!"

"Well, upon my word, if this isn't lucky," remarked Mr. Evringham. "Here is some sugar in my pocket, now." He passed some lumps to the child.

"Would it be right?" she asked, glancing down the ravine. "Had I better wait till the girl comes up?"

"She won't mind, I'll wager," returned Mr. Evringham; so the child, thus encouraged, fed the coal black steed, who, for all his poetical appearance, had evidently a strongly developed sweet tooth.

"Hello, what's this!" exclaimed the broker, stepping to the fence and taking up something black and folded. When he shook it out, it proved to be a child's riding skirt.

"She's left it there," said Jewel eagerly. "We ought not to touch it. It's very hard on clothes going down the ravine, and she's left it there. Don't you think, grandpa, you *ought* to put it back?" for to her great surprise her punctilious and particular relative was shaking the fine skirt about recklessly and examining it.

"Here's a name," he said, bringing his prize to Jewel and showing her an oblong bit of white cloth, much as tailors use inside dresses. "What do you make of it?"

The child, disturbed by such daring, and dreading to see the owner of these splendid possessions scramble up the bank, looked reluctantly.

The name was a long one, but so familiar that she recognized it at once. "Evringham."

She lifted her eyes to her grandfather. "It's the same as ours."

"There isn't another Evringham in Bel-Air," returned the broker. "The fairies dropped this for you, I guess, Jewel. It certainly won't fit me. Let's try it on."

He slipped it over the head of the dazed child and hooked it around her waist.

"'It fitted her exactly,'" murmured Jewel. "They always say so in fairy stories.

"Look here," said her grandfather. He put his hand into the stirrup and drew out a folded bit of paper. He handed it to the child, who began to wonder if she was dreaming.

DEAR JEWEL (she read),—I believe you expected Divine Love to send you a horse. I have come to belong to you, and my name is STAR.

It was astonishing what a large, round penmanship the pony possessed. There was no possibility of mistaking a word.

Jewel read the note over twice as she stood there, the long, scant skirt, making her look tall. Mr. Evringham stood watching her. His part in the comedy was played. He waited.

She looked up at him with eyes that seemed trying to comprehend a fact too large.

"Grandpa, have you given me this horse?" she asked solemnly, and he could see her hands beginning to tremble.

"Oh, am I to get some credit for this?" returned the broker, smiling and twisting his mustache. "I didn't expect that."

He knew her lack of motion would not last long, and was bracing himself for the attack when, to his surprise, she pulled up the impeding skirt and made a rush, not for him, but for the pony. Hiding her face on the creature's satin shoulder, she flung her arm around his throat, and seizing his rippling mane, sobbed as if her heart would break.

Mr. Evringham had not spent weeks in selecting and testing a horse for his granddaughter without choosing one whose nervous system would be proof against sudden assaults of affection; but this onslaught was so energetic that the pony tossed his head and backed to the end of his tether.

His new mistress stumbled after him, her face still hidden. She was trying heroically to stifle the sobs that were shaking her from head to foot.

"Jewel, Jewel, child!" ejaculated her grandfather, much dismayed. "Come, come, what's this?"

He drew her with a strong hand, and she deserted the pony, much to the latter's relief, and clasping Mr. Evringham as high up as she could reach, began bedewing his vest buttons with her tears.

"Oh, gra—grandpa, I c—can't have him!" she sobbed. "There isn't any roo—room for him in our—our fla—fla—flat!"

"Well, did you expect to keep him in the flat?" inquired Mr. Evringham, stooping tenderly, his own eyes shining suspiciously, as he put his arms around the little shaking form.

"N—no; but we—we haven't any bar—barn."

The broker smiled above the voluminous, quivering bows.

"Well, hasn't some good livery man in your neighborhood a stable?"

"Ye—yes." Jewel made greater efforts to stop crying. "But I—I talked with mo—mother once about cou—could I ha—have a horse sometime before I grew up, and she said she might buy the horse, but it would cost so much—much money every week to board it, it would be error."

Mr. Evringham patted the heaving shoulder.

"Ah, but you don't know yet all about your horse. In some respects I've never seen a pony like him."

"I—I never have," returned the child.

"Oh, but you'll be surprised at *this*. This pony has a bank account."

Jewel slowly grew quiet.

"Nobody has to pay for *his* board and clothes. He is very independent. He would have it that way."

"Grandpa!" came in muffled tones from the broker's vest.

"So don't you think you'd better cheer up and look at him once more, and tell him you won't cry on his shoulder very often?"

In a minute Jewel looked up, revealing her swollen eyes. "I'm ashamed," she said softly, "but he was—so—be—*autiful*—I forgot to remember."

"Well, I guess you did forget to remember," returned Mr. Evringham, shaking his head and leading the child to her pony's side.

He lifted her into the saddle and arranged her skirt, brushing away the dust.

"Grandpa!" she exclaimed softly, with a long, quivering sigh, "I'm so *happy*!"

"Have you ever ridden, Jewel?"

"Oh, yes, a thousand times," she answered quickly; "but not on a real horse," she added as an afterthought.

"H'm. That might make a difference." Mr. Evringham loosed the pony and put the white bridle in the child's hands; then he led the pretty creature down the woodland road.

"I'm *so* happy," repeated Jewel. "What will mother and father say!"

"You'll be a regular circus rider by the time they come home."

As the broker spoke these words Zeke appeared around the bend in the road, riding Essex Maid. His face was alight with interest in the sight that met him.

Jewel called to him radiantly. "Oh, Zeke, what do you think?"

"I think it's great," he responded. "Hello, little kid," he said, as he came nearer and perceived the signs in the child's face. "Pony do any harm, Mr. Evringham?" he asked with respectful concern.

"No; Jewel cried a little, but it was only because I told her she could not sleep nights in Star's manger."

The child gave one look of astonishment at the speaker's grave countenance, and then shouted with a laugh as spontaneous as though no tear had ever fallen from her shining eyes.

"See Essex Maid look at my pony, grandpa!" she said joyously. "She looks so proud and stuck *up*."

"Look away, my lady," said the broker. "You'll see a great deal more of this young spring before you see less."

Zeke dismounted.

"Now then," Mr. Evringham looked up at the child. "I'm going to let go your bridle."

"I want you to," she answered gayly.

Mr. Evringham mounted his horse. "We'll take a sedate walk through the woods," he said. "Zeke, you might lead her a little way."

"No, no, *please*," begged the child. "I know how to ride. I *do*."

"Well, let her go then," smiled the broker, and Essex Maid trotted slowly, noting with haughty bright eyes the little black companion, who might have stepped out of a picture book, but whose easy canter was tossing Jewel at every step.

"I haven't—any—whip!" The words were bounced out of the child's lips, and Mr. Evringham's laugh resounded along the avenue.

"I believe she'd use it," he said to Zeke, who was running along beside the black pony.

"I guess she would, sir," grinned the young fellow responsively.

It was not many days before Jewel had learned to stay in the saddle. She had an efficient teacher who worked with her *con amore*, and the sight of the erect, gray-haired man on his famous mare, always accompanied by the rosy little girl on a black pony, came to be a familiar sight in Bel-Air, and one which people always turned to follow with their eyes.

Eloise had her talk with Mr. Evringham one evening when Jewel was excluded from the library, and she emerged from the interview with a more contented heart than she had known for a year.

She endeavored to convey the situation to her mother in detail, but when that lady had learned that there were no happy surprises, she declined to listen.

"Tastes differ, Eloise," she said. "I am one who believes that where ignorance is bliss 'tis folly to be wise." Mrs. Evringham had regained a quite light-hearted appearance in the interest of expending a portion of her windfall on her own and Eloise's summer wardrobe.

"Well, you shan't be bothered then," returned her daughter. "You have me to take care of our money matters."

"I prefer to let father do it," returned Mrs. Evringham decidedly. "He is a changed being of late, and we are as well situated as we could hope to be. I don't feel quite satisfied with the lining of the brougham, but some day I mean to speak of it."

Eloise threw up both hands, but she laughed. She and her grandfather had an excellent understanding, and she knew that the mills of the gods were about to grind.

One evening the broker called his daughter-in-law into the library.

"I hope it isn't on business," she remarked flippantly as she entered. "I tell you right at the start, father, I can't understand it." Her eyes wandered about the room curiously. It was strange to her. She took up a woman's picture from the desk. "Who is this?" she asked.

"How do you like the face?" he returned.

The dark eyes and sweet mouth looked back at her. She frowned slightly. She did not like the situation in which she had found the photograph. It was far too intimate for a stranger, and made her a little nervous.

"If he is going to marry again, then good-by indeed!" she thought.

"I think it is rather sentimental," she returned, with an air of engaging candor, "don't you? Just my first impression, you know; but it's a face I shouldn't trust. Who is it?"

"It is Jewel's mother," returned the broker quietly, "my daughter Julia. Jewel brought it down last night, also a lot of little letters her mother had put in the pockets of the child's dresses when she packed them."

"Ah!" exclaimed Mrs. Evringham triumphantly. "Didn't I say she was sentimental? About that sort of thing my perceptions are always so keen."

"H'm. I read the letters, and I judged from them that one can trust her. Will you be seated?" He placed a chair. "I should like to ask your plans for the summer."

Mrs. Evringham looked up quickly, startled. "Oh, I haven't any. Have you?"

"Yes. I always seek some cool spot. You have an invitation to View Point, I understand. You could scarcely do better."

"I have reasons, father," impressively, "reasons for declining that."

"Then where are you going?"

"I would just as lief stay here and take care of your house as not," declared the lady magnanimously.

"Ha! Without any servants?"

"Why, what do you mean?"

"They are going away for a vacation. I am intending to have the house wired, and Mrs. Forbes and Zeke will hold sway in the barn. She doesn't wish to leave him."

Mrs. Evringham was silenced and dismayed. She felt herself being firmly and inexorably pushed out of this well-lined nest.

Her eyes fell before the impenetrable ones regarding her.

"How did Jewel ever win him?" she thought. The picturesque pony, with his arched neck and expensive trappings, had outraged her feelings for days.

"About the View Point plan," continued Mr. Evringham deliberately. "I think there are influences waiting for you there that will be of benefit. There is a new philosophy percolating in these days through our worldly rubbish which you and I would be the better for grasping. Your chances are better than mine, for you are young still. Your daughter is expanding like a flower already, in the first rays of her understanding of it. This young man whom you fancy you can avoid is a help to her. Mr. Reeves was talking to me about him last night. He says that so far as his business is concerned, young Bonnell is proving the square peg in the square hole. I don't know what Eloise's sentiments are toward him, but I do know that she shall be independent of any one's financial help but mine."

Mrs. Evringham lifted her eyes hopefully.

"I shall eke out the little income which is left to you with sufficient for you to live—not as you have done—but comfortably."

The eager light faded from his listener's eyes.

"Eloise and I have arranged that," he continued, "and she is satisfied. Take my advice, Madge. Go to View Point."

"I suppose Eloise doesn't need horses so long as Jewel has them," said Mrs. Evringham rising.

Her host followed her example. "She thinks not," he returned concisely; then he opened the library door, and his daughter-in-law swept from his presence with all the dignity she could muster.

CHAPTER XXVIII
AT TWILIGHT

It was Sunday, and Mr. Bonnell was dining at Bel-Air Park. Had Jewel thought of it, she might have contrasted the expression of Mrs. Forbes's face as she waited at table this evening with the look it wore on the day she first arrived; might have noted the cheerful flow of talk which enlivened the board, in distinction from the stiff silence or bitter repartee which once chilled her. As she responded to the smiles hovering now about Eloise's lovely lips, she might have remembered the once sombre sadness of those eyes. Even Mrs. Evringham had buried the Macbethian dagger, and wore the meek and patient air of one misunderstood; but nothing would have amazed the child so much as to be told that she had had anything to do with this metamorphosis.

Anna Belle,—deserted often now, perforce, on account of the pony, whose life was a strenuous one, owing to the variety of Jewel's attentions,— Anna Belle was petted with extra fondness when her turn came; and she sat at table now in a pleasing trance, her smile an impartial benediction upon all.

It had been a glorious June day, the park was at its best. After dinner the family strolled out toward the piazza.

Mrs. Forbes had attended her own Baptist church that morning, and the familiar Sunday-school tune that the children sang floated through her mind as she looked after the group.

"When He cometh, when He cometh,
To make up His jewels,
All His pure ones, all His bright ones,
His loved and His own.

"Little children, little children,
Who love their Redeemer,
Are the jewels, precious jewels,
His loved and His own."

"What is Mr. Evringham going to do without that child?" she thought.

The broker was invaded with the same problem as Jewel lingered with him on the piazza, while the others walked on toward a seat beneath a spreading maple.

He ensconced himself in his favorite chair. The thrushes were singing vespers. The pure air was faintly and deliciously scented.

"Grandpa, is it too late to bring Star out for a nibble?" asked the little girl wistfully.

"No, I guess not," returned the broker as he opened his cigar case. "Star may have a short life, but he's certainly experiencing a merry one. There's no moss gathering on that pony."

Jewel had not waited for more than the permission. She was fleeing toward the barn.

Mr. Evringham lighted his cigar, and then his eye fell upon the doll, too hastily set down, and fallen at a distressing angle. Her eyes were closed as if her sensibilities had been shocked overmuch.

"Anna Belle, Anna Belle, has it come to this!" he murmured, picking up the neglected one, who, with her usual elasticity and exuberance of spirit, at once opened her eyes and beamed optimistically on her rescuer. He set her, facing him, on his knee. "Such is youth!" he sighed. "When she throws you down, I feel that I'm not going to be so recuperative as you, Anna Belle. I have a plan, however, a plan of self-defense; but if it weren't for your discretion, I shouldn't tell it to you, for I'm an old bird, young lady, and can't be caught with chaff. There are many worthy persons who may rise to lofty heights in eternity, who nevertheless, meanwhile are not desirable to sit opposite a man at his breakfast table. A visit, Anna Belle, a short visit from my daughter Julia is all I shall ask for at first, and I shall test her, test her, my dear. I'll look at her through a magnifying glass. Of course, if they'd give me Jewel, it would be all I'd ask for; but they won't. That is self-evident."

Here the child came around the corner of the house, leading her pet by a halter, but with her hand in his mane as she pressed close to his side, caressing and talking to him. In fact it was the harassing problem of the pony's life to manage to avoid stepping on her. Zeke lounged in the background on account equally of his orders and his inclination.

Star began cropping the grass, and Mr. Evringham continued his disquisition to the bright-eyed young person on his knee:—

"My son Harry is turning out a pretty good sort, I fancy. I'm not particularly shy of giving him a trial, provided he'll do the same by me; but I suppose he will have to go West at first, anyway. Julia is a different thing. I can't whistle her on and off with the same frankness; and I must be careful, Anna Belle. Do you understand? Careful! And I'm going to be, by Jove, in spite of the way it makes me cringe to think of this big house, empty as a drum. It wasn't empty before, that's the mischief of it. What has happened to me? I thought things were well enough in those days. Nobody whom I knew was particularly happy. Why should I be?"

The thrushes stopped, for Jewel's childish voice floated out on the evening air.

Mr. Evringham knew what had happened. He knew that Zeke had asked her to sing. They two were sitting on the ground, while the pony cropped away at the sweet grass.

"From tired joy and grief afar,
And nearer Thee,
Father, where Thine own children are
I love to be!"

The broker listened for a minute.

"I'll take Jewel and her mother to the seashore somewhere; for I must leave the house, if only to let Madge down easily, and too, I wish to study Julia outside her atmosphere. Poor Madge, she's a light weight, but I think there are better times coming for her. At View Point she'll find friends."

Time passed, and at last Mr. Evringham called, "That will do, Jewel."

"Do you want Star to go in?" she returned.

The broker nodded, and the child sprang up and began patting and smoothing the little horse with energetic affection.

"It's your bedtime, Star," she said, "but morning's coming." She kissed his sleek shoulder. "We'll have such a good time in the morning. I don't bounce a bit now, do I, Zeke?" she asked, turning to him.

"Well, I guess not," returned Zeke scornfully. "You ain't the kind that gets bounced after a fellow knows you," he added, smiling. He took the pony's halter. "Good-night, Jewel."

"Good-night, Zeke." She ran across the lawn and up the piazza steps. "How kind of you, grandpa, to amuse Anna Belle!" she exclaimed gratefully, observing the doll on his knee. At the same time she most abruptly whisked that patient person into a neighboring chair and usurped her place. Cuddling down in her grandfather's arms, she nestled her head against his shoulder and sighed happily.

The light began to fade, the last smoke from the broker's cigar curled out into the summer air. He tossed it away and pressed the child more closely to him.

"Sing once again the song you sang for Zeke." he said.

And she began softly in her true, clear voice:—

"From tired joy and grief afar,
And nearer Thee,
Father, where Thine own children are
I love to be!"

"Amen," breathed Mr. Evringham.